CLUB 13

A NOVEL

BRISTOL ROSE

To all the mysteries in this world that have kept my mind wandering.

Quiet, Inanna, the ways of the underworld are perfect
They may not be questioned.

-*The Descent of Inanna*, an ancient Sumerian poem translated by
Wolkstein &
Kramer, 1983

My dear Greg, Elise, and Liam,

I'll try to keep things short and sweet, even though we all know I'm a ranter.

When I left initially, I did it because I thought I knew what I *needed*. My soul was searching for something bigger, something more grandiose in the spiritual sense. I tried to pretend for years, and I hope each of you understand that I tried my very best. To be a good mom. To be a loving wife. To provide a nurturing home. To survive. I tried my very best to fit the mold that society created for me. It's not that I didn't love being a mother and a wife, it's just that it wasn't what I was made for. It was slowly suffocating my soul. So, I left it all behind to find what I needed. In the end, though, I realized that what I was searching for isn't here on this Earth. It isn't on this plane. I leave now, knowing that my soul is where it needs to be, where it can thrive.

I'll be waiting patiently for each of you. Live long, prosperous lives. I love you to the moon.

Yours truly,

Gina

CHAPTER 1

Sirens blare up the street as flashing red and white lights come into focus. The emergency vehicle barrels through the middle of the road towards us. We pull over to the right to let the ambulance through. The urge to know what happened and to whom always hits me. "I hope everything is okay," I say as I crank my neck to follow the direction of the mysterious crisis. "Want me to follow them?" my husband asks with a cackle. I shrug off my nosy intrigue and lower the car visor to peer at myself in the mirror. Round, dark eyes stare back at me. I poke at the outer corners. My mother nagged at me to use a daily SPF throughout my early twenties, which I didn't. Now I'm staring at the consequences. I'm reaching the end of an era. The end of my glory years. Subtle crow's feet settle into my brown skin. The thought of turning thirty has haunted me ever since I turned twenty-six. On that birthday, an ex told me, "It's only downhill from here babe". And I never forgot it. With little less than a year left, my youth practically seeps out of me.

My eyes shift to the man beside me in the driver seat. He hit his thirties a few years ago but you'd never know it. His unblemished, porcelain skin, dirty blonde hair, and muscular physique is just as impressive as the pictures I've seen of him from a decade ago.

Why is it that men age in reverse?

My attention drifts back to the mirror and I fiddle with my loose curls, cursing their lack of moisture.

"What's on the menu for tonight, Lula?" Jason asks as he loosens his grip from the steering wheel and places his hand on my thigh with a squeeze. I whip up the visor and come back to the present, relishing in his touch.

"You pick tonight, babe. I chose last night," I say with a whine.

"That's not how this works. Happy wife, happy life, remember? You run this show," he says, throwing a wink my way.

The corners of my mouth rise. He always knows how to make me smile. It's one of the many reasons that I love him. It's never a crazy, grand gesture. I have always appreciated the little things. Simplicity is a beauty all its own.

If you asked me what I want out of life, I'd tell you that I've crossed just about all of it off the list. A loving husband, a stable job, a beautiful home, a sense of safety and security. Check, check, check, check. Sometimes, it's just nice to have a life that's easy.

Despite this, my mom's words ring through my head every now and then.

You're settling, Lula. Vivez la vie pleinement!

"Live life to the fullest" has been forced down my throat since before I even made it to middle school. If it were up to my mother, I'd be single until fifty, traveling the world and soaking up different cultures all while tasting the variety of flavors of men that the Earth has to offer.

Just a glance at the sparkling, pear-shaped diamond on my ring finger is enough to push those thoughts aside, though. This is how life is supposed to be. Easy. So, what if I haven't seen the Eiffel tower, crossed the narrow sea, or hooked up with a sexy Brazilian man? This is what I want. And I am happy. One day, my mom will understand.

Jason catches me staring at the bling. It's not the biggest diamond, but I couldn't be more obsessed with it.

"Ready for an upgrade already?" he asks, chuckling.

"Of course not. I'm just admiring it. It's been nearly half a year, and it still mesmerizes me every time I look down. You did good," I say and return the wink he gave me earlier.

Jason and I met shortly after he moved to Garden Valley. I went into the liquor store for a bottle of raspberry Smirnoff, and he went in for a bottle of Blanton's. My poor choice in alcohol quality caught his attention and he made jokes about it all the way up to the cash register. "You're going to be in for the world's worst hangover with that bottle of garbage," he said. As the clerk bagged my vodka and he stood behind me in line, he asked if he could have my number. "I'll take you out for a *real* drink," he said. It felt like perfect timing. I had just gotten out of a long-term relationship, but my heart had been ready to move on for some time. To my mother's dismay, I jumped in with both feet and it all went so quickly after that.

She told me once that my incessant need for love and safety has led to my endless cycle of relationship after relationship. She once even called Jason my crutch. I didn't talk to her for weeks after that.

What she doesn't realize is that Jason is different. His interest in me is what really drew me in. The men from my past loved to talk about themselves. I would listen, feed egos, and fulfill needs. But in the end, I was always left empty. I wasn't special. It could have been any girl who was willing to put in the effort, that girl just so happened to always be me. But from day one, Jason made me the focal point. The attention to detail, the "I miss you", "I love you", and "I want you" that always come when I need them the most, and the willingness to meet me in the middle spoke volumes. I always feel heard. I'm never left wanting.

So far, he's been my greatest accomplishment, which if I ever said out loud, my mom would probably disown me. I've always been jealous of people like my mother who have intense passion and aspiration, who strive to reach for the stars, but that's just not me. Contentment has always been my goal.

"Our first anniversary I'm getting you something bigger. Something that will make a statement," he says.

"You don't need to do that. I love my ring," I say.

"I know you do. You would have loved any ring. That's just who you are. But now that I can afford it, I want you to have a big rock to show off."

Jason made partner about a month ago at Stellar Capital. He's used to having money; his parents both came from old money. Now he's finally on the road to making them proud. But I'm not used to it. I grew up with parents that struggled to make ends meet.

The Jeep screeches to a halt in our driveway. The home that Jason and I moved into six months ago isn't luxury, but it's far from modest. We decided on a three bedroom, which his mother declared would give us space to expand our family in the future. Jason insisted on creating an "Italianesque" feel in the front yard complete with fully mature cypress and olive trees and a finely crafted pergola in the entryway. I got to choose my upgrades inside the house. I was just happy with crown molding, a kitchen lined with marble, and a bathroom with his and her shower heads. Either way, I would have been perfectly fine with simple suburbia in a cookie cutter home, but Jason's mother wanted to gift us our dream home. Something that made my mom feel insecure after she offered to buy us the stainless-steel toaster we put on our registry.

Jason puts the car in park and kisses my forehead before getting out and grabbing the bags of groceries.

Walking to check the mail, I catch a scent of freshly cut grass and the blooming lavender bush next door. Spring is starting to fade into summer and the crispness of the morning air has been replaced with a muggy warmth. The daily paper is shoved into our mailbox, not quite compact enough to slide in neatly. Newspapers are practically nonexistent in the modern world, but here in the small town of Garden Valley, California, we do a good job of holding onto random customs from simpler times. There are some things we just can't let go of.

The damp paper threatens to crumple in my hands but the headlines gleam off the page.

SUCIDE LETTER LEAKED

UPPER-CLASS MOM OF TWO ENDS IT ALL

The Reeses have been on the front cover of the newspaper for the last week. The husband, Greg, is high up in a Fortune 500 company, so of course the wife's death was publicized by every local news outlet within a hundred-mile radius. Even a few national outlets picked it up. Although, I'm sure it isn't what the family wants to be remembered for.

The reported story is suicide. I've heard all sorts of rumors from a bottle of pills to a noose around the neck. Everyone is dying to know why a gorgeous, rich woman with the world at her fingertips would take her own life.

In other words, everyone wants something to gossip about.

"You brought all the groceries in?" I ask as I set the pile of mail and soaked newspaper on the kitchen counter.

Jason is glued to his phone. Something that I've been noticing more and more lately.

"Babe?" I ask, trying to pull his attention away from the screen.

"Huh?" He looks up from his phone and hurriedly slides it into his pocket.

"Sorry. Work has been crazy lately. Feels like I can't catch a break," he says, running his hand through his hair.

"What you need is to relax," I say and inch closer, grabbing his hand. "How about I make us some chicken Alfredo? Maybe you could use a bit of comfort food," I say.

He pulls me in close to him and the look of concern on his face changes to one of amusement. "Well, you know I'd never turn down a good pasta," he says.

I'm relieved at the thought that I could help at least a little. I bury my face into his chest. The smell of his woodsy aftershave lingers on his t-shirt, and I breathe it in. I wish he knew just how much comfort he provides me.

"Hey, I've been meaning to tell you that I'm going to be working late these next few nights," he says, rubbing my back to ease the blow.

My heart sinks. I dread the late nights. I find myself waiting around for him, passing the time with trash tv and mindless scrolling through social media, just counting down the minutes until he gets back. It's not intentional. I just can't seem to help it. But I would never let him know how his absence affects me.

"Sandy gave me a bunch of paperwork to take home from the office, so I'll be pretty preoccupied this week, anyways," I lie.

"That works out well then. But I can make it up to you. Derrick is having a poker night at his house Saturday night. It's a couple's thing. You want to join me?" he asks, shooting me a devilish smirk.

Jason has made a lot of friends since moving here, most from work. I've been here my entire life and only have a few close friends to show for it. Most have since moved away. I suppose it's just the magnetism about him, and the wallflower in me. I never get invited to anything involving his work friends, so it feels good that he is thinking of me. Even though he knows how I feel about large social gatherings.

"I know it's not your idea of a good time, but I could use a pretty lady on my arm," he says.

I roll my eyes and chuckle.

I'm not much of a "people person". I had a terrible stutter as a child, courtesy of what the doctor assumed was social anxiety disorder. The impediment made me hate speaking. The more I spoke, the dumber I would sound, so for many years, I stayed quiet. I stayed so quiet that making friends was damn near impossible. I grew out of the stutter, thank God, but my aberrant fear of social interaction has never left me. I do have to give credit to Zoloft, though, for keeping me functionable.

"Derrick is married to Cheyenne, right? Who else is going to be there?" I ask.

I've heard about some of his friends but haven't met many. I try not to force myself into his social circle. Not only do I appreciate not having to socialize with people I don't know, but I also don't want to overstep. I don't want him to feel like I have to be involved just because I'm his wife.

"Just some other guys from Aspen Financial and their wives. Ellis, Greg, Atlas, Wyatt, and some others. I think you've met a few in passing."

One name catches my attention.

"Greg? Greg Reese? Isn't he the one that just lost his wife?" I ask casually, trying to avoid sounding like I'm prying.

Jason nods and his voice gets low. "Yeah… Gina. Poor guy."

"I almost forgot that your company works with him," I lie, "How is he managing?"

"He's handling it pretty well," he says.

I shake my head. "Pretty well? I can't imagine it. Will this be the first time he's getting out since she passed?"

"Um, yeah. I think," he says.

"Do the kids— "

He cuts me off, "I think he just wants to move past it. It's not something we bring up." Jason's tone stiffens.

Silence ensues for a few moments after that. Each of us trying to figure out where we left off after the conversation snaked its way to the Reeses.

I kick myself for mentioning it at all. If Jason wanted to talk about it, he would have. It isn't any of my business anyways.

"So, you'll go?" Jason asks, killing the silence.

"I'll go," I reply, praying that I don't regret accepting the invitation.

Jason's mouth curls into a smile and he leans down to press his lips against mine. They are warm and my mouth melts into his, the subtle hint of citrus erupting from his breath. He tugs at my waist and presses my body into his, kissing me harder. I wince as his teeth clamp down on my bottom lip.

"You like that?" he asks in a whisper.

I nod and lick my lips, a tinge of blood tickling my taste buds.

"Good," he says and lifts me onto the granite countertop.

I can't imagine my life without this man.

CHAPTER 2

"Just how fancy do I need to be?" I yell out to Jason from my closet. Piles of clothes are strewn across the bedroom. Nothing is just right. It's either too frumpy, too small, or too plain. I haven't been *out* in months. I've lost my sense of style.

I've been dreading this night the entire week. I willed the days to slow down. But time never seems to be on our side.

"What about this?" Jason holds up a slinky black mini dress. I can't even remember where or why I bought it, but I notice that I haven't even taken the tags off yet.

"I'm sure I bought that for some college party I naively thought I'd attend. It probably won't even fit me anymore," I laugh.

"Come on. Just try it on. I think it would be perfect," he says.

"You don't think it's too much? Too risqué?" I ask.

I can just picture the classy, sophisticated wives grouped together, gossiping.

Who does Jason's wife think she is?

Jason laughs. "It may be risqué. But I'm not opposed to it. I'll have the hottest wife there."

He comes over and wraps his arms around me as I hold the dress up against my body. I haven't dressed in something this skimpy since I was 19. I place it next to a pair of heels and shrug. "If they hate me, I'm blaming you," I say.

"Hate you? I don't think that anyone could ever hate you, Lula."

We pull up to 99 E Geranium Pl as the sun is starting to fall in the sky, casting stripes of orange and purple throughout the clear sky. As we park and I turn to face the home, my jaw drops. This isn't actually a home at all. It's a damn villa. The gigantic house wraps around a courtyard of lush greenery and various flowers. A glowing fountain sparkles in the center of it all. Jason must notice my mouth agape.

"These people have money dripping from their fingertips. Just wait until you see the inside," he says, ushering me to follow him onto the cobblestone path.

Derrick made partner at Aspen ages ago. He has built the kind of wealth that I'm sure Jason is striving for. With our salaries combined, he and I are comfortable, but this is a whole new level of comfortability.

The soft chirps of crickets pervade through the warm, late spring air. At this point, I would give my left pinky finger to stay out here and soak it all in instead of going inside to be bombarded with social interaction.

With each click of my heel on the pavement we move closer and closer to the front door, all the while my stomach clenches tighter and tighter. A security camera in the upper right corner of the doorway is aimed in our direction, I look down at my feet, pretending not to notice it.

"Ready?" Jason asks.

"As I'll ever be."

I should have taken an emergency Xanax or at least a few shots of vodka. I take a deep breath as Jason's knuckles rap on the wood. The door swings open almost immediately, wafting an ambery gush of air into our faces.

"J!"

My husband is pulled into the arms of a curvaceous blonde. She kisses him on both cheeks as her freshly blown out hair swings in his face.

J?

"Honey, this is Cheyenne Wright. Cheyenne, this is my wife, Lula." Jason gestures towards me.

"It's so nice to meet you. You have a beautiful h—" Before I can finish my sentence Cheyenne pulls me into the same all-encompassing embrace.

"I've heard so much about you! It's about time Jason brought you around!" Cheyenne winks at Jason and leads us down the hall donned with framed artwork that I have no doubt cost and arm and a leg.

The hall opens to a foyer decked with velvet furniture, marble tile, a crystal lined chandelier, and a built-in bar in the far corner. Perpetual hosts.

A group of well-dressed men and women stand around with drinks in hand, conversating. The wives are not nearly as modest as I imagined them to be. Diamonds, satin, cleavage; glamour in a nutshell. I can't spot a single unattractive individual. Plenty of resting bitch face to go around, though.

"Jason!" A burly man with a full beard shouts and makes his way over to us, causing a few heads to turn.

"Hey, Calen." They give each other pats on the back and Calen turns his attention to me.

"Now who is this lovely lady? You've been hiding her from us, Jason?" His voice is thundering as it reverberates off the walls.

My cheeks get hot.

"Hi. I'm Lula," I say softly and reach my hand out to shake his. Instead, he pulls me into his arms, squeezing me tightly. He reeks of bourbon. Or maybe it's scotch. His hands start to drift down my back, and I tense. He must be able to feel it because he quickly releases and backs away a few steps.

I need a drink. And fast.

"Derrick! Get these two something strong!" Calen yells to a man in a black button up and maroon tie. I recognize him from Jason's office. The man of the house.

He can sense my sobriety. Is it that palpable?

"There's a full bar. The bartender will make you whatever you'd like," Derrick calls out and directs us over to the bar.

"Babe, will you get me a gin and tonic? I'll be right back." Jason says and walks away before I can protest. I suppose he must have forgotten his promise not to leave my side.

"New here?" the bartender asks.

"Is it that obvious?" I ask, my face falling.

"I always recognize a new face. The Wrights have a large circle, but it stays pretty constant."

"Do they have you on retainer or something?" I chuckle.

"Something like that. It's always a party with this bunch," he grins. The man barely looks old enough to drink. His baby face and dimpled cheeks give him the look of a cherub. "Anyways, what can I get you?" he asks.

I order Jason his drink and get a Midori sour for myself. I chug it. Willing the calming effects of the alcohol to settle in. I could stay at the bar all night and chat it up with the young bartender, but instead I take the drinks and position myself next to an empty table near the clusters of chatty guests.

A lady in a black pantsuit with a pixie cut keeps glancing in my direction. We make eye contact a few times and I can't help but think I must have a hair out of place or a gigantic piece of spinach in my teeth from dinner. I pull out my phone and try to glance at myself in the dark reflection.

Searching the large room for Jason, I spot him near a hallway that appears to lead to another section of the home. His suit fits him like a glove like everything else in his wardrobe. His hair is perfectly styled but all I want to do is run my fingers through it. My heart swells and I move to head his way, but two women beat me to him, leaving me to sulk back to my original spot. A blonde and a brunette. Both are gorgeous and both have their hands on his shoulders, throwing their heads back as laughter erupts from the three of them. My heart rate ramps up and my eyes dart away. Jason has always had a thing for blondes. In fact, that's all he dated in high school and college. He switched things up for me. I am so far from that.

In attempts to push aside my insecurities and resist the urge to find the nearest bathroom to hide in, I plant myself on a loveseat nearby, abandoning Jason's drink at the table.

One leg crosses over the other and I fiddle with the hem of my dress, picking at the threads. My drink is mostly ice now, but I sip it anway.

"Hey, doll. Are you Jason's wife?" A petite redhead in stilettos struts over, trailed by another man I recognize. Tall, dark, and handsome. I can't remember his name, though.

"Yes, I'm Lula," I say and stand to shake her hand. Mine is clammy and I immediately regret it, but she doesn't squirm away.

"I'm Meagan. This is my husband, Atlas."

He flashes me a pearly smile that sends butterflies fluttering inside me. "I think we have met before," he says, and I nod in agreement.

She's pretty. With sleek, long, fiery hair, emerald eyes and a slender body offset with perky cleavage. It's no wonder she was able to bag a man like Atlas. His chocolate skin is completely unblemished, and his muscle tone shows through his cotton button down.

"Take a shot with us?" she asks.

I don't refuse.

Meagan whispers something to the bartender and turns back around with the shots.

"What is this?" I ask as she hands me a small glass full of brown liquid.

"Come on now. Don't spoil the fun," she replies.

Our glasses clink. The alcohol burns as it goes down my throat, but a warm sensation soon washes over me.

"So, what has taken you so long to come around our bunch of crazies? Meagan asks and makes herself comfortable on the loveseat next to me. Atlas grabs a barstool and drags it over to sit across from us.

My shoulders shrug. "I didn't realize this was such a close-knit group. Jason has always made it seem like just a bunch of colleagues. Do you work for Stellar also?" I ask Meagan.

"I don't. Just Atlas. Not all of us do, but many connections were made through the company. You sure look as though you'd fit in with us, though," she says, turning to Atlas with a bat of her lashes.

"How so?" I ask in a light tone.

She ignores my question. "Another shot!"

As she walks away to gather the drinks Atlas speaks up, "These people can be a bit much but don't let them scare you off. Take a deep breath."

I do as he says, thankful to have someone who understands how overwhelming this all is.

The second shot hits even faster than the first and the tension in my body evaporates. Meagan's body has drifted closer to mine, so close that our legs brush against each other a few times. Hers are silky smooth.

"You're so exotic looking! I love it!" Meagan twirls her fingers around my hair. "Look at her hair babe, it's beautiful. I'd kill for this volume."

"Just let her know if she's violating your personal space," Atlas laughs, "she gets a bit handsy when she's tipsy."

"Thanks. You're so sweet," I tell Meagan, trying to keep my voice from wavering, uncovering how uncomfortable I am. "Yours is gorgeous. Is that your natural color?"

She ignores my question again and continues to study my features.

"Ugh and your lips! Even with filler I can't achieve that pout." I'm used to the fetishization of my Black features, courtesy of my father, especially growing up in a town with a lack of diversity. Meagan leans in, her pursed lips aimed for mine and I swear she's about to plant a kiss on me. Before she reaches my mouth, a giggle rings out. She backs away and gets up to straddle Atlas on the barstool, her long bare legs draping over his. She cranks her neck to give me a sly grin before smooching him. Instead of closing his eyes, Atlas' gaze locks with mine. His eyes lock with mine as the lip smacking ensues and for some reason, I don't dart my focus away. Neither of us blink, but once her tongue slides into his mouth, I snap back to reality and quickly break eye contact.

Weird.

"Lula!" Cheyenne pops up out of nowhere and I'm immediately grateful. She grabs my arm and pulls me away from the makeout session. We walk past the chatter and out a pair of tall double doors that lead outside towards the back of the house.

It's quieter out here. Another thing to be grateful for. The sun has completely set now, leaving the sky a dusky blue.

"Do you know where Jason went?" I ask as she guides me.

"I'm sure he's in the other room playing poker with the rest of the competitive bastards," she says.

A glimmering pool spreads far and wide on the side of us. It must be heated, otherwise it wouldn't be quite warm enough for the woman that floats on her back.

"What a gorgeous pool. Oh—" The woman's bare breasts poke up out of the water and I look away, feeling my cheeks warm again.

"Don't mind, Clara. She has a mind of her own," Cheyenne says, chuckling. I let out a laugh too, hoping it didn't sound too fake.

Concrete pavers are strategically placed between lush green grass in a fancy diamond pattern. The kind of landscaping that takes months to complete. Nearly every section of the yard is made complete with a bed of flowers, giving the area vibrancy. The faint scent of lilacs is in the air, and I take a deep breath in.

I'd kill to live in this paradise.

"There are a few people I'd like for you to meet," Cheyenne says.

I follow her to a large cabana with sheer curtains that flow in the breeze. Multiple people sit on an outdoor sectional with drinks in hand, sharing in conversation.

"Okay, this is Rasheeda, Ellis, Wyatt and Haven," she says, pointing each one out as she introduces them, "This is Jason's wife, Lula."

I give a small wave. I recognize Haven as one of the women who was rubbing on my husband earlier. They all wave in unison.

"Come sit!" Wyatt scoots over to make room and I plant myself onto the soft cushion. Someone hands me another drink. I don't know if I need it. But I start sipping anyway.

"So, Lula, what do you do for work?" Rasheeda asks, her eyes pinned on me.

"Oh, uh. I'm just a receptionist at a dental office here in town," I say shyly.

"Good for you!" Haven shouts, "Most of us women don't have the willpower to work. I for one wouldn't be caught dead sitting at a desk all day, taking orders. But I admire the resolve." They all laugh, and I nod, unsure if I was insulted or not.

"Speak for yourself, Haven," Rasheeda says, "Some of us actually have passions that extend deeper than just lip filler and Louis Vuitton bags."

Rasheeda winks at her and Haven sticks out her tongue.

"I'm actually a professor at UCSC. Mesopotamian Studies," Rasheeda says.

"Wow. That sounds interesting," I say.

"Interesting for sure; to put it lightly. I've been studying the culture for over 20 years now. Sometimes I dive so deep I'm scared I won't make it out. I could study it for the rest of my life and never be satisfied, never feel like I have it all down." Rasheeda's tone gets more intense as her passion shines through.

Silence ensues until Wyatt, the guy with the bald head and ill-fitting khakis, pipes up. "So, Lula, has Jason filled you in on our little club?" He looks up from his glass at me. Rasheeda waves to shush him.

"Club?" I ask.

"Oh, it's just a little group we formed a few years back," Rasheeda replies.

"I'd love to hear about it," I say.

I can feel this drink hitting me hard as I try hard not to slur my words.

Wyatt continues, "It's definitely a good time. I'm not trying to start any arguments, but Jason is doing you a disservice by not filling you in. We need someone like you." He raises his eyebrows and smirks. I return the smile.

I don't know what the hell he's talking about, but the liquor is causing my head to swim, and my confusion turns into a disillusioned flattery.

His hand grazes my thigh.

"Well, I may have to have a discussion with him tonight," I say, the smile still plastered on my face.

I finish my drink as the conversation changes and turns to gossip about schoolteachers, bosses, and Pilates instructors. Wyatt's gaze keeps coming back to me. But for some reason I yearn for it.

Before long, the sky turns to a bluish-black, and the air cools, leaving a slight chill in the air.

"Sorry babe. I was just playing a game of poker in the back. Looks like you've gotten acquainted with everyone." Jason's voice startles me as he walks in our direction. I immediately scoot a bit farther from Ellis on the couch, realizing that my lowered inhibitions pulled me a little too close. Jason doesn't seem to notice, though.

"Took this fucker for all he's worth!" Calen walks up behind him and smacks him on the back, jolting Jason forward.

"You didn't tell us that your wife was so stunning, Jason," Haven says, batting her long, thick lashes.

My cheeks hurt from smiling so much tonight.

"Haven can't stand someone being prettier than her!" Calen scoffs and she gives him the middle finger.

"You ready to head out before Calen bleeds me dry?" Jason asks. I nod and stand up, swaying a little as I do so. Hurrying to him, I steady myself on his arm.

I definitely drank too much.

"Was it your plan to avoid me the entire night?" I whisper as we walk away from the group.

"I figured you'd get to know everyone better if I wasn't around. Plus, it looks like you enjoyed yourself anyway." Jason kisses the top of my head.

A man stumbles up ahead of us. I instantly recognize him as Greg Reese, the widower. I don't know how we didn't cross paths all night. From the looks of it, he must have spent the entire night glued to a bar stool. He wobbles towards the entrance as his keys jangle in his hand. We make our way back through the house and out to the car. He continues a few paces ahead of us, almost tripping into the fountain.

"There's no way he is going to try to drive, right?" I ask Jason, softly. He shrugs and I look at him, furrowing my brows. He sighs in concession.

"Hey, Greg. Let us give you a ride home, buddy!" Jason speeds up and reaches for Greg's arm. Greg whips it away.

"I'm fine!" He spits out his words.

"We really don't mind. Better to be safe than sorry, right?" I call out.

He turns around and glares at me, eyes like daggers. Maybe I shouldn't have said anything at all. He doesn't know me. The last thing I'm sure he wants is some stranger telling him what to do.

We stand together and watch as Greg gets in his Audi and speeds off, leaving a trail of exhaust in his stead.

Jason shakes his head, "I'm sure he will be fine."

As I climb into the Jeep, I try to brush off that uncomfortable encounter. The hum of the engine is the only noise that fills the car as we head towards home. I'm ready to debrief but Jason seems ready to decompress.

"So, Calen was interesting." I say, breaking the silence in the car.

"What do you mean interesting?" he asks.

"I mean, he practically grabbed my ass when you introduced us. I was surprised you didn't notice."

He turns his eyes from the road and glances my way, shaking his head. "That's Calen for you. Loves the pretty girls."

Gotta love men with no boundaries.

I roll my eyes and continue, "And I met Meagan. She was interesting too. Very… bold?" I struggle to think of the right word to describe her.

In the darkness of the car, I can't tell if this sentiment garnered a smile.

"I also heard a bit about some club you're all supposedly a part of. What's all that about?" I ask.

There's a brief pause before Jason responds.

"Those people love to talk, don't they?" He keeps his tone light, "It's nothing crazy. Just a group of some of the people that were at the party tonight. I guess a few of them started it years ago, just to get together and share philosophical views and ideas. Real deep stuff when they actually get into it. They say it is all for the betterment of mind and soul, or some sappy shit like that. Most of it goes over my head."

"How'd they rope you into it?" I ask.

"It was mostly the free drinks," he says, and we both have a fit of laughter.

"But really, Derrick convinced me that I needed to open my mind up a bit, loosen up. I was at a work function a little later than usual one night when Rasheeda showed up. Derrick called her 'an old friend'. They sat down and started talking crazy. All sorts of ancient knowledge she's into. I was intrigued and fell down the rabbit hole with them. Before I knew it, there was no crawling back out," he says, finishing with an odd noise in between a snort and a cough.

I resist the urge to nag.

Why is this the first time I'm hearing of this?

"Sounds enthralling. Who all is a part of it?" I ask.

"The folks you were sitting with tonight and a few others," he says.

"What about Greg? And… Gina?" My voice lowers at the mention of her name. Both have been on my mind since Greg drove away.

Jason's eyebrows rise, like he's questioning my curiosity.

"Uh, yeah. Them too," he says.

CHAPTER 3

Poker night was a few weeks ago. The Monday following the party, I got a Facebook message from Cheyenne.

It was so nice to meet you! You're welcome at our house any time. Thank you for coming.

-Cheyenne Wright

Since then, I haven't been invited to any of the other gatherings. Last weekend they had a wine tasting event. Jason went, but there was no invitation extended to me. I spent the night curled up on the couch with a bowl of popcorn drenched in melted butter and reality tv, my guilty pleasures. I can't say I wasn't offended. I thought maybe I'd be invited to the outings now since I'd become acquainted with everyone. A thousand thoughts went through my head. Was I too awkward? Did I make a fool of myself? Is Jason embarrassed of me? After letting the negativity fester for a few days and working myself into a frenzy, I noticed two friend requests on Facebook. One from Cheyenne and one from Meagan. These small gestures of acceptance settled my fears, and I decided that I was overreacting. I chalked up the lack of invitation to Jason just needing time with the guys.

Tonight, I get to finally have a proper evening alone with my husband in what feels like ages. He's been so busy with the company that we barely get in a few words and a kiss before bed. Today, I got home from work and shaved every square inch of my body. I probably used half of the perfume bottle spritzing my skin and hair with his favorite perfume. And I repainted both my finger and toenails in the deepest red I could find in my nail polish basket, which is his favorite color on me. He says it makes my skin color stand out.

Spaghetti Bolognese is the choice for dinner. It's the meal that Jason orders at every Italian restaurant we've ever been to. The garlic is fragrant and fills the home with a comforting scent. I'm just finishing up sprinkling the basil over the dish when keys jangle at the front door.

"Hey baby! I'm in the kitchen," I call out.

Jason walks through to the kitchen, already unbuttoning the collar of his shirt, like he always does when he gets home. There's a giddiness about him as he ruffles his dirty blonde hair.

"Good day or what?" I ask.

"Do I smell my favorite meal cooking?" he asks.

I open up the lid to the pan and bring it up to him. The steam seeps out and he inhales it. His face brightens even more.

"And this is why I love you," he says. His lips press against my forehead.

"Why don't you grab us some wine glasses and I'll plate this up for us," he says, grabbing the pan from my hands.

Jason shovels the pasta into his mouth like it's the first meal he's had all day.

"Did you not get a chance to eat lunch today?" I ask, motioning at his animalistic eating behavior.

"Sorry," he wipes the red sauce off his mouth with a napkin, "I barely had a chance to breathe today let alone eat."

"I get the company is busy, but they can't keep overworking you," I say, sipping the last few drops of the wine in my glass.

"No work talk tonight," he says.

"That's fair."

"Family talk instead," he says.

"Oh goodie." I pour us both another large glass full. We both know we need it when the conversation switches to our parents.

"My mom wants to know if we are spending Christmas with her this year. She said she would have the guest quarters made up for us."

"Do we have a choice in the matter?" I say.

"Probably not," he laughs.

By the end of our meal, the entire bottle of Pinot is gone. We are both left loose, blissful, and slightly woozy.

"I'm going to go hop in the shower. And then I want you on the bed. Clothes off," Jason says with devilish eyes. He gets up from the chair and then bends down to kiss my lips. His hand drifts to my lap and he rubs me over my pants. I push my lips harder against his and lean in, willing it to continue. He stops just as my mouth opens, leaving me wanting more.

The dishes are easy to clean. I scoop the leftovers in a container for Jason's lunch tomorrow, start the dishwasher, and turn off the lights. Once I get upstairs to the bedroom, I light a few tea light candles to set the mood, casting a faint glow across the bed. My panty and bra set are red to match my nails and I undress to reveal them. With a whiff of my wrist, I can still smell the perfume lingering.

Our bed conforms to my body as I fall onto my back. Each of my muscles relaxes as the wine continues to circulate through my bloodstream.

On the bedside table next to me, Jason's phone flashes. Once. Twice. My attention is captured, and I allow my eyes to drift over to the screen, flipping onto my belly. Two text notifications pop up, but the sender is hidden.

The shower stream still flows loudly behind the bathroom door. I don't like to snoop but curiosity gets the best of me tonight. My stomach clenches as I tap the passcode onto the screen.

The contact is Haven Emery.

Think of us tonight (; XO

I recall Haven. The cute, slender blonde from poker night. The one with perky double D's spilling over in her low-cut dress.

An incoming image struggles to load. The shower still runs. I'm running out of time. My heart thumps loudly,

The image pops up onto the screen and I gasp. I can't believe what I'm seeing. This has to be a mistake.

But the longer I stare at the phone, the more I'm certain it's no mistake. The photo before me sends vomit creeping up my throat. Three individuals, bodies entangled. And there he is, his head thrown back in ecstasy as Haven and Meagan share his dick, their tongues on his shaft. Haven manages to hold the camera up high, ensuring she catches all the right angles as she stares at the man she is pleasuring. The man that is unquestionably my husband.

I'm going to be sick. I swallow down the wine that threatens to come back up.

Questions flutter in my head. Why? When? How?

The shower stream sputters to silence.

Shit.

I swipe out of the messages and place the phone back onto the table. There are so many ways to handle this. But I can't settle on one now. Too many emotions. And my mind is too foggy.

With a hard puff, I blow out the candles. Needing the safety of the dark.

When Jason steps out of the bathroom, his silhouette is illuminated by the little bit of moonlight shining through the curtains. His towel drops to the floor as he makes his way over to the bed. Feeling for my body, he grabs at my waist, pulling me towards the edge of the bed.

"Why are these still on?" he asks as he tears off my panties, throwing them off to the side. Then I'm bent over the bed, face pressing into the comforter as he shoves himself inside me from behind. With each stroke, my stream of tears gets heavier and heavier.

I can't control it anymore and my sobs become audible, muffled only slightly by the blanket.

"What's wrong? Am I being too rough?" he asks, whipping me around. His blue eyes are filled with such concern, such care.

All I can muster up the strength to do is point to his phone.

"Is it my mom?" he asks.

His face twists in terror and he rushes over to the bedside table. As he swipes, searching through, it doesn't take long for him to realize what I saw. There is a click, and the phone goes dark. It takes a few moments for Jason to look up at me.

"Lula. Baby," he pleads, a slight whine in his tone.

"No! You don't get to call me that!" I scream so loud it echoes off the walls.

"Lu, you don't understand." He's back over, reaching for my hand, but I scoot to the opposite side of the bed, creating distance from the disgust in front of me.

"How many women have you fucked since we got married?" Saliva flies from my mouth.

"I haven't—"

I cut him off. "So, you never actually fucked them?"

"I mean—"

"How could you do this to me, Jason? I look so stupid!" My throat burns as I overexert my vocal cords.

"You don't look stupid. There's so much more to it than what you're thinking. Just relax and let me explain," he says.

"Relax?" I scoff.

My breath is heavy as my sadness turns to a hot rage, my tears drying up in streaks on my cheeks.

"Baby, I know this feels like a betrayal but that's just not it. It's purely spiritual," he says, hands outstretched.

"Oh, don't give me any of that bullshit! Is this why you never invite me to hang out with you and your friends? It's just a big free for all?" I ask.

"You have it all wrong. I was going to tell you once I felt you were open to it. You're framing this all wrong," he says, his tone soft but firm.

I shake my head at the stupidity. "Tell me then, Jason. How should I be framing it?"

I want to strangle him. To knock some sense into him. This isn't the man I know. This isn't the man that I love, the man that loves me.

"There is a whole new way of existing, Lula. And it's magical. You just have to open your mind and trust me." He inches closer to me on the bed.

"Your 'whole new way of existing' is fucking half of the women in Garden Valley? You sound insane, Jason! I'm not as gullible as you think I am."

"It's a form of worship. An ancient tradition the club has been practicing for some time now," he says, finally grabbing a hold of my hands.

"Oh," I rip my hands from his grasp, "so this is the enthralling talk you and Rasheeda had that night at Derrick's? These are the 'rabbit holes' you fell into?" I throw up aggressive air quotes with my fingers.

He shakes his head vigorously. A man trying to convince himself that he didn't commit the most egregious sin. "Sexual pleasure shouldn't have limits, Lu.

"Who are you?" I ask, my voice now low.

"I'm the man you married. I'm sorry if it was all a little jarring for you, but none of it was meant to hurt you. I just need you to hear me out."

I grab a t-shirt from my drawers and pull it over my head. Crawling under the covers, I bury myself away from it all. It feels like I'm in a bad dream. A bad dream that I can't rouse myself out of. Jason's presence lingers on the edge of the bed. The room envelopes in quiet, my ears only registering the soft hum of the air conditioning circulating through our home.

After a few minutes, Jason moves to kneel on the floor beside me, his face only inches from mine underneath the covers.

"Don't allow this to break us," he says.

I let him peel the covers back to expose my head.

"What are you asking me to do, Jason? Allow you to continue on this ride of infidelity?" I can barely speak between my pitiful whimpers. The sorrow has started again as the anger dissipates.

"I'm asking you to take this jump with me. When have you ever stepped outside of your comfort zone, Lula?"

The question feels like a sharp stab to my side. I know he's right. But this doesn't seem fair.

My deep breaths turn shallow, and I struggle to get in enough air. A suffocating grip overtakes me and I'm unable to shake it. I whip the blankets off and jump out of bed. Jason sits on the carpet with his back against the bed, head hanging down like a sad puppy. He lifts his head with puzzled eyes as I pull on my pants. He doesn't have time to ask me questions before I rush down the stairs to our entryway, throw on my worn sneakers and head out the front door. I haven't run in months, not since we moved in, but it's the only thing that feels right at the moment.

"Lula?" Jason's voice travels from behind the door. I don't answer. I don't turn around.

My feet hit the blacktop and take off down the road, with no thought of direction.

Am I going to let this break us? Can I stand to lose him?

The streets are empty. Only a few houses are lit, most dark with curtains drawn. I'm supposed to be in bed right now too. Drifting off in a boozy, satisfied slumber.

I sprint, as fast as my legs can take me.

My pace continues to pick up until my lungs are on fire and I feel like I'm sucking in air through a straw.

I couldn't even say how far I've gone, but nothing looks familiar anymore.

Out of breath, I stop and choose a spot on a curb in front of an old Victorian house to sit. Gulps of the fresh air slow my breathing along with the beat of my heart. A dog barks in the distance, probably aware of my unfamiliar presence.

Images of women all over Jason's body flash in my head. His cock in their mouth. His moans as he reaches the climax. I shudder, feeling sick all over again. The anticipatory, one-sided dialogue following my mother's discovery of his infidelity rings through my ears.

He's making you out to be the fool. The man doesn't love you. Have some self-respect and leave.

She's right, though. I can't allow this to continue. I can't sit by and allow myself to be a joke, the laughingstock of his so-called "club". No matter how much I love him.

I have to let him go.

With this clarity, I make my way back home. But this time, I walk. I contemplate what I will say to him when I return. I teeter between graceful and pacific and harsh and enraged. In the end, I think I'll settle for something in the middle.

When I open the front door, Jason is the first thing I see.

"Lula, I know you're angry but it's not safe to be roaming the streets at night. I've been worried sick." His tone is stern.

I ignore the comment and throw my sweaty shoes behind me, letting them hit the wall.

As I walk back up the stairs, Jason trails behind me. Once we reach the bedroom, I turn to face him. This is my chance to take charge. To stand my ground.

My mouth opens up to speak, but as I look in his eyes all of the negative emotions fade away.

He stares at me. Waiting for me to react. Waiting for all of the built-up emotions to explode out of me. But I can't bring myself to say a word.

Numb and confused, I grab his hand, pulling him to the bed. His clothes come off first, then my own. My body ends up on top of his and I position myself over his groin, allowing the tears to flow again as he penetrates me.

I'm making a mistake. I just know it.

"Come on this journey with me." His whisper tickles my ear as he pushes further into me.

It was at this moment that all logic flew out the window. It was at this moment that I had the craziest thought. Maybe this is it. Maybe this is my shot to "Vivez la vie pleinement".

CHAPTER 4

I spent a few days giving Jason the silent treatment. He came home with flowers three days in a row. Red roses on the first day, yellow tulips the second, and purple orchids on the third. Each day he has reassured me that everything is going to be okay, that none of this is going to change us and the life that we have built. Since the day I uncovered his secret, I've visited the websites of 22 local divorce attorneys. I even filled my information out in the "contact me" box of a woman with numerous five-star reviews who looked promising. But when she phoned the next day, I declined the call. By the fifth day, I realized all of this feigning anger was pointless. I'm not angry. Yes, I'm hurt and shocked, but there isn't fury anymore. More than anything, I want to get back to the way we were before I ever opened that text. The way I felt when he'd walk into a room or kiss me on the forehead. I almost regret even snooping to begin with. Naive? For sure. Pathetic? Probably.

At first, I looked for ways to make sense of and justify his behavior. When we first started dating, Jason would lament about his father and their damaged relationship that worsened right up until his dad died of brain cancer. His father was a complicated man, or at least that's what he used to tell me. His past was full of sin, greed, and debauchery. "His proclivities for young men always put a wedge between us," Jason had said. I didn't push any more on the subject. I figured it was better I didn't know the dark side of my husband's parentage.

Is this what has led Jason to dabble in these morally questionable practices? Is he yearning to better understand his late father?

After trying to psychoanalyze my husband, I turned my inquisition inward.

Am I doing this for myself? Or am I forcing myself because the only other alternative is losing my husband? I still can't quite answer that. But regardless, I know that I'm ready for a little more excitement in my life.

I've spent too much of my life stagnant. Average and predictable. Once, not too many years back, I passed up a promotion at Aspen Dental. From lowly Receptionist to Head of Sales and Marketing. I suppose I wasn't fully offered the position, but the owner made it entirely clear that she'd like me to apply and that I was "an excellent candidate for the position". The night before my interview I laid in bed and contemplated my life as Lula, the Head of Sales and Marketing at Aspen Dental. Sure, it was an extra $3 an hour. Sure, it came with a greater sense of respect within the company. And sure, it would add more *pizazz* to my resume. But was any of this worth the irrevocable change that would ensue? Ultimately, I decided it wasn't. I suppose you could call me lazy, boring, or timid. My mom had quite a few "nicer" adjectives that stick with me. But I guess it has always just been simpler to stick with what I know. And herein lies the problem. No one should die with the word "simple" chiseled into their gravestone.

"Ready, baby?" Jason walks out of the bedroom rubbing his wrists together and the seductive scent of bergamot and amber fills the air. The smell comforts me and the butterflies swimming around in my belly settle just a bit.

"Same people as before, right?" I ask. I want to be sure I'm not going to be blindsided tonight.

"Same people, same vibe, just a bit more excitement," he says. He pulls me in and kisses my nose, something he used to do when we first started dating.

I caved. And tonight, I've agreed to join him for a meeting with the club. For a meeting that includes women that I have every right to smack across the face. I don't know exactly what I'm doing. But I decided to go with the flow. To let life, let my husband take the reins and guide me.

He picked out my outfit for tonight. My ensemble better resembled Mother Theresa at the poker night when compared to what I've got on now.

He got home from work last night with a white box tied with red, satin ribbon. The box contained pink tissue paper that revealed a black, lacey catsuit. It looked so sheer that I could see my fingers through it.

"For tomorrow," he had said with a smirk on his face.

I was hesitant at first. Told him that I'd look more like a hooker than a sexy housewife, but he insisted. Insisted that I'd look amazing in it and that it would give me confidence to embrace this new experience.

After sucking in and slowly inching it up my body, I stare at my reflection in the bathroom mirror. He's right. I do look good. The lace hugs my slender curves just right. But the confidence is still wavering. Especially considering the fact that I'm going to have to face the two women who had their way with my husband.

"I can't wait to get you out of this tonight." Jason slaps my ass. "I'll meet you in the car," he says as he heads out of the bedroom.

I've googled "orgy", "sex party", "swingers", and just about a hundred other related terms to try and prepare myself for what I might be witnessing tonight. I asked Jason so many questions, but he was pretty tight lipped. Supposedly secrecy is all part of the experience. "You'll see soon enough. Just relax and enjoy the experience," he said.

But he knows just as much as anyone that I don't do well with the unknown.

I take one last look at myself, flip my waves to the side to add more volume to my hair, and add extra gloss to my lips, perfecting my pout. A deep sigh relieves pressure from my chest.

You'll never be as pretty as you are right now.

Words from my favorite reality dating show ring through my head. I think I've peaked. It's only downhill from here.

When I get into the car, Jason has a mini bottle of Grey Goose for me.

"For your nerves," he says and hands it over. I chug it and pray for its numbing effects.

As the tires crunch on the gravel out the driveway of our home, I make a point not to look back and yearn for the comfort of home. Oddly enough, we take a different route than usual, passing the old Victorian house that I came across on the night of my run. I try to shake the feeling that I should have done things differently when I got home that night. Should have packed up my things and left. It's too late for that now, though.

After a solid twenty minutes on the road, I'm confused as we pass landmarks that I don't recognize.

"Why are you taking a different route to Derrick and Cheyenne's?" I ask.

"Oh, we aren't going to Derrick's. They wanted a more private space for tonight," he says.

"How does it get any more private than their 3,600 square foot villa?" I laugh.

"We just don't like to deal with any constraints. Plus, you're able to clear your head a little more out here." He gestures to the barren landscape in front of us. Nothing but dirt and sparse brush for miles.

"Yeah, if you aren't axe murdered first," I reply.

I understand the "out here" sentiment as we turn onto a road that looks like it's from a scene in *The Hills Have Eyes*. There is no one out here to hear you scream. No houses, no sign of civilization. There aren't even streetlights to guide your way.

"Oh stop. It's perfectly safe out here," he says.

I resist the urge to pester him with questions throughout the drive and our banter is uncomfortably mundane. Neither of us want to bring up the events that are about to transpire.

Before long, we pull into a long driveway that pops up out of nowhere. Jason turns on his high beams and I can make out a log cabin in the distance, which looks spacious enough to sleep multiple families. The property could easily be missed by passersby in the dark as there is barely any light shining through the covered windows.

We park at a patch of concrete on the property, next to a band of luxury vehicles. I recognize a few from the poker night.

I point out a pearlescent BMW. "Let's trade in my Fusion for one of those."

Jason chuckles. "Yeah, once my paycheck starts looking a little more like Haven's does," he says.

I cringe at the mention of her name. Of course, that's the car she drives. Bile rises in my throat, and I swallow it back down.

The click from Jason's belt unbuckling fills me with dread. One step closer to walking through the door to the unknown.

We get out of the car and walk the long pathway to the cabin. As summer gets closer, the nights turn warmer, no longer holding a striking chill. The area is silent aside for the sound of our feet crunching on the dirt path. My heels dig into the earth. The combination of my footwear, the terrain, and the vodka send me tumbling down into the gravel.

"Woah, there," Jason says as he catches my fall.

"Sorry. I didn't realize we'd be out in BFE," I say, and we both laugh, breaking the calming silence in the dark night.

When we reach the door to the cabin, it doesn't appear any different from any other rustic home I've ever been to. A brown slab of wood with a white frame and a metal knob—just like any other door. So why does it feel like it may as well be the entrance to hell?

"You ready?" Jason asks.

I suck in a deep breath and pull out another vodka mini bottle I stuffed in my purse before we left the house. I chug it before turning to face Jason.

"Let's go," I say.

The door is unlocked. It opens up to a dimly, warm lit room. Mood lighting, I assume. The soft beat of an instrumental version of a song that I can't quite recall the name of fills the room and this, combined with the lack of lighting, gives me a mild sense of comfortability, and eases the tightness in my stomach.

"Where is everyone?" I whisper. My whisper is more like a faint breath, but Jason hears me anyway.

The front room is bare aside from a couple of couches, a coffee table and one of those fancy electric fireplaces lit with a purple hue.

"Just follow me." Jason's voice is also a whisper. He grabs my hand and as we walk farther into the house, he uses his thumb to trace circles around my sweaty palm in attempts to ease my tension.

I wonder if he can feel my pulse quickening through my hand.

The cabin looks so minuscule from the outside but as we creep down the corridor past the front room, I'm getting that feeling you have in a dream. When the hallway appears to stretch for miles, and you relentlessly follow with no end in sight.

Maybe that shot is really kicking in.

We move closer to a closed door at the end of the hall with deep orange light shining underneath the crack.

"Babe. Wait," I say. I stop and let go of his warm grasp.

Jason's eyes are pleading. He knows how deep my hesitation runs, but he silently begs me not to shut this down.

"I just don't want to be blindsided. Promise me something," I say.

"Lula."

"Please," I beg.

"Alright. What do you need?" he asks. His voice is calm, reassuring, and he grasps my hand again.

"No sex. I—" My voice stammers as a vision of my husband's cock in Haven's mouth swirls in my mind. "I'm just not quite there yet," I say.

Jason nods and squeezes my palm. "We are in this together," he says.

And with that, hand in hand, we open the door at the end of the hall and walk through.

CHAPTER 5

As the door creeps open, the rich smell of frankincense is released. It instantly makes me think of my mom and the forever burning of incense in her home. I don't hate it, but I don't love it either. The aroma smacks me in the face along with a thick cloud of smoke that pervades the dimly lit room. I hold a cough in my lungs that threatens to escape.

"The fog provides a little more discretion. It won't bother you for long," Jason mutters.

The room is made maneuverable by two smoked glass light fixtures hanging on the front and back walls. Still, the deep amber lighting makes it hard to perceive anything except for what's in front of you. The room appears to be about the size of four primary bedrooms put together. Much too big to be a living room. More like some type of large rec room. Maybe the owner tore a few walls down in the cabin to make one large space. Either way, it seems to serve a purpose. My ears perk up at the faint whispers filtering in from just about every corner. Tri-panel room partitions are set up alongside the outer walls, hiding the club members behind them, however the occasional silhouette comes in and out of focus through the fog that appears to be getting only more dense.

"J, it's good to see you. Glad to see you're bringing around your other half," a voice says. A man with a short, but muscular build, and a well-groomed beard appears from a partition on the side of the room. I recognize him as Ellis from the other night. His shirt is completely unbuttoned, and his fly unzipped.

"I guess I just couldn't keep her locked away," Jason says.

I give a wave but instead of returning one, Ellis walks over and pulls me into a tight hug. He's sticky from sweat but the sour mixes well with the intoxicating woodsy musk soaked into his skin.

"It's nice to see you again," he says, releasing me from his embrace.

"Ellis!" a girlish voice yells out from the same direction. As the petite woman emerges from the fog, I remember the topless chest from the pool at Derrick and Cheyenne's house. The name Clara rings through my head. Her breasts are exposed again tonight, with only heart shaped pasties to cover her nipples. Her bottom half is clad in a lacey thong and garter belt.

"Get back here," Clara says as she grabs Ellis's waist and pulls him back to the dark abyss, giving us a wink as she does so.

"Are they a couple?" I ask Jason.

"Nah. Ellis couldn't handle a commitment like that to save his life. But Clara seems to have staked her claim."

Soft giggles emanate from afar. I yearn to be Clara. Seemingly carefree, comfortable in her skin, and vibrant. She seems to be the epitome of this world. Everything that Jason hopes I'll be.

I'm led to a table filled with platters of an assortment of berries, decadent pastries, glasses of wine, and a silver tray filled with small paper cups, each containing tiny, bright pink pills.

Jason grabs two cups and hands me one, without an explanation. Inside, I notice the pill has been stamped with a smiley face. My brows furrow. I may be naive, but I'm not stupid. Jason ignores my hesitation. He takes the pill from his cup and presses it to my lips. I shake my head, keeping my lips pressed together.

He sticks the pill on his tongue instead and kisses me. When my mouth opens, his tongue swirls around mine. The pill disintegrates as our saliva mixes.

What did I just take? Could it have been laced with anything?

A smirk brandishes his face, and he reaches down to smack my ass.

"I've got to go find Calen. He owes me some money," Jason says.

"You're leaving me?" I ask, panic rising in my throat.

"I'll only be a minute, I promise."

That's what you said last time.

He gives me his usual kiss on the forehead and walks back towards the door we just came through. I'm left to stand here alone like an idiot. This experience didn't come with an instruction manual. I need Jason to guide me through this.

Goosebumps scatter throughout my skin and I fold my arms across my chest. The strawberries look perfectly ripe, but my stomach is too queasy to eat anything.

"I've been waiting to touch this ass ever since it took a seat next to me at poker night." I jump at the voice that creeps up out of nowhere and as I whip around to see who it is, Wyatt grabs a handful off my ass, squeezing it painfully tight.

"It's Lula, right?" he asks, his breath reeking of cheese.

"Yes, I'm Lula." I take a step backwards from him, knocking into the table.

"Woah. Careful," he says and attempts to grab my hand.

Instead pull it away and make my revulsion by tucking my hair behind my ear.

"Sorry. I'd better find Jason," I say and scurry off in the opposite direction, rubbing my sweaty palms off on the lacey fabric glued to my thighs. My heart races as though I'm walking the plank to my death. I don't know where I'm going, but I have no desire to go any farther with Wyatt.

I go through the middle of the room, passing all the partitions, as I wander aimlessly. My eyes threaten to wander as well, but I keep them focused straight ahead. I'm sure that not all swingers are voyeurs.

"Gah!"

The noise stops me dead in my tracks and I turn to see who made the painful cry. Squinting to my left, my eyes focus on a man. It only takes seconds to realize that he is completely nude, and only a few more seconds to realize that the cry wasn't in pain, but in pleasure. Greg Reese breathes heavily, as his dripping penis hangs down between his legs. Our gazes meet.

"I'm so sorry," I say and take bigger strides towards the back of the room, cheeks on fire.

None of this is what I signed up for. I think this was a mistake.

A tall figure stands in the back of the room, too still to be human. I may have found my only solace. As I near, the smoke lessens, and the life-size bronze statue of a voluptuous woman comes into view. She is surrounded by candles, which allows the metal to give off a glistening shimmer. It's captivating. Her breasts protrude from the body and the wings that flank her sides accentuate her slim waist and broad hips. She stands atop a lion, her head adorned with an 8-point star. My hand reaches out to touch her, but I pull back when someone appears next to me without warning.

"Isn't she absolutely magnificent?" Rasheeda asks, staring up at the statue.

"She is," I say.

"I paid a pretty penny to have her handcrafted." There is pride in her voice.

"Who is she?" I ask.

"She's the goddess, the warrior, the embodiment of love. She's Inanna. Stick around and you'll come to know her like we do," she says.

Rasheeda places her hand on my shoulder and leans in close, her whispering breath hot on my ear. "She doesn't mind if you touch her. She actually prefers it."

Her voice sends shivers down my spine and as Rasheeda walks away, I reach my hand out again and cup the statue's right breast. It's cold but perfectly shaped.

I've never done drugs before. Unless you count alcohol or the few puffs of weed I tried with an old boyfriend in college. But this is different. Much, much different. That little pill has definitely kicked in.

My other hand goes out to trace along Inanna's other breast. I can't seem to control my hands as they rub the smooth mounds. Almost instinctively, I press my whole body up against hers, my cheek gliding along her chest. The metal cools the fire that has started burning in my body and a tear rolls down my cheek.

She's just so beautiful. So perfectly crafted.

My lips brush over the subtle bulge of her lower stomach and I feel my tongue connecting with the slight indent of her belly button. My taste buds tingle with a bitter metallic taste. My tongue begins to travel farther down when I'm pulled away by smooth fingers.

"So, I see you've met Inanna."

I whip around as Atlas' lips curve up to the left in a sinful smirk. I don't know how everyone keeps creeping up on me without my noticing.

"I was hoping I'd see you again," he says.

I can't bring myself to respond. My gaze is glued to the suppleness of his face. The hairs on his cheeks have been shaved down so precisely, leaving baby bottom smooth skin. Without permission, my hand reaches up and strokes it, my thumb softly pinching the apples. My eyes travel up to his and they stare directly into mine, their dark chocolate hue radiating in the low amber lighting.

I want to tell him how captivating his eyes are. The way the different shades of brown all melt into one, magnificent, solid color. The words don't form in my mouth, though. As our faces move closer together, it's like our minds are meshing into one. I don't need to tell him. He already knows exactly what I was going to say.

Our lips connect and pressure builds up in every inch of my body. As he opens his mouth wider, I taste him. A swirling combination of mint and sweet saliva fills my tongue as I move my way through every section of his mouth.

His fingers wrap around the waves in my hair and the slight tug emanates through my scalp. My fingers begin to trace the buttons on his shirt and before I know it they are all undone, leaving his abdomen exposed.

The ridges of his muscles are firm underneath my hands. Each ab seems to be perfectly carved.

Jason's stomach doesn't have this much definition.

The thought fills me with desire. My hand drops down to tug at his waistband until his hand stops me.

"What's wrong?" I ask.

"You're sure you want to do this?" he asks. His light tone is now more intense.

"Why not?" I shrug my shoulders and grab at his waistband again to pull him closer.

I want this. I want this experience. I *need* it.

Maybe it will make up for all of the missed opportunities throughout my lifetime.

As his lips sink back into mine, my hand lowers into his pants. His warmth sends heat waves through me.

"Tell me what you want," he says.

"I want you. I want you inside of me," I say, my voice barely above a whisper.

Atlas doesn't think twice. He leads me to a loveseat behind one of the partitions. The seclusion and lack of light lends to a warm sense of comfort.

"I need to feel all of you. Every single inch," he says.

His fingers hook around the lace that covers my shoulders and as he pulls down, I yank out my arms and allow the rest to slide off my body, dropping the catsuit to the floor. I move toward the couch, but he shakes his head.

"Those need to go too," he says.

Tingles prickle throughout me as his eyes trace the length of my body.

As he stares, I undo my bra and throw my panties to the floor. The tingling has been replaced with a burning as he examines my fully naked body, like I'm straight out of a million-dollar painting.

"Is that better?" I ask in a seductive voice that doesn't quite sound like me at all.

Before I can blink, I'm thrown onto the loveseat. The smooth velvet caresses my skin. I slide my legs up and down the fabric.

Atlas kneels onto the couch. He grabs both of my legs and pulls me into his waist. His fingertips dig into my thighs.

A deep moan can be heard from across the room. Atlas' mouth curves up into that same smile again.

"You hear that?" he asks.

I nod as he pushes himself against me. His slacks rub on my bare lips.

"I want you to be even louder," he demands.

Before I respond his pants are down and his dick bounces out. He slides inside of me with zero resistance. A groan surfaces from deep within me.

"There you go, baby. Let them hear you," he says, letting out a soft groan of his own.

I push air through my vocal cords and howl in pleasure. My toes curl at the sounds flowing from my mouth. I'm stretched wider as his erection strengthens. With each motion, he seems to grow, filling me up. My own fluids leak out, causing a cold puddle on the velvet beneath me. If I've ever been this wet before, I don't remember it now.

"Holy shit, you're soaked," he says, eyes wide.

"It's just so good," I whine.

"Get on your hands and knees," he commands.

My palms plant onto the couch. Atlas presses his lips down my lower back until he gets to my ass. I resist a shriek as his teeth clamp down, sending a wave of pain through my backside. He grabs my hips and slides back inside of me. His strokes are slow, as if he's savoring every inch of my insides. I tighten my muscles and grip him, never wanting to let him go.

With each stroke he reaches deeper and deeper and soon my cervix is screaming for a break. I realize that my own moans have become ear piercing as he pulls out of me, leaving me empty.

"What's all this commotion?" A voice breaks my trance.

It's Meagan. Atlas' wife.

I bolt upright and cover my exposed body with my knees at my chest. Shame nags at the back of my mind.

"Don't be shy," she says. "Stick out your tongue."

I do as I'm told, and she puts something tiny and bitter in my mouth.

I scoot as far as possible to the side, giving the couple space. Meagan sits in between us, turns to Atlas, and grabs his face. Her lacey red bra and thong hug her just right. Their eyes flutter in my direction before they shove their faces together, his hand tugging at her auburn hair.

Her scent wafts over to me and I breathe in deeply. A spicy vanilla.

"Join us, Lula," she says in between kisses.

Meagan rubs her hand on my thigh, and I allow my knees to fall, regaining a sense of comfortability. Her hand is soft, and I want more of it.

I grab it off my thigh and spread my legs. Their kisses get louder and more intense as I lean back and rub myself with her palm, moving her warm fingertips up and down. Up and down. Up and down.

Until the world around me starts to blur. And everything goes black.

"Lula."

My vision clears. Jason, shirtless and hair tousled, lays in bed next to me.

I look around and squint at the bright sunshine that seeps through the curtains. "We're home?" I ask. I'm shocked to see my bedroom. And to feel my bed sheets surrounding me.

"Of course, we are. Where else would we be?"

"I just don't…" I rack my brain for memories of last night. Images start to flood, and I shudder at the thoughts. I sit up and pull the blankets around me as if they can hide me from the shame of my choices.

"You were really tired. That place can do some weird shit to you if you aren't careful. Do you remember any of your time last night?" he asks.

"Some," I say. Which is the truth. I don't remember all of it. And the parts I do remember, I can't take the time to process right now.

He sits upright and pulls me close. His skin smells clean, like he just got out of the shower.

"Jason, I—," my voice falters. As last night's events start to reemerge in my mind, guilt sets in.

"Babe. We don't have to talk about it," he says. His hand caresses my hair as my head rests on his chest. "Last night was all about you letting loose and having fun. About you exploring and embracing pleasure. The way it was meant to be. I would never fault you for that, Lu."

Pleasure. Atlas. He made me feel like I was the only woman in the room. That much I can remember.

Jason lifts my chin.

"I had sex with another man last night, Jason." My tone is soft, timid. I search his face for anger, sadness, revulsion, any kind of emotion. I did what I asked him not to do. He should be upset with me but he's a blank slate.

"I know. I heard," he says.

My vision starts to blur again as tears well up in my eyes.

I took things too far. Was it the pills?

You know better than to blame your actions on a drug, Lula.

Jason's brows furrow and he grabs my cheeks, pulling me into a kiss that feels as if it lasts minutes. The tears flow down my face but our faces don't part.

"You were beautiful last night, Lu. You were the real you." His breath tickles my lips.

Before I can speak, he lays me back down on the bed and leans over.

"I am so in love with you, Lula Jane."

His kisses graze my entire body, starting from my forehead. Once he reaches my chest, he pulls off my t-shirt and continues down my breasts and to my belly. I try not to squirm as my overstimulated skin is tickled by his lips. His mouth grazes below my stomach and my night shorts are thrown across the room. He plants the longest kiss on my vulva, heating my body from within.

"I want you inside of me," I say, echoing my words from last night, but in a different place, with a different man.

We make love for close to an hour. And it's more beautiful than it has ever been.

CHAPTER 6

Gina Reese: 2 Months Before Death

Greg sat me down again today to talk. For what feels like the millionth time. He told me he's done. I told him I'm not. We are in too deep.

The club isn't something you can just quit. It's not a subscription to cancel. It's a lifetime membership.

He makes it sound so easy. To let go of all those bonds and connections. To let go of the freedom that's so rightfully ours.

This isn't the first time we have had this talk. Yet he seemed more insistent this time. I wince as I think back to his fist slamming against the dining room table, the dishes rattling.

He didn't see how depressed I was before devoting my spirit and body to Inanna and to this club. He didn't see my swollen eyes after spending night after night weeping into my pillow so as not to wake him. I'd have to cover up the darkness with makeup in the mornings before going off to work a 9-5 for barely over minimum wage (just enough to put the kids into daycare) and face the day with the most strained smile I could muster.

It was torture. I couldn't live another day like that again. I'd rather be dead.

I knew from the beginning that Greg was only in it for the sex. That would entice any man. But I see the way the girls look at Greg. It isn't the same way they look at the other men. And I think he's beginning to notice that too. Most of the time he's just *there*. And he's jealous. I thought after months of exposure to this new life he would mellow out, but it seems as if he hasn't.

He can't keep me all to himself. They wouldn't let him even if he tried.

CHAPTER 7

Jason and I have made love every night since the party. I let go of my guilt and decided that if it's going to make my marriage stronger, then I'm willing to fully dive in. He's never been more gentle, more passionate, and more obsessed with me. We didn't talk much about our time there. I didn't ask him what he had been up to that night. But I don't think either of us need to know. We got the release we needed and that's all that matters.

Porn Hub has become the most visited site on my browser. If these parties are to be a regular thing, I want to be sure that I'm experienced enough. Meagan was the first girl I've ever been intimate with. The drugs made me daring, but sober Lula needs some guidance.

We sit at the dinner table tonight with bowls of French onion soup and the red roses Jason had delivered to my work this morning as our centerpiece.

"How was work?" I ask.

"Shit," he says. "I'm tired of not being taken seriously."

"You only made partner a few months ago, babe. Your time will come."

"I've proven myself time and time again. Derrick fucks around all day while I bust my ass and he's making over triple what I'm making." Jason's voice rises. I don't think he realizes how hard he's gripping the spoon. His fist is white.

I stay silent and continue sipping my soup. Unsure of how to make it any better.

"If only everyone knew how the Wrights really made their fortune," he adds.

"What do you mean?" I ask.

"Never mind," he says, finally letting his spoon clank back onto the table.

I always knew that Jason was a bit jealous of Derrick's success, but I didn't think there was any animosity between them. Derrick is the whole reason Jason was promoted in the first place.

My husband has always been an overachiever. His father drilled it into him at a young age. For better or for worse, it made him who he is today. He won't be satisfied until he's at the very top. It is one of the things that I love about him. I often wish that I had the same drive.

I get up and grab a bottle of red wine from the fridge and pour us each a glass. Malbec is too dry for my liking, I much prefer sweet, but Jason loves it, and I can sacrifice for tonight.

"For your tension," I say as I hold my glass up and take a sip. He does the same and I finally get a smile out of him.

"Enough about me. How was your day at work?" he asks.

"Utterly uneventful," I say.

"Well let's change the subject to something more eventful then. Initiation night." His eyes glisten.

The wine almost flies out my nose as I chuckle. "Initiation night?"

"It sounds silly, but Rasheeda takes this stuff very seriously, as do most of the other members. You'll swear your devotion, prove your loyalty. She loves her rituals."

"It sounds extremely silly. You participated in this?"

"I did. It was mind opening. *Soul* seducing," his face stays straight, "It drew me into the club, has kept me committed. Purpose is an enigma. So when you find something that provides you some sense of it, you hang on tight and refuse to let go."

I find myself staring at him with my mouth agape and quickly pick up my jaw. How was all of this was happening completely unbeknownst to me. Why have we never been able to reach these depths in our discussion before. My pride attempts to take over. He's *my* husband. As his wife, I deserve to know all the intimate corners of his mind, all the fleeting thoughts and the burning questions. I fight the urge to turn this into a fight.

"If I'm being honest, it kind of sounds like a cult," I say, circling my finger around the top of my glass.

Jason raises his glass now. "Well, what's so bad about that?"

It's initiation night.

I feel stupid. This all feels stupid.

But Jason has stressed the importance of this night, so I'm going to try to bite my tongue and play along.

He says it's at the same cabin from the last party, which makes me feel a bit uneasy. I spent all day at work trying not to vent to my coworkers about it. We aren't close, but I would have liked to have gotten it off my chest. I also thought about calling my childhood friend, Macy. But she would have told me I'm batshit crazy and would've probably called my mom or gotten on the next flight to come see me. I also don't think this is something Jason wants me discussing with others. He has made it very clear that this is an exclusive club and that the group prides themselves on privacy. And I don't blame them. The thought of my boss or my grandma finding out that I've been experimenting with random men and women at the whim of my husband makes me want to melt into the ground.

I honestly don't know whether to cringe at the thoughts of that night or to relish in them. As uneasy as I am, I'm also excited. I loved the way I felt seen, sexy, and worshiped. And I can't deny that I'm looking forward to seeing Atlas again.

Jason asked me to wear red tonight.

The dress is long, form fitting, and satin. I look like I'm going to some sort of red-carpet event. I'm not used to dressing up. My version of fancy is a sundress on Easter Sunday. But the red does complement my bronze skin. I pair it with a red lip and sleek, straightened hair, something that I don't usually take the time to do. A short, gold chain with a dainty rose pendant adorns my neck. Attention is drawn to my breasts where the stem of the rose ends. My head is held high with an air of confidence. I usually prefer to be out of the limelight but tonight there is a burning desire to be seen.

"You are the most beautiful girl in the world."

Jason twirls me around and pulls me into a kiss. He looks phenomenal. Unlike me, Jason is used to dressing up. He spent his young adulthood at cocktail parties and company dinners. Even in his youth he was expected to look nice for church and his family's many formal events. I guess that's a given when you come from money. You always have to play the part.

He told me once that his mom waxed his unibrow at just a year old. Couldn't have a hair out of place. It makes me happy that he moved away from her, which is something she will always despise me for. She'd much rather have him in a house right next door to her, at a fingertips reach.

On the other hand, my mother would let me out of the house in a sundress and snow boots in the heat of the summer, my unbrushed hair flowing in the breeze. As long as I felt comfortable, she had no qualms, no matter what events we were attending. It's not like we ever went anywhere fancy anyways. We didn't have the money, especially with my dad being months behind in child support payments.

It's crazy how two people can be raised so differently.

His red button up makes his steel, blue eyes pop. I stare into them with longing for him to remember me, the way I am now, the way we are now, before we go on this crazy adventure together.

"Just allow your mind to open tonight, okay?" he says, more of a command than a question.

CHAPTER 8

Gina Reese: 6 Weeks Before Death

The more Greg pesters me about leaving, the more I think back to our initiation night. Together. I had never seen him more excited. Not even when our children were born. Pussy and painkillers have always been his definition of a good time. He heard that these ran rampant throughout the club. Greg wasn't the only one who was excited, though. I needed a change in my life. I needed the dark cloud above my head to stop following me around every second of the day. Rasheeda promised me a different life. I'd give anything for that promise to be fulfilled.

We took the oath to Inanna without much thought about what that actually meant. I was born and raised Methodist. The act of taking the oath could be considered sacrilege in the eyes of my parents. And I won't sit here and say I wasn't a believer because it's not the truth. The Methodist in my blood ran strong and seeped into many avenues of my life. My kids prayed every night and the sentiment "Oh my God" always made me cringe. In the grander scheme of things, the oath was a risky move. I definitely didn't know the extent to which my life would change.

I know now, though. That night I gave my soul. Not to Inanna, not to some distant Christian god, but to myself. I'm in control of my pleasure, my fortune, my morality. And that's what this club is all about. To move away from the restrictions of society and indulge the way we were meant to.

Greg couldn't have cared less about the meaning behind it all. To this day I don't think he ever did. He has given his blood but nothing else worthwhile to this club. It makes sense why he feels he can so easily split. But he obviously didn't read the fine print.

Once you free your soul, there's no getting it back.

CHAPTER 9

We drive down the same barren road as before. This time, there's no conversation. Jason eyes the road the entire time, clenching the steering wheel with what appears to be all his might. Judging from the last time we were out here; I sense we are getting closer, so I break the silence.

"Is everything alright?" I ask.

He nods.

"Can you give me more than just a nod, please?"

He looks away from the road for a good five seconds to look into my eyes. "Tonight is more important than I think you understand," he says.

"Okay, so help me to understand." I try to stay level, even though my nerves have me increasingly agitated.

He doesn't shout, but his tone is firm. "These people are expecting your full cooperation tonight. Once you're in this, there's no backing out. And if you can't take it seriously— if you don't want to take it seriously, then we should probably just turn around now," he says.

"You're kind of scaring me," I say.

"Do you want to do this, Lula?"

Once again, I get the feeling that my husband is pulling away from me. Like he's moving just out of my reach. We have been so close the past few weeks. Is this silly charade the only way to pull him back in?

I take a deep breath. "I'll do it for us," I say. Dread sweeps over me. I plead to the universe that this isn't a mistake. That this won't ruin my marriage.

Jason only nods. We continue to the cabin. Relief fills me as Jason takes one hand off the steering wheel and grabs mine, squeezing it tight.

We pull up to the cabin. The same cars are parked around as before. The sun set long ago and now there's a bite to the air that makes me shiver. Jason said no liquid courage tonight. I recoiled at the thought of going into this sober but maybe it's better to stay levelheaded anyways.

When we get to the door, Jason stops me.

"Stick out your tongue," he says.

He holds a tiny white sheet of paper in his fingers. I have a faint idea of what it could be.

"I don't know. I don't want to feel messed up again," I say.

"Do it." His command catches me off guard. I stick out my tongue and say a quick prayer to a god I don't necessarily believe in.

Please let me live to see tomorrow.

A bitter tang fills my mouth but the paper dissolves quickly.

The doors open up. The room is dark except for the same fireplace in the front room, which is now lit with a bright crimson. Two red hooded robes are draped over the couch.

"One for you and one for me," Jason says.

He reaches for the one closest and helps me put it on. I know better than to ask what it's for or why it's necessary. He places the hood over my head. I watch as Jason puts on his own, his face so dim now that I can barely make out his features.

Our hands meet and we walk to the same door that we did the night of the party. The thud of my heart rings through my ears. Before opening the door Jason grabs my face.

"Expand your mind, Lula."

Next thing I know the door is opening to another gush of fog. Instead of amber lighting it's red, as if we are in the deepest depths of hell.

I'm beginning to sense a theme.

We make our way through the fog and as it clears, my heart drops to my stomach and a scream escapes my lips.

The partitions are gone, and the room is practically empty, aside from a woman dangling from the ceiling by her ankles. She is completely naked. Her skin is so pale that it's tinged with blue, and I question whether or not she's alive. My first instinct is to run out of the room but when I see her eyelids flutter, my heart rate slows a little. Jason squeezes my hand tight.

"Breathe. Relax," he whispers.

My gaze finally drifts from the hanging woman to what's in front of me. Eleven cloaked individuals stand in a circle below her with the life size statue of Inanna directly underneath. The bronze glitters in the red hue. The room appears to be frozen in place. Each has their hoods up and heads down. Each is as still as can be. Like they are waiting for something.

Jason leaves my side and moves to an open spot in the circle.

Here they stand as a club of twelve. I will make thirteen.

My stomach clenches as I stand to the side, unsure of what to do next. Worried to make the wrong move. I can't help but to study the naked woman top to bottom. Her ankles must be on fire. And the blood rush to her head must be nauseating.

What are these people doing?

"I give you permission to speak through me, goddess." A voice booms within the circle.

A cloaked individual steps out of the circle and stands right next to Inanna. As she lifts her head, I can see that the thundering voice is Rasheeda's.

She motions to a spot in the circle, and I squeeze in between the bodies, unaware of the faces beneath the hoods.

I jump as a piercing scream escapes Rasheeda's lips. The shriek is deafening but it doesn't seem to faze any of the other still bodies in the room. As the shriek switches to a low groan, I follow suit and hang my head.

"I have journeyed to hell and back. From the depths of the underworld, I was called. Called to be stripped down to the flesh, barren in front of all. Called to be hung, like swine up for slaughter. And called to be flayed, my flesh sliced and torn from the bone. From death, freedom was born. The ultimate price paid for the ultimate reward."

Her words are sharp and measured. I wonder how many times she has recited this. Tingles move along my back as she speaks. Like an electric current rushing through me.

Rasheeda turns around and kneels in front of Inanna. The glitter radiating off of the goddess' bronze skin appears to dance in the red beams. I reach out to feel the sparkles floating in the air, emanating from Inanna. They escape my fingertips.

In a trance, I fail to realize that everyone else has knelt too. I do the same, nearly ripping my dress in the process.

The wood floor is cold, and I tug the cloak tighter around my body.

"Made new in Inanna, made new in Inanna, made new in Inanna."

Chanting rings out throughout the twelve individuals. Over and over. It takes me a minute to decipher exactly what it is they're saying. The words sound like a melody in my head.

Their heads lift and twelve pairs of eyes become visible, like galaxies to explore. Haven's eyes are particularly entrancing. I picture dolphins riding the waves in her turquoise irises.

No wonder my husband fucked her.

Soon we all stand again, and the circle slowly closes in on the woman hanging six inches above us. I almost forgot she was even here, dangling in the middle of the room. We don't seem to faze her, as if she's in a deep slumber. Rasheeda stands directly underneath the body and reaches for the woman's arm.

Her body is frail, ribs exposed, and hair thin. She looks a bit like a druggie in the throes of addiction. Her body ravaged by her substance of choice, her appetite for food diminished. A shell of a woman.

Piercing screams fill the air again but this time it's not coming from Rasheeda's mouth. It's coming from the hanging girl. Rasheeda has sliced her arm with a long, silver blade. My mouth drops as the blood flows down, splattering onto the floor. The rich smell of iron fills my nostrils. The girl's eyes have opened now, veiny and bulging. I move to help her but a hand stops me, pulling me back. On my side, Atlas shakes his head and leans in close to my ear.

"Keep your cool. We have her consent," he says. His voice is barely audible.

Who the hell would consent to something like this?

I keep my feet planted, resisting the urge to yank the knife away from Rasheeda to cut her down from the ceiling.

"Made new in Inanna, the freedom of the world is yours to take," Rasheeda yells.

She proceeds to bring the blade to her lips, licking off the crimson until the knife is a shining silver once again.

What the fuck?

She hands the knife to the person next to her. Clara. My stomach swirls as Clara follows suit. The hanging lady is cut on the other arm causing more blood to spill. Clara then takes her turn lapping up the liquid on the blade.

Clara hands it off to a man I recognize as Greg. He's a bit scruffier than when I saw him last. His hand fumbles with the knife as he inches closer to the woman. I'm surprised to see tears streaking down his face. But despite this he doesn't hesitate. A slice is made under the woman's armpit. His eyes close as his tongue moves across the knife.

He then hands it off again.

With each slice a scream ensues. With each scream, blood pools on the ground underneath her. Arms, stomach, thighs, breasts, ass. Her whole body is covered in carvings. Twelve to be exact. I'm frozen in bewilderment as each member takes their turn. The sour stench pervades every inch of air in the room.

Her face is crumpled, her eyes narrow and heavy. There is a nudge to my arm. Haven eyes me with the knife outstretched.

It's my turn.

My hand trembles as I grab the handle from her stained hands. I hold it in front of me and see myself in the glossy reflection. It's not me. I can't be me. I don't look like Lula.

My feet drag towards the woman. I reach up and caress the first cut on her arm with my thumb. She whimpers. The blood has already started to dry.

Bile rises up my throat. I turn to Jason in the group of individuals behind me. He nods and I know what he expects. I know that I'm being tested.

I can drop the knife and walk out now, or I can jump in with both feet and get this over with.

Rasheeda can sense my hesitation.

"Do you need a second, Lula?" she asks.

My head shakes but so does my hand, the knife close to slipping through my fingers.

"Lula?" Jason pleads.

I don't want to embarrass him. I can't betray him like that.

"I'm sorry," I whisper as I turn back towards her.

Standing on my tiptoes, I glide the blade diagonally across her waist. The knife is so sharp that it gives no resistance, slipping right through the flesh as if it's jello. I close my eyes as the blood flows out. At this point she is no longer wailing at the bodily abuse. Her eyes are completely shut now but her chest moves up and down as she breathes. The blood on the knife appears almost neon in the red lighting. Everyone waits in silence for me to finish my turn. After a deep breath my tongue slides along the blade. A sharp tang overpowers my taste buds as I lap up every last bit. I swallow hard and resist the urge to throw it all back up. The knife falls from my hand and drops to the floor with a clank.

I did it. I'm done.

Without warning, cloaks come off and bodies drop to the widening puddle on the floor. Maegan and Atlas paint each other in the blood. His soiled hands smear her cheeks and move down to her breasts. Clara rolls around in it, like a pig in the mud on a hot summer day. Calen runs it through his hair. Everyone bathes in the blood of the hanging woman. Like feral animals.

Everyone except for two.

Jason and Rasheeda stand behind me, cloaks still on.

"It's time for you to swear your devotion in written form." Rasheeda hands me papers, probably around 10 pages, and a pen. Paragraphs of small copy fill the pages with a huge line at the end which I can only assume is for my signature. The words jump off the page, letters swirling around and around. I look at Jason, as if awaiting his permission. Like we are signing the deed to a home.

"I'm supposed to sign this?" I ask. My voice crackles like I haven't used it in weeks.

Both Rasheeda and Jason nod. I don't know what I could possibly be agreeing to. Regardless, I don't take the time to read it. I don't think I could read right now even if I tried. And it's not like any of this is legally binding anyways. I take the pen and glide my signature across the line then hand it all back to Rasheeda.

She tears off the first page and hands the rest of the pages back to me.

"Read through these when your mind clears up. There are some things that are important for you to know. Some rules that will be crucial to follow. But we are so happy to have you here with us," she says. She grabs my hands and squeezes them tight, then turns me around to face the group who by now have covered their entire bodies in the blood. The hanging lady is being taken down and carried away by two men in dark clothing and balaclava masks. Nobody seems to notice them, and nobody seems to be concerned about the wellbeing of the woman they just practically drained the life out of.

I feel like I'm in a dream. These types of things don't happen in real life.

Jason takes the pages from my hand, setting them aside, and guides me to the stained floor. He presses his lips against mine. As I lick his lips an explosion of flavors bursts in my mouth. I kiss him deeper. My senses are on fire. I can't get enough.

While I'm lost in a trance with my husband, hands remove my cloak from behind me and rub on my bare shoulders. They are soft and warm. And wet. I don't care, though. The hands move from my shoulders to my hips, and someone pulls me into them. An erection presses up against my ass. Our lips stay locked as Jason grabs the front of my dress with both hands and rips it apart, exposing my entire top half.

I twirl around to see Atlas. A red handprint runs down his handsome face. He rips off the rest of my dress and lays kisses up and down my body. Soon the three of us are down on the floor with the pile of bodies, every one of us entwined. Palms touch my exposed skin from all directions. Moans thunder through the room. Our bodies glide along the soaked floor. I allow myself to lay there in the mess, relishing in the pleasure.

CHAPTER 10

Blood, bodies, and cloaks fill my dreams after initiation night.

"Lula."

Jason's voice shakes me from slumber. My head is fuzzy as I try to piece together the events of last night, how I got home, and how the night ended. Just like last time.

"What time is it?" I ask, rubbing the sleep from my eyes.

"It's three in the afternoon. I figured you could use the extra sleep," he says.

I don't think I've slept past 9 am in years. Maybe even a whole decade. I pull myself up to sit, which feels like an enormous task. My body and my brain are moving slowly, like some cables are only loosely connected.

"I'm going to go out for my Sunday jog. You should probably look these over."

He tosses the stack of papers from last night onto the duvet.

Nausea builds at the thoughts of last night, of what I took part in. It's hard to believe that any of it really happened at all. If the papers weren't in front of me, I would have doubted the whole thing. But here is the evidence, strewn across my bed. The hanging lady pops into my mind and fear crawls up my skin.

"That woman. The one from last night. Is she okay?" I ask him.

"What woman?"

"The one that was hanging—"

Jason cuts me off, "I think it's best if you stop right there, Lula. Read the documents. I'll see you in a bit."

And with that he leaves the bedroom, shutting the door behind him. His curt response stings and only leaves me with more questions.

CLUB 13 headlines the packet in thick, bold lettering. Thirteen? Squeezing my eyes shut, I try to remember how many robe-laden people were in the circle last night, how many cuts the pale body had endured. Bodies fade in and out of my mind along with faces and bloody hands. After multiple counts, I reach the number twelve. Club 13? My own shaking hand comes into view. Thirteen. There were twelve members before me... once Gina had died. I've taken her place, slipped in as her replacement as if she never existed. I rub my bare arms as goosebumps form.

I spend the rest of the day in bed, shuffling through Rasheeda's pages. I'm shocked with how thorough she is. The whole packet must have taken her ages to type up. And even longer to plan. The first few documents consist of historical dates starting with the world's creation, continuing with ancient Mesopotamia, and leading up until the present time. Early texts of the goddess Inanna precede a detailed manifesto,

Since the wave of Christianity began in the first century and spread throughout the world, humanity has never been the same. We have lost connection with our true spirits and have become a society that forces us to inhibit our natural instincts and attempts to ban us from indulging in the desires that are so rightfully ours to take. In the midst of all the smoke and lies we have forgotten why we are here. We must let go of the pressures and limits that society sets against us and live without fear of sin or damnation. We were meant to chase the euphoric pleasures of the world and through Inanna we can attain the freedom to do so. In the end we will be left to embrace our impulses and find divine fulfillment.

When I reach the "rules and regulations" page, the intricacy of it all is a bit absurd.

There is a numbered list, but the first line is bolded and underlined.

1. ***<u>The group thrives off of the closed lips of its members. Bonds are built, safety is ensured, and limits are endless with the practice of secrecy. There is nothing more important than this rule.</u>***

The rest of the rules don't seem to be in any specific order of importance even though they are numbered. It's as if Rasheeda just typed as things popped into her mind, although she states that all contents were inspired by Inanna. I can picture her standing with her statue, eyes closed and hands on Inanna's solid head, willing ethereal information to fill her mind.

2. *Proof of regular sexually transmitted disease testing every six months*

3.   *Proof of up-to-date birth control prescription or IUD insertion*

4.   *No phones or cameras during club meetings or events*

5.   *No transparency on social media*

6.   *Forty percent of your time shall be designated to furthering the club's efforts and/or affairs*

7.   *Keep clear of mind inhibiting propaganda (i.e., religious churches and texts, counseling services, family interventions)*

8.   *Must be open to all forms of pleasure, regardless of previous stigmas or misconceptions*

9.   *Must report any new relationships (platonic or other), which are outside of the club members, to a higher official*

10.   *Must use discretion when conversing with family, friends and acquaintances outside of the club*

11.   *Must provide a monthly sacrifice to Inanna either bodily or monetarily as designated by a higher official*

12.   *Must report a member with wavering loyalty to a higher official immediately*

13.   *Must delete text messages, emails, and voicemails sent to and from club members at the end of each day*

14.   *Must relay any questions revolving around the club, ideals, or loyalty to a higher official*

15.   *Must relay any issues to a higher official*

16.   *Must report any medical appointments or visits to a higher official*

17.   *Must remember that ethics are both pliable and subjective and moral dilemmas need to be reported to a higher official*

The higher officials appear to be Rasheeda Edwards and Derrick Wright, their names etched at the bottom of the paper.

The list goes on with a total of fifty-two rules we are required to follow. Some, sort of make sense for a sex club, some don't, and others are downright ridiculous. I can't imagine these rules are actually followed. Thankfully Jason isn't here, or he would have heard my fits of laughter from the absurdity of it all.

The next page, I recognize, is a non-disclosure agreement. And at the very end lies the sloppy signature that I wrote with frazzled, strung-out fingers last night. A notary has signed the line under mine and left an official red stamp next to the name.

Calen Banks.

I don't remember Calen even being near when I signed the document. Could this actually be legally binding?

The material exhausts me, and I'm left with unease. My entire life may soon be consumed by what was once my husband's extracurriculars. And now I have made them my own.

Am I stupid for thinking that any of this insanity is a good idea? Probably.

Jason comes back to the room only once to bring me a greasy cheeseburger and fries. He tells me that he knows how brutal the come down can be and insists that I need my rest. I don't mind it. I feel like I was hit by a train. Worse than any hangover I've ever had. Even that time when I was 19 and slammed five shots and 3 beers in an hour, waking up to a mix of drool and vomit on the sidewalk in front of the dive bar my best friend and I snuck into. And my mind spins. Men, women, blood, and that imposing statue. It all comes in waves of vivid images. Especially Atlas. He always seems to stick out amongst the rest. I try not to wince at some moments. But I do have to admit that not all of it was bad. Maybe it was just the drugs, but I felt so good, not just physically but also mentally. I broke out of the little box my mind usually finds impossible to get free of. The experience was pleasurable and that's the whole point of this club, embracing your pleasure.

I lost my virginity at seventeen. I wasn't really a "hot girl" in high school. My hair was frizzy, teeth were crooked, and knees were wobbly. By the time I hit senior year, I was ready to get it all over with. My friends had all had sex, and I was the odd one out. I was tired of the backhanded comments, "You might as well wait for marriage at this point" and "Maybe you'll have more luck in college." When I finally found myself alone with Carson Jennings after a home football game, I made sure the deed was done. It didn't hurt, but it wasn't good.

I didn't orgasm until I was twenty-two. My boyfriend at the time had insisted on it. But once he had accomplished his goal he didn't try anymore. Sex ended when *he* got his rocks off. My completion from then on was irrelevant. And the story stayed consistent throughout my relationships.

Last night I was able to focus on *my* body, not on tending to a man's. It was liberating. Maybe I needed this club and its ludicrous rules more than I knew.

CHAPTER 11

Gina Reese: 5 Weeks Before Death

Last night Greg had an outburst at dinner with the group. I didn't want them to know his feelings. I thought I could talk him out of them before needing to bring the club into it, but I guess I was wrong. I should have gone to them the moment Greg's hesitation arose.

When I got up to help Cheyenne serve the dessert, he went through my phone and read my texts. He saw messages between me and another man. And this wasn't the first time. He had asked me to restrict my contact to club events only. But now he knows I haven't.

He went off on everyone at the table. I wasn't shocked at his behavior, but they were.

"He's just drunk, Gina. I'll talk some sense into him," Calen said.

Greg stormed out of the house and Calen followed him. What Calen doesn't understand is that he's *always* drunk. Or always high. There is no sober Greg anymore. And no excuse for his behavior. But I can't be held responsible for his spiraling. I don't want to end up spiraling myself.

How can he expect me to love just one man? That isn't the way we are meant to be. It's too suffocating and I have every right to my own freedom to love. I think he's hurt that it isn't just all about the sex. His ego is bruised that I'm feeling emotional passion for someone other than him.

He has made his frustrations clear to everyone in the club. Now I'm left to pick up all of the pieces, just like it has always been.

CHAPTER 12

I stare at the reflection of my naked body in the mirror. The bruises I earned from the passion of initiation night are just starting to fade. For the first time, I don't cringe at what I see. I notice the perkiness of the B cups I used to be embarrassed by. And the small curve of my hips that I never thought were defined enough. A smile creeps on my face as I remember the way I was touched that night. Like I was a goddess, meant to be worshiped and ravished.

But even though I'm empowered by this new sense of confidence, I can't fight the unease nagging in the back of my mind. It all stems from that woman. The hanging woman. There are so many questions that I don't have the answers to. Who in their right mind would give their consent for something so demeaning and horrific? And does her consent make the abuse legal? I know that some people get off on sadomasochism, but it was so extreme. Way crazier than anything I've been able to find in porn. I'm worried about her. She didn't look well after we were finished with her. I just need to know that she's okay.

I don't dare ask Jason again. He made it clear that it wasn't up for discussion. I'm trying to push it out of my mind, but some things cannot be unseen.

I'm pulled out of my head when my phone chimes.

"Hey mom," I say as I finally pick up her call.

She has been calling me nonstop for the past week and I've been texting her with excuses as to why I can't chat. Today, I answer. I know I can't get away with it for too long before she comes pounding at my door, forcing her way into my private life.

"You need to start answering my calls, Lula Jane. You only do this when you have something to hide. So, what is it?" Her caring tone always comes off as patronizing.

"I'm a grown adult, mom. I don't have to hide anything," I say.

"You're right, you don't have to. Yet you do it anyway."

"Is there a reason that you called other than to pry?" I ask.

I love my mom to death but that doesn't change the fact that she is nosy, opinionated, and forward. We are quite opposites. I know she just wants the best for me. Sometimes she's just too much.

"Do you follow those community groups on Facebook? Pleasant Valley Crime, Moms of El Dorado County, and others like that?" she asks.

"I don't know. Probably not. Why?" I ask even though I'd rather not hear the answer. She's a notorious drama seeker and lives for the theatrics, even though she preaches tranquility.

"You know I have a sixth sense about this stuff, Lula. Maybe it's from watching too many episodes of 60 Minutes back in the nineties. Or maybe it's truly a gift given to me from the universe. Anyways, I went to grade school with this frizzy haired lady, Liza Cooper. She's going on and on in the posts about her fourteen-year-old daughter going missing. A runaway. Or maybe not. Either way, it had me thinking about my own kid. I'm worried about you." Her tone becomes increasingly paternalistic, which has me rubbing at my temples to soothe the headache that I know is bound to start at any moment.

"What are you talking about?" I ask.

"It's not creepy, unshaven men in white, windowless vans offering candy anymore, you know? These poor moms having to worry sick about their girls. I can't fathom it. I really can't."

"Keyword, mom, *girls.* Like I said before, I'm a grown adult. I can handle myself."

"You can never be too careful, Lula. Remember a few months back when I was followed at that janky supermarket off of Seventh and Pine? The son of a bitch trailed me down every aisle, pretending to look at pickles in aisle two, marshmallows in aisle five, and apple cider vinegar in aisle seven for god's sake! My guard is always up. And you need to do the same with yours."

"Stay off those fear mongering groups before you give yourself a heart attack," I say, only half listening to her rantings.

"With as much as I meditate, there is no heart attack in my future. Anyways, I want to come see you. It's been too long. Does Saturday night work?" she asks. Mallory's mind is always going a mile a minute. A thought that is there one minute will be gone the next. A bundle of overbearing energy.

"It does not. Jason and I have dinner plans with friends," I say.

"Friends? What friends?" Her question is innocent, even though it comes off as offensive.

"*Our* friends. You don't know everyone in our lives, mom." Exasperation fills my voice. I'm sure she can sense my irritation from miles away.

"Well can I come to dinner? I'd like to meet these so-called friends," she says.

"You may not. But we would love to have you over on Sunday," I lie.

"I suppose I can wait one extra day," she says.

"Next Sunday," I clarify. Her eye roll is perceptible through the phone.

"Fine, Lula. See you next week."

Jason is going to be less than thrilled that his mother-in-law is visiting us next weekend. She has never truly approved of him, and he can sense it. "All that man wants to do is dull your sparkle, Lula," is what she told me after she met him for the first time. She has always felt that way about men. As if you're bound down by shackles the second you say, "I do". It's why she never fully committed to my dad.

According to Jason, Saturday night is supposed to be much more laid back than the previous club meetups. I could never be seen by my mom the day after a night like that. She would sense the air of non-monogamous sex seeping out of me. Hopefully by next weekend she won't be able to perceive that anything is off. Just her boring daughter with her boring son-in-law. It's supposed to be just a casual dinner with friends. And I'm praying that no women are hanging upside down over a dish of baked mac and cheese.

Saturday rolls around and when we pull up to Derrick and Cheyenne's this time, I don't have as many butterflies in my stomach. Jason seems much less tense than last time as well. He holds my hand the entire drive and we actually talk. For once, he doesn't talk about the stresses of work. He kisses me before we get out of the car.

"I love you, Lu," he says.

"I love you, too."

I'm not doing this alone. The past few weeks he has consistently reminded me of that. This is a journey that we are navigating together. I think the weight of hiding the club from me was putting a strain on him and now that it's lifted, he can be open and truly himself. I'm starting to see cracks in his perfect facade that I never noticed before. As we laid in bed the other night he began to cry. He had shed a few tears at our wedding, but it was the first time I had ever seen him sob. Tears flowed down his cheeks as he confessed his dad's vices and the awful things he had witnessed and experienced when he was a child. His dad had a thing for young boys and while he never laid a hand on Jason in a sexual manner, he didn't hold back on the violence. The man would take all of his hatred and shame for his own actions out on Jason. I had only been around his dad a few times, but I never would have guessed. He was always so polished, poised, and successful with his just as refined wife on his arms. I tried not to ask Jason too many questions and just listened, holding back my own tears. I feel bad that he felt he couldn't tell me sooner but maybe by us diving deeper into the club together, he is feeling a sense of closeness between us that wasn't there before. And a sense of freedom in our marriage.

When we open the door. The smell of garlic and lemon rushes out. My stomach grumbles at the thought of what could be cooking. Cheyenne must notice me sniffing the air.

"I had our chef whip up some chicken piccata with lemon sauce. It's to die for!" She rushes over to hug both of us.

It must be nice to have a personal chef.

We head to the dining room, which I've never been in before. The space is taken up by a massive white quartz dining table with fourteen purple, velvet chairs. Above the table hangs a glittering crystal chandelier that I can't keep my eyes off of. I had always dreamed of having one on the ceiling in my bedroom as a child. The room is something out of a luxury home magazine.

"I'll let Gustavo take it from here! Make yourselves at home." Cheyenne says and drifts back off towards the front of the house.

A man in a black apron guides us to our seats. We must be the first to arrive because every other seat is empty. The man pulls out each of our chairs and we sit.

"Can I get you each a glass of wine? Chardonnay? Pinot Blanc?" he asks.

We both go with the Chardonnay.

Soon familiar faces fill the room. I stay seated and give a subtle wave to everyone as they sit. Jason gets up and shakes hands or gives pecks on the cheek. Haven walks in with her fresh blowout and juicy lips. I look away as her and Jason embrace, ignoring the stab in my stomach.

There are some things I may never get used to.

Across from me sits Clara while Atlas and Maegan sit on my other side. Atlas bends down to hug me, and I catch a whiff of his intoxicating smell once again. Maegan gives me a wave that I return with a cheesy grin, an awkward response as I just reveled in her husband's aroma.

Once we are all seated, Derrick stands and clears his throat. The room falls silent in an instant.

"Like always, I'm so grateful to see you all here tonight. Let us just forget about the pressures of the week and enjoy this night," he says.

"Eat, drink, and be merry!" Calen yells as he lifts his wine glass. We each do the same and the chef comes around with our plates, each neatly arranged with a medley of steaming food.

As we eat I can't help but notice the stark contrast between this night with the club and the other night. How these individuals went from practically barbaric to civilized overnight is beyond me. How can we be on the floor fucking in a stranger's blood one minute and then eating chicken piccata with a fork and a napkin the next?

At the far side of the table sits Greg. His wine glass is already empty, and I can only assume he is impatiently waiting for another. An empty seat sits next to him, and I can't help but think it's a cruel joke. I feel sorry for him. He's been through so much and I wonder why he still attends. What joy can he find in being here without her?

"So, Lula, I've asked just about everyone here to come do hot yoga with me and no one seems the slightest bit interested. I tell them that it's great for the skin, but no one seems to care," Clara pipes up from across the table and twirls her cappuccino hair in her fingers, "But you're a fresh face so I'll try one last time. Care to join me tomorrow morning? I promise it will be life changing."

"I'd love to try it," I say, shrugging. My response puts a huge grin on her face. I could use a bit of physical activity anyways. Although I'm thin, sitting at the front desk of the office all day hasn't done me any favors.

Atlas' hand brushes my thigh underneath the table and my body warms. I'm unsure if it was an accident, but when I glance over at him, his eyes meet mine and I realize he meant to touch me. The thought speeds my heart rate so much that I'm sure we could all hear its thud if the room went quiet. I gulp down the rest of my wine in an attempt to settle the tension inside of me.

Atlas' focus moves to his wife as he brushes her hair out of her face. A pang hits my stomach and I remember that he isn't mine to have. Whatever sexual tension there is between us, it's purely just that. Sexual. And nothing more. I turn to my own husband and give him a smile. I need to remember what I have and why I'm doing all of this to begin with.

Gustavo clears our plates after we finish with dinner.

"Care to join me out by the pool? I'd love to chat," Clara says, winking at me.

We make our way to a couple of striped lounge chairs by the pool. The sun is just starting to sink lower in the sky and the temperature is perfect.

"So, you're single?" I ask the only question that I can come up with after racking my brain with conversation starters.

"For the most part," she says with another wink, "But I do hope to have a big family one day. I'm only twenty-seven but sometimes I feel like my biological clock is tick, ticking away."

"You've still got lots of time," I tell her with a wave of my hand.

"Well, what about you? Any kids in your future? You know that you and Jason would make the most gorgeous babies."

I shake my head. "I'm not so sure children are in the cards for us. I carry a few hereditary conditions that I'm not comfortable with passing on."

Clara covers her mouth and gasps, almost spilling the glass of wine she holds in her other hand.

"No, no, it's okay. I've come to terms with it. And Jason has known from the beginning. He's barely got time for kids anyways."

Clara nods like she understands but her eyes flash with pity.

She's probably running over the numerous conditions I could possibly have that would necessitate my womb being bare for my entire life. But it isn't something like Cystic Fibrosis or Huntington's Disease that's keeping me from having kids. I've always blamed it on my fear that my son or daughter might grow up with crippling anxiety, needing to be medicated by either a pharmaceutical drug or a recreational one to feel normal. Just like their mother. So, in this sense, I suppose it could be my fear of passing on a hereditary condition. But if I'm really being honest with myself, I simply don't want them. It's hard enough to manage my own life. God forbid I have to manage the lives of other little beings. And I lied about Jason. The only time he has discussed offspring is when his mother brought up grandchildren the last time, we had family dinner with her. His response to her was short and curt.

"You won't be getting any."

A tightness I had felt inside for so long finally released upon hearing his answer. We had been on the same page all along, even if we had never actually talked about it.

Clara throws back the rest of her wine. "Well, enough about that. Let's get intimate." She sets down her empty glass and clasps her hands together. "What's the craziest thing you've ever done?"

I let out a shaky laugh.

"To be honest, Clara. I'm a pretty dull person, if you take out the whole 'joining a sex club with your husband' part."

She holds up a finger. "First off, we do not label ourselves as a 'sex club'. Rasheeda would lose her shit if she ever heard you say that. And second, that wasn't an answer to my question."

I give her an apologetic look. "In college, I smoked a joint and got really high for the first time. I was so messed up, couldn't think straight, and thought I was going to die of a heart attack. I pulled out my phone and texted a message to who I thought was my mother. I said 'I need help. I'm stupid and smoked with Claire in my dorm room and I think I did too much. I don't know what's happening and my heart is about to stop. Should I call an ambulance?'"

Clara bursts out in laughter.

"Turns out I actually sent that message to my sociology professor. But she took pity on me and replied, 'I'm just going to assume this message was meant for someone else and pretend like I never saw it… see you Monday, Lula.' I was mortified! I couldn't look her in the eye for months," I say.

"For fucks sake, Lula. You've got to get out more. But don't worry, that's what I'm here for," she says.

She reclines the lounger and leans back. "Anyways, I want to know what you are doing *here*." Her grin turns devilish.

"Well, I–"

"Can I pull Lula away for a few minutes, Clara?" Atlas walks up to us and I'm relieved to have a distraction from my pending answer. Swarms of butterflies begin to flutter in my stomach.

I half hope she says no.

"No, stay! I'll leave," she says, "don't forget about Sunday, Lula!" Clara walks back into the house, leaving Atlas and I alone.

I shift in my chair and pull down on my skirt which has started to ride up my thighs.

Leaning back in the chair next to me, he crosses one leg over the other and turns his head in my direction, a wide grin spread across his face.

"What?" I ask, chuckling.

"You know there's just something about you, Lula Carson. Something enthralling. What was your maiden name?" he asks.

"Why would you want to know that?" I cock my head to the side, genuinely curious.

"Well because I'm curious about you. The first step to uncovering the true Lula is to at least know your name."

"It's Ames," I say.

"Middle name?"

"Jane."

"Lula Jane Ames. Lula Jane Ames. Lula Jane Ames." I try not to break eye contact as he repeats it. I don't want him to know how nervous he makes me. But my name in his mouth has never sounded better. The way it rolls off his tongue makes me want to melt.

"You like it?" I ask.

"I like you," he says.

The sentiment makes me giggle. I want to take him seriously. He's so believable, so forward.

"You don't know me," I say, trying to come back to reality.

"Can't you see I'm trying to change that?"

The stark reminder of Meagan sends me soaring back to real life. Why does this banter feel so wrong? She can't possibly be okay with her husband forming actual connections with another woman. I'm not okay with Jason doing so. What can Atlas get from me that he can't get from Meagan? What is Jason not getting from me?

Or maybe I'm just reading into it too much. I can't presume to know his intentions. For all I know he flirts like this with all the new members.

"Can I ask you a question?" I ask.

"Fire away."

"Who made the decision to join the club first? You or Maegan?"

He squints at me like he can see the gears turning in my head.

"I didn't force Maegan into this world. Hell, I was raised Catholic. When she proposed the idea to me, the ideology, and the expectations, I just about threw a gallon of holy water on her. I figured that this was just an early midlife crisis. I decided I'd ride out this life phase with her. And what could be so bad about getting to watch your wife hookup with hot women every now and again?”

“You make it sound so easy,” I say.

“Don’t get me wrong. It hasn’t been all sunshine and daisies. This club is no joke. But I’ve found my place in it and I don’t regret it,” he says.

I gaze in the direction of the house and can see Haven sitting on Jason’s lap in the foyer. Her head is thrown back in laughter. Her blonde hair close enough to touch Jason’s nose. I’m sure it smells like strawberries. The giddiness on Jason’s face makes my stomachache. I suppose it’s a sight I need to get used to seeing. This is what I signed up for.

“Okay Atlas, what more do you want to know about me?” I ask.

“Let’s take a walk.”

We leave the property and walk towards a grove of trees. I never realized their home backed up to a wood. The sun is now starting to set, leaving a brilliant sky of purply orange above the foliage. In this lighting, his caramel skin gives off a golden hue. Our hands brush against each other as we walk, and I quickly bring my hand up to tousle my waves.

The rich smell of dirt and oak swarms us. Sticks and debris crunch under our feet. The peace in the woods is intoxicating. If I lived at the Wright’s, I would be out wandering every day.

“You from here?” he asks.

“Born and raised. How about you?”

“No, I only moved here a few years ago. I grew up in Atlanta. Got a job opportunity here in California and took the first ticket out. I needed a change.” He kicks a rock out of his way.

"I get that. I love it here but sometimes I wonder how my life would've been if I got out when I had the chance," I say.

"Well don't go running away on me just yet," he says, nudging me with his shoulder, "What do you do for fun? On a weekend with nothing else to do?"

"Is this 21 Questions?" I sneer.

"It can be," he says.

"I like to write," I say.

"Poetry?"

"Mostly just journaling. Since I was younger, I have found that putting my thoughts to paper is cheaper than therapy."

"I'm the same way with drawing. I've been doing it since I was a young boy. There's something about gliding that graphite across the crisp white page that is therapeutic."

"Are you any good?" I ask.

"I'll let you be the judge of that," he says.

We find a stone bench next to a small pond and sit.

The sun has set quickly as the sky settles into a dark blue. A chill fills the air and a frog croaks somewhere close. Atlas' deep voice pervades through the woods as he speaks.

"You know, I'd like to read something you've written," he says.

I scoff. "It's all just rants and ramblings. Nothing that you'd be interested in, I'm sure."

"I think you underestimate my curiosity with you. What I wouldn't give to have a peek into the private diary of Lula Jane Ames."

His eyes study my face and tingles prickle my body. I look to the pond, avoiding his piercing gaze.

As the conversation lulls, we are left listening to the crickets chirp. I'm surprised that the silence isn't uncomfortable. I don't feel like I need to force any small talk.

Atlas' hand creeps over to my fingers splayed over the bench. He locks his pinky with mine and the butterflies start up once again. I turn away from the pond to look at him, only to realize that he has been staring at me. He moves in and kisses me but this time the kiss is different. There is no tongue, no swapping of saliva, just a kiss. Our lips linger there for a moment, lightly caressing each other. When he pulls away, he brushes my hair behind my ear.

"It was lovely getting to know you, Lula Jane."

When the dinner is over and we walk through the doorway of our home, the door has barely closed before Jason lifts my skirt and shoves himself inside of me. My body folds over the back of the couch in our front room and my hips ram into its solid frame. His strokes are hard and fast, forcing my body to open up to him. It isn't the gentle love making I've become accustomed to with my husband. This time it's rough, animalistic. There isn't any kissing or staring each other in the eyes. It's detached. But I don't mind it. My face mashes into the couch cushions, drowning out his presence. Flashes of Atlas fill my mind, the way his hand brushed my fingers, the way his voice deepened as he said my name, the way his lips felt on mine.

And then I cum. Hard.

CHAPTER 13

I wake the next morning with a sunny disposition. I'm excited to get to know Clara a bit more and sweating out the tension that has been building the last few weeks isn't a bad idea. It would be nice to have another woman to talk to who knows this world. Lord knows I can't go to my mother.

The yoga session kicks my ass. I know I won't make it through the rest of the day without a dose of caffeine. I suggest a nearby coffee shop once we finish and Clara excitedly agrees, thankful to have more time to chat. I order a blonde iced latte and Clara orders a Frappuccino. There's a shaded spot at a table outside where we sit. The breeze picks up and cools the sticky sweat covering my skin. Clara's brown hair flutters into her face.

"Okay ma'am, now that we are free from sexy, chocolate distractions, give me the lowdown. Why are you in this club?" she asks and takes a sip of her drink.

Her question catches me off guard and I stammer over my words for a second.

"It wasn't a trick question, Lula," she says, tapping her fingers on the lid, waiting for my answer.

"I know. I just don't quite have a clear answer yet. The quick answer would be because of my husband," I admit, sheepishly, "But it's not just that. I don't think I've done this solely for him. I think that I need it too," I say.

She nods. "Your needs come first. If it's working for you, then go all in. Honestly, Lula. Fuck what Jason wants. You can't please anyone else except for yourself. Don't even try. It's not worth it."

"I'm starting to see that," I say.

"You have so much potential, babes. You're gorgeous, seem to have a good head on your shoulders, don't sell yourself short. I won't sit here and tell you that you don't need him. Because you won't listen to me. But I've seen what men can do. I wouldn't say that I'm jaded but I'm not new to this life. Don't let anyone walk all over you."

"I don't know about other girls. But I think you've misjudged me and my husband. We just aren't like that," I say.

Clara smiles but I see pity strewn across her face. She nods in an appearance of agreement and then shrugs her shoulders. "Well, I won't argue with that."

I had so many questions for her, but they fade now. I don't want to look like a complete, blindsided idiot. I don't think my husband is getting one over on me. He has been clear and open since we started this journey together a few months ago. He hid things from me earlier this year, sure. But all that matters is the page we are on now.

I do appreciate Clara's concern though. This world is hard to navigate, and Clara has shown me that it's not all so straightforward. There are so many ups and downs. I'm lucky that Jason and I have only had one snag since this chapter in our lives started. I can't take that for granted because not everyone is as lucky.

"Can I ask why you joined the club?" I ask.

"Rasheeda gave me her spiel. You know the concept of the whole divine fulfillment and releasing the grip of societal pressures that she goes on about? Well after hearing all of that I was hooked. Instantly. I've always been one to go against the status quo. This club serves my needs," she says with an air of temptation to her voice, batting her thick eyelashes.

Clara is beautiful. Her chocolate hair looks freshly blown out even though we just sweat our asses off. Freckles splatter her flushed face.

"Oh, and before I forget, I was asked to give you this," she says and hands me a folded piece of paper. "Secrets are always fun." She winks at me as she gets up to leave.

I unravel the note.

Atlas 714-655-0917

My heart races and I shove it into my pocket. It feels like a scorching piece of coal ready to burn through my clothing. I don't know why I feel the need to hide it. I don't know why it feels wrong. And I don't know why the urge to type the number into my phone is so strong either. For now, it will stay right where I've put it. Tucked away. I'll address it with Jason once he gets done with work later tonight. If I expect honesty from him, then I must do the same. That's the only way this whole experience is going to work.

After heading home from the coffee shop, I shower and prepare for my workday tomorrow. My mind keeps drifting back to the piece of paper in my pocket. I wonder if Atlas is waiting for me, squirming in anticipation for his phone to light up with an unknown number. Or if he does this with every new member, opening up a line of communication for the betterment of the group. I haven't been passed a secret note since high school and while the whole ordeal should only make me laugh, it doesn't. It's riveting.

I've set the note on the counter, awaiting Jason's arrival. We have yet to bring up boundaries. I can't assume that he's okay with me forming an emotional connection with anyone else. I don't know for sure if I'm even comfortable with it. I also don't know what exactly Atlas' intentions are. Jason might have more insight on this. I'm lost in the flurry of it all and I need my husband to make everything less blurry.

When my phone chimes, I half expect to see Atlas' number on the screen. But it isn't.

"Hello, Sandy," I say, trying not to sound annoyed that I'm being called on a Sunday evening.

Sandy is my boss who rarely calls me outside of work hours unless she is in dire straits.

"I know you're probably busy with your day off and it's not fair of me to ask for your help, but at this point I don't have a choice. I'll clock you back in and I need you to go into the database and finish filling in the new patient information paperwork. They are due early in the morning, and I wasn't able to have Rita finish them," she says.

She's not asking me. It's an order. Rita never gets anything done. Soon after she first started, I caught her sitting at the computer playing solitaire while she was supposed to be hard at work learning the system. Like always, the neglected work falls back on me.

I let out a highly audible sigh. "Will do."

Sandy never bought me a work laptop for home like she had always promised, so I'm left navigating Jason's Mac, which is an operating system that I'm not used to.

I boot up the computer and enter Jason's passcode, the same one he uses for everything despite my constant pleas to diversify a bit for the sake of safety.

The screen immediately opens up to Jason's email account. I move the cursor over the 'x' to close out of the browser, but something catches my eye. HayEmery@outlook.com, accompanied by a bold number 6. Six unread messages. The tiny profile picture by the address tells me all I need to know. Haven's teeth shine in her professional headshot. I know I shouldn't open them. It isn't any of my business and for all I know it could be about work. But six is a lot. I move the cursor over it, hold my breath, and click.

Pages and pages of emails from Haven. None of them are about business. One makes my heart hurt more than the others.

To: JCarson@gmail.com
From: HayEmery@outlook.com
Date: Monday, June 6, 2023, 09:15:33 PST
Subject: Needing You

From the beginning you said that you didn't want to fall for me. You said that you'd fallen for a woman in our circle before and it went south. Your words were, "All business and pleasure, no feelings". And now you say that you're in love with me.

I'm sorry I left as soon as you said it. You shook the ground underneath me, Jason. I was scared. Terrified. I've put a lot of thought into it and weighed my feelings. I've written a list of pros and cons, which was promptly tossed in the trash. I never wanted to be just another girl in the club that you've fallen for. But here we are. And when it comes down to it, none of that matters. The logistics don't matter. I'm ready for whatever this is. I need to see you. Let me know a time and a place. The sooner the better.

Yours forever,

Haven

My blood is boiling, and I feel like throwing up. How could this relationship have formed right under my nose? How have I been so blind to it all? We have only been married a little over half a year. At what point did this even start? And who is this other woman? How did he have the time to fall in love with *two* women while also being committed to me?

I thought it was all about the sex. But turns out I was wrong. Turns out that not even my love has been good enough for my husband.

My eyes swell and threaten to burst. I pick up the closest thing to me, a picture frame of Jason and his mother, and throw it across the room. It shatters as it hits the wall, sending a million shards of glass to scatter on the carpet below it. A scream escapes my lips before my hands cover my mouth.

I won't let this ruin me.

My body shakes with rage, but I wipe my eyes and get up to grab the vacuum. Placing the cracked picture frame back onto the desk, I clean up my mess, half hoping I miss a shard and Jason steps on it later. Before finishing my task from Sandy, I head to the kitchen to get the folded note. My finger taps the number onto the phone screen, and I type.

Hey, Atlas. I got your note. It's Lula.

CHAPTER 14

Gina Reese: 4 Weeks Before Death

Greg put his hands on me a few nights ago. Thankfully, the kids were off in dreamland, unaware of his meltdown. I was roused out of a dead sleep by hostile shouts. He stood next to my side of the bed, hovering over me, arms flailing like a mad man. "What the fuck did you tell them, Gina?" he screamed over and over as I struggled to adjust my sleepy eyes to his blurry figure.

It took me a minute to understand what the hell he was asking. And when it clicked, I groaned. "I told them that you were wavering. That you were trying to pull me out with you. I told them the truth, Greg."

"Since when did you become such a fucking cunt?" Saliva flew from his mouth and splattered in my face. With that, I sat up straight in the bed and spit back with force, returning the favor. Not even a second later, his hand swung, his palm connecting with my cheek in a loud smack.

My jaw dropped. I stayed like that, in a stupor, until he walked out of the bedroom thirty seconds later.

I packed a bag and left the next morning. Rasheeda has offered up the cabin to me. It has kept me safe from Greg's wrath and his influence. Whenever I'm around him, he tries to taint my mind. He has threatened to take the kids from me permanently, which is silly because he is the one who is an addict and unfit to parent. I feel bad leaving them with him but I can't survive suffocating in that home. I can't be a decent mom while I struggle just to get out of bed in the morning.

Rasheeda says that I can stay here for as long as I need to. She understands what it's like to have a man distract you from your potential. If Greg doesn't want to be a part of this life anymore, then so be it. But I won't have him drag me down into the depths of misery with him. He's jealous. I get that. It's hard to see your person fall for someone else, especially if your mind is as closed off as his is. I can't revert to the way things used to be. I can't undo the commitments that we have made. And even if I could, I'd rather die.

I've made connections that cannot be broken. And now that I'm no longer living at home, distracted by marital conflict, I can deepen other relationships. Greg is not entitled to my sole focus and energy. Inanna has made that clear for me. I'm not the same person I used to be. I've made too many sacrifices to give up now.

CHAPTER 15

I'm in bed by the time Jason comes home. My ears pick up the switch of the deadbolt, then the jangle of the keys as they're thrown onto the kitchen counter. He'll think I'm just tired from a long day of sitting at the computer during working hours. No thoughts of notes or emails or texts will even cross his mind.

When he comes creeping into the bedroom an hour later, I pretend to be asleep. I close my eyes and slow my breathing. The floor creaks softly underneath his feet as he attempts to keep quiet. His footsteps tread to the bathroom to wash the day away. As soon as the door clicks shut, I whip out my phone from underneath my pillow. The soft buzzing underneath my head has been making me anxious. After I texted Atlas, I waited for a response. When it didn't come right away, I doubted the whole ordeal. Maybe I had it all wrong.

But now I tap into my messages. There is one from my mom, one from Sandy, and one from the 714 number that has suddenly become familiar. I'm filled with excitement as I open the message.

Lula. Thought I'd be waiting forever.

I shove my face into the pillow to hide my giddy smile. He knew good and well that he wouldn't have to wait long. I should wait to reply. Play coy. But I don't.

You wouldn't have given me your number if you thought you'd be waiting forever. So, what are you wanting from me, Atlas?

Three bubbles pop up but are gone just as fast, leaving me staring at the bright screen, waiting for his response.

The shower water stops running and I shove my phone back under my pillow. As I slow my breathing, Jason opens up the bathroom door. My eyes closed tight but I can still feel his gaze, scanning my body from top to bottom.

Not tonight. Not tonight.

Since when do I dread my husband's touch? The thought makes me sick. This is the man I promised my life to. This isn't how it's supposed to be.

Reluctantly, I shift a little, giving him an opportunity. And he takes it.

Jason flips me from my side to my back. His towel drops to the floor, leaving him bare. I pretend to rouse from a deep sleep, grunting a bit to play the part. His mouth connects with my neck, and he begins to suck. His teeth graze the veins. I ignore the pain and decide that I'll cover the anticipated marks with foundation in the morning.

His erection pushes into my thigh, and I slide my pajama shorts down, ready to get it all over with.

"You're mine," he says and forces himself into me, leaving me to wince at the burn from the lack of moisture.

I ignore his words but move my hips to his rhythm.

"Say it," he demands.

The sweet smell of whiskey radiates from his breath. We make eye contact but the lack of passion that stares back at me is numbing.

His palm reaches down to slap my cheek. The sting makes me gasp. I try to sit up, but he presses my chest back down and pushes further into me. I'm too shocked to put up a fight.

"Say it!" He screams, his voice echoing off the walls.

"I'm yours," I say. My voice is a whisper as I rub my warm cheek. He asks me to say it again and I don't hesitate, unwilling to get hit again.

He turns me over and pushes my face into the pillow. I try to lift my head, but he only presses down harder. My phone buzzes under the pillow below me. Atlas flashes into my mind.

Jason thrusts into me over and over again. And with each rough stroke, my mouth and nose smash further into the pillow.

I need air.

The urge for a breath of oxygen becomes overwhelming and my arms and legs start to flail. Panic rises in my chest. He has to know that I need to take a breath. He fights my movements as he continues his.

Just as I think I can't hold off any longer, Jason groans as he finishes inside of me. He releases my head and I roll over, panting for air. He rolls off the bed to go clean off in the bathroom. Tears burst from my eyes as soon as the door shuts. I take what feels like a million deep breaths, thankful that I'm able to do so.

I don't understand what just happened. I don't understand where that came from.

Jason comes out of the bathroom and is snoring as soon as his head hits the pillow. I watch his chest rise and fall as he breathes in and out. He looks so peaceful, like the events from ten minutes ago never even took place. His effortless breaths make me think of my face shoved in the pillow. The terror of feeling like oxygen may never reach my lungs again. The thoughts consume me and I have to focus my respiration to keep from hyperventilating.

Atlas' reply stands out on my dim phone screen.

I want to see you again. Soon. If that's okay.

I wouldn't dare reply to him tonight. Not with Jason lying in the bed next to me. His presence is all encompassing, suffocating.

For the rest of the night I fight back tears as I Google search topics like "smothering fantasies" and "sudden violent sexual acts". According to Reddit threads and WebMD, Jason's newfound tendencies could stem from a number of things including deep seeded anger or sociopathy. And while I know that none of it is normal behavior for Jason, there must be some way to explain this drastic shift. Our sex has always been gentle, easy, and honestly, vanilla. Before I knew the lifestyle Jason was into, I figured he was pretty boring when it came to his sexual preferences. Our sex was always good, but it was never freaky or taboo. I wonder now if I should have been more explorative. Or at least open to it.

Has he been scared to show me what he's into?

I'm scared that I don't know my husband like I thought I did. Maybe now I'm slowly learning the real Jason Carson.

Better late than never.

CHAPTER 16

Atlas has invited me to dinner at a small Bar and Grill a few towns over. I'm assuming we have to go farther because he doesn't want anyone that we know seeing us out together. But he says it's because this place has some of the best buffalo wings that I'll ever eat. It feels scandalous, like I'm a teen again sneaking out past curfew. But this time, instead of stressing over being caught by mom, I have to worry about being caught by my husband.

I'm a married woman, leaving my house at 7 pm on a Friday to have dinner with a man who is not my husband.

I considered asking Atlas what Meagan is doing tonight, just to ease some of my reservations about this whole ordeal. But I decided against it. It's none of my business and Atlas rarely brings her up anyways. Almost like she doesn't exist. Maybe it's easier that way for him to separate the two of us.

Jason and I haven't talked much after our eventful night in the bedroom a few days ago. Neither of us spoke about it. It's like it never happened. Tonight, he is working late to finish up a big project that has been consuming him for the past few weeks. I'm not sure if this project is actually work related or consists of a petite blond with fake boobs but I try not to let it bother me.

Those who live in glass houses shouldn't throw stones.

Either way, I'm happy I won't have to make up an excuse as to where I'm going.

"I'll be home later tonight," Jason says as he grabs his keys off the counter.

"How late are you thinking?" I ask and hand him his travel mug of coffee. Black. The only way he'll drink it.

"No need to wait up. I can call in some Chinese for delivery if you want that for dinner," he says.

"That's sweet. But I'll probably just have some canned soup or something. I haven't had much of an appetite lately," I lie.

Jason's eyebrows rise. "You alright?"

"I'm fine. Don't worry. It's just a phase, I'm sure. I'll see you in the morning," I say.

We walk together to our cars in the driveway, and he opens my door for me.

"Are you sure you're okay?" Jason asks.

I smile. "I'm fine."

Jason pecks me on the lips and brushes a loose strand of hair behind my ear. A caring gesture, although I don't feel the adoration.

When pulls his car out of the driveway, his phone is already up to his ear. Already off in his other world. Following behind, I head to work, anxious of what this day might bring.

When the clock hits 5:30 pm, I've already clocked out and have all my belongings packed up and ready to go.

"Well, you're out of here quick! Got a hot date tonight?" my coworker asks.

"You know my life isn't that exciting, I've just gotta get home to my can of tomato soup!" I shout as I walk out the door, lying through my teeth again.

Option 1 or 2? Or neither? Be honest.

I text Clara pictures of two separate outfits for tonight. One is a pair of mom jeans with a simple beige tank top and the other a black mini skirt with an old band tee that I got from the thrift store ages ago. Clara is the only person who knows about this little planned rendezvous. I had to tell someone just in case I happen to be walking into the trap of a serial killer or something. I don't know Atlas as much as it feels like I do. And I've always been taught to err on the side of caution when it comes to men. But I also just wanted someone to discuss it with. Clara is easy to talk to. She doesn't judge and I know that she likes to keep things hush hush. I've almost considered talking to her about the other night with Jason, but I should probably keep it between me and my husband. This club may share partners, but it doesn't need to share the intimate parts of a marriage.

Atlas will be here in thirty minutes to pick me up and I'm sweating as I run around the bedroom like a mad woman trying to finish sprucing myself up. By the time Clara has texted back, it looks like a tornado has flown through my closet and bathroom.

Option 2, obviously! Have fun babes! Can't wait to hear all the dirty little details.

At 6:55 pm my phone buzzes as I'm adding a few more coats of mascara. It's Atlas.

I'm outside but no rush.

My heart skips a beat and I almost smear the wand onto my eyelid. I spritz myself with Flower Bomb and give myself one more look over in the mirror. One more quick tousle of my wavy hair and I'm heading to the front door, stomach tense.

Atlas stands with his back leaning up against his Range Rover. I think this is the first time I've seen him dressed so casually. He looks just as good in jeans and a t-shirt as he does in his formal wear. Maybe even a tad bit sexier. His jeans are just the right amount of tight and I never realized before how nice his backside is.

He pulls me into him, and I breathe in his usual intoxicating smell.

"You hungry?" he asks.

"I can definitely go for some buffalo wings," I say.

He smiles at my response, opens the passenger door, and ushers me in. Barry White plays on low volume. Just being in his car gives me a better sense of who he is. There is a silver necklace that swings from his rearview mirror.

"What's this for?" I ask as I hold the chain still in my hand.

"It was my mom's. She passed away when I was 18. She wore it every day. I've had it in every car since. I want to have a piece of her every place I go," he says.

"I'm sorry. That must have been so hard," I say.

He nods, shifting the car into gear and pulling away from my house. "There isn't a day that has gone by for the past seventeen years that I haven't thought of her."

"I'm sure she would be proud of the success you have achieved so far," I say, unsure of the right words to use.

He laughs, lightening the mood. "I don't know about that. I'm not so sure that this is what she envisioned for me. But she isn't here to bite my head off, which is nobody's fault but her own. So here I am, living a life of debauchery."

His face has an air of optimism that shows me that he's healed from those wounds. It's something he is able to discuss freely. I'm not the biggest fan of my mother. But I can't imagine losing her. Especially at such a fragile age. I wonder how many milestones of his she missed.

"Well, I can't imagine she's up there disappointed," I say.

"Oh, I'm sure she's thoroughly appalled."

We both laugh now. He rubs the chain between his fingertips and then grabs my hand, caressing my palm. It sends shockwaves through me.

"So, you like Barry White?" I ask.

His eyes light up and he chuckles. "What do you know about Barry White?"

"A lot, actually. He was my dad's favorite, along with Marvin Gaye and Diana Ross."

"I think I'd like this guy," he says.

"I might too if he hadn't left. I was around eight when my mom assured him that she had no desire to settle down. He became practically transparent after that. I got a few calls on birthdays and Christmas for the first few years. And then it all fizzled out. I haven't heard from him since I was thirteen."

His tone darkens. "I'm sorry. I know the damage that losing a parent can cause. But I can safely say that he's the one who's missing out."

"Thanks. I've got my mom, though. For better or worse," I say.

"Tell me more about this lady."

"She's great. She really is. I suppose that she just spends so much time crossing things off her never-ending bucket list that she barely even remembers she's a woman in her mid 50's with no priorities and no man to grow old with," I say.

"Well, that can't be such a bad thing, can it?" he asks.

I shrug.

Atlas gives me his full attention. He doesn't try to steer the conversation back to his own experiences and he gives my hand a gentle squeeze anytime the topic gets more serious.

When we finally pull up to the restaurant, I don't want to leave the privacy of the car. A warmth has spread through me having just been heard for the past thirty minutes.

"Sorry that we had to come all the way out to BFE. But I promise it'll all be worth it," he says.

"It better not disappoint."

The wings are to die for. Atlas wasn't lying. And by the time I'm finishing up my eighth, my fingers are sticky, and my stomach is screaming at me to stop.

"Looks like I'll have to bring you back here," Atlas says.

I blush as I use one too many napkins to clean up the mess I've made.

"Shall we have one more drink before we head out?" he asks.

I agree and he calls the waitress over.

"Hey, can I get another whiskey coke? And then she'll have…"

"I'll have another Midori Sour," I say.

"We might actually be out of limes, hon. But I can check–Savannah, do we have any lime for a Midori?" she yells to a woman behind the bar.

I glance at the woman searching behind the counter. Pale skin, gaunt face. She looks so familiar. Where have I seen her before?

"We've got a few! I can make a Midori," the woman blurts out.

All of the sudden it hits me like a ton of bricks. Flashes of a frail woman hanging from the ceiling flare in my mind.

It's her. The hanging lady.

"I'll be right back. I'm going to use the bathroom," I tell Atlas.

Except I walk past the hallway to the bathroom and go straight to the bar. I'm not one to strike up conversations with strangers, but there is a burning curiosity inside of me that I can't put out.

"Hey," I say over the counter.

When she glances up, her eyes widen, and her pale face goes even whiter. She knows exactly who I am.

"Can we speak in private? Please? It will be quick," I plead.

She moves her head towards a secluded hallway next to a door labeled "employees only" and we both scurry over.

"I shouldn't say anything," she says as she glances over Atlas' way.

"You don't have to worry about me. I won't tell a soul," I say.

"You seem sweet…" she says.

"I'm new to it all, which I'm sure you could tell. I'm not trying to overstep. I'm just trying to understand."

"Why don't you ask him?" She motions over to Atlas.

"Honestly, I'm still trying to figure out who to trust."

She glances around for a minute, seeming to contemplate my reliability.

"What do you want to know?" she asks, her tone one of frustration.

"Did someone hire you?" I ask.

"It was a gig referred to me by a friend of a friend. I strip on the side. Bartending doesn't pay all the bills. I thought that it might be a good niche to get into. 'Niche' being one hell of a way to describe what you all requested."

"You all?" I ask.

"The whole damn cult," she says.

I frown and she can see that she offended me. She can see that I took her comment personally.

"Listen," she motions me in closer, "I've been asked to do some fucked up shit by clients before. I'm used to it. It's part of the profession. But this shit was next level. I was paid well so I followed through, but you can bet your ass I won't be back for more. It took me over a week just to recover."

I can't say I blame her. I think back to the initiation night and shivers run down my spine. I rub away the goosebumps on my arm.

She wears a full long sleeve and pants. I can only guess it's to cover the scars that may always be there. At least she looks a little less strung out than she had been that night. She looks younger now too, probably barely over twenty-one. They preyed on someone so vulnerable.

'I should have known, though. I have some girlfriends who have dabbled in that business and have never come back through. There's no telling where they are now. I can't say I'm surprised. There's evil within that group. No offense," she says.

"None taken."

"Look. I don't know how deep you are into all of this, but if I were you, I'd leave it all behind. Or at least keep your eyes and ears open. Some of those folks… some just aren't right," she says.

"Some? Which ones?" I ask.

"Savannah! Table 12 is waiting!" A voice calls from a distance, breaking her focus on our conversation.

"Just don't say I didn't warn you," she says as she walks away back towards the bar.

Atlas is probably wondering if I ditched him and caught an Uber back home. I make my way back to the table, not feeling any better about the whole ordeal.

"Your drink is probably watered down by now," he says and gives me a wink.

"Sorry. I just had to take an off the clock work call. Love it when my boss does things like that," I lie.

The rest of the evening is filled with smiles and laughs. I'm so giddy my cheeks hurt. Savannah stays at the back of my mind. I keep reminding myself that she agreed to it. And I just hope that she was paid well enough.

Atlas gives off a genuine energy that I can't help but to be drawn to. He takes my mind off of the worry in my marriage and the stress of this new venture I have decided to dive into. Which is quite the coincidence seeing as he's a major part of this whole world.

After one more drink and a slice of creamy raspberry cheesecake that we split, we get the check and head out.

As we drive back, my eyes drift to the glow of Atlas' phone lighting up with a picture of Meagan, her fiery hair tousled in front of half of her face. He glances down and hits the lock button, sending her to voicemail.

"You can answer that, you know. I don't mind," I say.

"Nah, she can wait," he says, and he grabs my hand to hold.

I'm both flattered and uneasy. She's his wife. I'm his... well I guess I don't really know what I am to him. But his loyalty to his wife should come first. I'm just a woman he met a month ago.

"I don't mean to overstep, but where does she think you are tonight?" I ask, half wishing I didn't.

He takes his eyes off the road to study my face. "Where does Jason think that you are?" he asks.

Touché.

I take the hint and drop the subject. His avoidance of the topic makes it clear that he doesn't want to talk about his wife. Compartmentalization. I get it. Maybe I should learn to do the same.

"No clouds tonight. I know of a pretty cool spot down the road where the sky lights up like a Christmas tree. Care to join me?" he asks.

There's a creeping feeling in the pit of my stomach telling me I should just go home. The time on the dash reads half past ten. I look at Atlas, ready to decline the offer but then he furrows his brows as if he knows he's about to be disappointed and I change my mind. I don't have it in me to let him down.

"It sounds beautiful," I say.

I was right. We pull into an empty dirt lot and Atlas puts the car in park. As soon as his headlights shut off, the sky above us shines. Hundreds of stars twinkle through the moonroof. I hurry out of the passenger door and turn my head upwards.

"The big dipper. There." I point to the vivid constellation.

"Come over here and I'll show you more," he says. Atlas lays out a blanket in the dirt. It isn't the most comfortable, but we both lie on our backs anyways and stare up at the sky.

"There is Cygnus. Crazy enough it was found to contain the first ever discovered black hole. And that one to the right is Lyra, which was also the name of my childhood Pitbull." He connects the dots with his finger.

"You sure know your stuff," I say.

"I had an astronomy book that I checked out from the library and never returned when I was like eight years old. I read that thing like crazy during the day and laid out in the little patch of grass in front of our house every night, staring up at the sky, for weeks," he says, "My mom would have to drag me back inside the house at bedtime."

We both laugh. I love learning all his little quirks and what makes him tick. There's something new to learn about him each time we are together. Our conversations have yet to get stale.

"How did you even find this spot?" I ask.

"I take drives when I have shit on my mind. I end up running into some pretty cool places," he says.

He rolls over onto his stomach and props himself up his elbows, his head hanging over mine.

"You can't beat this view though," he says.

It takes me a second to realize that he isn't referring to the view above him. He's referring to the view below him.

He leans in and presses his lips against mine. They are still sweet from the cheesecake we shared after dinner. The kisses continue and become heavier. Soon both of our mouths are open, my tongue swirling around his.

His fingers tangle in my hair as he pulls my head closer into his. The smell of our saliva mixes with the scent of his cologne. He is intoxicating. Soon I find myself on top of him, grinding my body into his. He hikes up my skirt and slips off my panties, throwing them aside to the dirt. When he slides inside of me, I let out a moan that travels through the desolate plain. I throw my head back and stare at the stars as our bodies move in perfect rhythm. We both finish hard, and our sweaty bodies collapse back onto the blanket. It takes me a second to catch my breath.

"What time is it?" I ask, panting.

"This must mean my time with you is up," he says.

He kisses the tip of my nose, and we head back to the car. I'm nervous to see how much time has passed. Jason will be out late, but he has to come home eventually.

11:35.

Shit.

It's going to take us at least 45 minutes to get back to my house. I can only hope that Jason's "work" has less to do with financials and more to do with a big breasted blonde. He may not stay out past midnight for paperwork, but I'd bet he would for his mistress.

As we get closer to home, I start to second guess my decision. What if he really was just working late and I've been out traipsing around like a tramp with a married man. I didn't mean to be out this long. I don't know what I'll tell him if he's home. Will he recognize Atlas' car? Will he believe that I was at my mom's having a drink?

My heart thuds in my chest as we pull onto my street.

"Is something wrong? You look like you're about to be sick," Atlas says.

I shake my head. I don't want Atlas to know that I'm scared of my husband catching me. He doesn't need to know the current state of mess my marriage is going through.

From a few houses down, I can see Jason's black Jeep is parked in the driveway. My stomach churns like I'm going to vomit.

"Stop the car!" I startle Atlas and he slams on the brakes.

He looks at me like I'm crazy, his eyes spread wide.

"I'm going to walk from here. Sorry. I'll explain later," I say and hop out of the car before he can say anything.

My legs move fast. My mind races with excuses. I inhale deep breaths of the warm air to steady my heart rate. If I'm hyperventilating, he will know that it's all bullshit.

I creak open the front door and shuffle to the kitchen. A glass of water might help before I go to the bedroom to face him. When I turn the corner, I'm in shock at the scene in front of me. White powder sits in a neat line on the countertop and my husband holds his sniffling nose. He jumps when he sees me standing quietly in bewilderment.

"Lula," he says, still wiping at his dripping nose.

"Coke, Jason? Really?" I ask, exasperated.

"Where have you been? I thought you were upstairs sleeping." he says, ignoring my question.

My voice thunders through the room. "What on Earth are you thinking?"

"It's just a little something Calen gave me to get through this damn quarter at work. Calm down." He crosses his arms over his chest.

"It's a hard drug, Jason. You can't just brush it off like you just popped a Tylenol."

"I'm going to shower," he says firmly and pushes past me.

He brushes the rest of the powder into a baggie and stuffs it in his pocket.

I'm at a loss for words as I watch him traipse up the staircase.

"You should probably rinse off as well," he calls back.

CHAPTER 17

Jason's arms are wrapped around me when I wake. His morning breath is sour, and oddly comforting. I turn my body to face him. His eyes are closed, and a quiet snore emanates from his nostrils. His dimples and long eyelashes remind me of how sweet and gentle my husband is. Like this man lying next to me now and the man from the past few weeks cannot possibly have existed on the same plane. The slight signs of age are present in his smooth skin. A few forehead wrinkles. Barely perceptible smile lines. I know his work is stressful and maybe I haven't been tending to him like I should be. He takes such good care of us. If it weren't for his hard work, I wouldn't be able to get away with my cushy, mindless job.

I kiss his nose and his eyes flutter open.

"Morning," I say.

Relief fills me when a smile spreads across his face.

"Good morning, my beautiful," he says.

"Want some bacon and eggs? I'm going to make some breakfast and then get the house ready for mom to come tomorrow," I say.

"That sounds amazing," he says as he stretches out his arms.

I jump out of bed to get things started, but before I leave the room, he stops me.

"Lu, I just want to let you know that I'm sorry for last night. Work has been kicking my ass lately. It was stupid. And I dumped the baggy in the toilet and threw it into the trash. You don't have to worry about it anymore."

And just like that, I remember why I married this man. But now guilt washes over me. Atlas is great. But he's not Jason.

"There's my girl."

My mom shows up at our doorstep on Sunday afternoon with a bottle of wine, a small black book, and a handful of daffodils.

"I picked these from my sweet little neighbor lady's garden. I thought they'd look cute in your kitchen," she says as she marches through the doorway before I'm even able to greet her.

"Good to see you, mom." I follow after her.

She heads straight for my kitchen cabinets and searches through my glasses for a vase. The woman has no sense of boundaries. I lean into the island, putting my elbows onto the granite, and watch her take over my home.

"Oh, and I brought you this book. I swear I finished it in less than a day. You have to read it. It's so enlightening." She hands me the book. *The Art of Being Alone* is scrawled across the cover and I refrain from rolling my eyes.

She finds a tall, skinny vase and sets the arrangement on my countertop, as if she's decorating her own home.

"Beautiful. Thank you," I say.

"So, what's new? Why have you been avoiding me?" she asks, putting a hand on her hip.

"I have not been avoiding you."

"Where is my son-in-law?" she asks.

"He's out grabbing us some sandwiches for lunch. He should be back any minute."

"Okay so we don't have to be so secretive. *What* is going on?" she asks, commanding me to fill her in. She takes a washcloth from the basin and starts scrubbing at the handle of my refrigerator.

My mother's passion for prying and gossip will probably always outweigh her pursuit of zen. Two odd obsessions for someone who considers themselves to be highly enlightened. I often find myself biting my tongue when she's around. I hate to fight with her and it's much easier to just ignore the annoying comments that she makes. It's also much easier to keep her out of my private life. Although she would love it if she could know every little, juicy detail.

"Same old, same old. Work and home. That's about it," I say and take the washcloth from her hands, placing it back in the basin.

"See and that's the problem, Lula." She slaps her now empty hand against her thigh.

"I'm in a phase in my life right now where I just want to chill, to be at peace," I say.

"Let's not sit here and pretend you haven't always been in that phase. And there is a difference between peace and stability." Her voice is condescending, judgy.

I clasp my hands together and attempt to change the ever-present topic. "How have you been?"

She shakes her head, begrudgingly accepting that I don't want to have the same conversation we have every time I've seen her for the past two years.

Her demeanor changes in an instant. "I've been absolutely wonderful. I signed up for a membership at that yoga studio on 6th and 10th St. Hot yoga twice a week. I feel so rejuvenated each time. Sweating out all the negativity. You know, you really should join me. It's not too far from here," she says.

"I just might have to do that."

"Got some negativity you need to be rid of?" she asks.

"Mom, stop," I say, throwing my head back in frustration.

The front door swings open and Jason walks in with a bag full of sandwiches.

"Provolone or Swiss?" he asks as enters the kitchen and moves in for a hug from his mother-in-law.

She embraces him like she wasn't trying to dig up the dirt on him less than thirty seconds ago.

"I'm off dairy, Jason. So, I will be picking it off either way," she says.

I bite my tongue. Hard.

We eat a nice lunch, sans cheese, over glasses of wine in the living room. My mom talks about her plans for a trip to Belize and the hot forty-something at the yoga studio who asked for her number and was affectionately rejected. Jason bears it all with laughs, nods, and commentary. I'm appreciative that he humors her, even though he knows she's not his biggest fan.

"Well, ladies. I've got a golf date that I'm due for in about an hour, so I'd better get going. Thank you for coming, Mallory," Jason says, a few hours into her visit.

"Thank you for having me. I'll be happy to have some alone time with my girl," my mom says and rubs my knee.

I know that Calen enjoys the occasional game of golf, but I can't help but to wonder if Haven is an avid golfer. Jason says his goodbyes, tells me he will be back in time for dinner, and leaves the house.

"Well shall we finish the bottle of Zin?" my mom asks.

I go to the kitchen to refill our glasses. This privacy allows me to check my phone, which I haven't looked at for the past few hours.

I need to talk to you when you get a chance.

My stomach clenches at Atlas' words on my phone screen. I wait a few seconds, then glance back at the empty wine glasses.

"I'm thinking of getting you one of those kubaton keychains. I put a few in my Amazon cart. You can't be meandering around town without protection these days." My mom's words filter in through the other room.

"Uh-huh, okay," I say, not caring if my voice travels far enough for her to hear.

My fingers fly across the keys as I type a response to Atlas before splitting the last bit of wine into both glasses.

Is everything alright?

When I get back to the living room, my mom is absent. I take a gulp of wine and stare at the phone screen, willing him to reply quickly.

"Lula Jane. What is this?" My mom pops up from the hallway. She shakes a plastic bag filled with a white substance in front of her.

It's not foreign to me, I recognize it immediately. The small baggie of powder that was supposed to be at the bottom of the garbage. Except this one is much fuller, like he's had a refill since the last time he was caught.

"Looks like you're having quite the spiritual awakening yourself," she says, peering at the powder.

"Where did you find that?" I ask, my tone curt.

I'm livid. At her for being a busybody and at Jason for being a liar. The air conditioning is on in our home but I'm suddenly roasting.

"I'm not judging you. Trust me, I've had my fair share of experimentation," she says, thoroughly amused.

"Mom, where did you find it?" I ask, ripping the baggie out of her hands.

"Calm down, Lula. I'm not going to snort your stash. I found it under the guest bathroom sink," she says, gesturing towards the hallway.

"So, you're snooping now?" I ask.

"I was looking for an extra roll of toilet paper, actually." Her voice rises.

I rush back into the kitchen and shake the bag over the sink. My mom follows after me.

"Lula, what the hell is going on? It's not yours then?" she asks.

"No, mom. Of course, it's not mine!" I don't mean to yell. I hate raising my voice at her.

"So, Jason is a junkie now?" She folds her arms across her chest.

"Seriously, mom? You were fine when you thought it was mine," I say, shutting off the faucet, hoping every last bit is gone. Untraceable.

"That's different. With you it would have been experimentation. You don't have an addictive personality. Never have. But with him, well that just worries me," she says, her head shaking again as she takes a seat at the table.

"It's not your job to worry about him, mom. It's mine," I say and take a seat across from her. Suddenly I'm tired. Both physically and emotionally. These past few days I've been forcing normalcy. Maybe it's something I'm stupid for striving for anymore.

Her tone softens. "It's my job to worry about you, Lula Jane."

I sigh. Long and hard.

"I think it's clear that I've overstayed my welcome. I'll get out of your hair," she says and scoots out of the chair.

She places her wine glass in the sink, comes back to me, leans over, and pulls me into a hug. Her usual perfume of jasmine and peach swirls in the air around us. I let the scent fill my senses. I love her. But sometimes it's easier to love someone from afar.

"Just keep your wits about you, honey," she says, squeezing me tight, and leaves out the front door with her head held high.

I stick Jason's baggie into my pocket. Scenarios of confrontation consume my mind. I'm at a loss for which approach to take.

A message from Atlas comes through but I swipe it up before I read any of the words. I can only handle one issue at a time. Right now, the coke issue takes precedence. This is a habit that can't continue.

It hits half past nine and Jason still isn't home. I call him twice but get his voicemail each time. Both times I leave a message.

"Jason, just wondering when you'll be home," I say in the first message.

"It's almost ten o'clock Jason. We need to talk. Where the hell are you?" I say in the second, my tone is firm and accusatory.

I scrunch myself up on the couch in the front room. Curtains are drawn but all that's left to see in the dark of night is the massive tv in the neighbor's living room, lit up with some sports game. My fingers drum my knees as my mind drifts to the plastic in my pocket. The lack of light in the room allows the moon to cast a white streak across the walls.

By the time the door inches open shortly after eleven, I've already drifted off to sleep, my head resting on the cushions.

The faint noise stirs me awake as Jason stumbles in, tripping over the rug in the doorway.

"Shit," he mutters and steadies himself on the coat rack.

"Drink a bit too much?" I mumble. Jason jumps, unaware that I'm on the couch waiting for him.

He grunts and I can sense he doesn't want to talk. He ignores me and trudges through the room. Drowsy and sluggish, I drag my feet and follow him to the kitchen, determined to address the issue at hand. He sways to the sink, clearly heavily intoxicated.

"We need to talk," I say.

Fumbling in the cabinet, he finds a glass and fills it, gulping it down in seconds.

"Not tonight, Lula. Just go to bed." He slurs each word.

"My mom found this in the bathroom cabinet." I hold up the empty baggie.

He points his finger at me. "Why the hell was that bitch even going through our things?"

I gasp. My mother is a lot of things, but not a bitch.

"What is wrong with you?" I ask, unable to keep my cool.

Jason swipes the baggie from my outstretched hand and throws it back at my face, the plastic grazes my cheek. "Maybe if you weren't turning out to be just like her, I wouldn't need to use that shit anyway."

I stammer for words. "You—you lied to me. You said you threw it out."

"For the love of God. Drop it, Lula!" he yells.

I stand there like a fool, tears welling in my eyes.

"You're drunk. This isn't you," I say with a whimper.

"You're drunk. This isn't you." Jason mocks my words in a high-pitched tone.

The tears flow now, and I wipe them with my arm. "We can talk about this in the morning. It's clear you're in no place to discuss this tonight."

I turn to leave him to his drunkenness, but he grabs my arm, yanking me to face him. The sour stench of beer flows from his ragged breath.

"Don't you dare bring this up again," he says.

I yank my arm out from his grasp and walk up the stairs, rubbing the spot his fingernails dug into.

Savannah's warning rings through my head.

Just don't say I didn't warn you.

CHAPTER 18

Gina Reese: 3 Weeks Before Death

He is getting the kids involved now. Elise has called me three times today, begging me to come home. My heart hurts for her. What she doesn't understand is that her father is the one making this separation necessary. He's not allowing me to be both a mother and a woman with her own needs and wants. She has it in her head that I've left for another man, which I'm assuming is Greg's doing. That couldn't be farthest from the truth. I assured her that I have not, and would not ever, leave her and Liam for something so small as a man.

Once I get back on my feet and get my own place, I'll be taking them to live with me. And Greg can be alone with his liquor and pills. As long as you remain loyal, the club will provide. And once Rasheeda gets things set in motion, I won't have to worry so much about funds. Money is the only thing that Greg has to dangle in front of my face. But I don't need to rely on it anymore.

The club has shown me nothing but care and devotion. Just about every member has come by to see me and talk me through this difficult time. Things will only go up from here.

CHAPTER 19

The sun rises early Monday morning as light filters through the curtains. I stretch out my limbs and realize the space next to me is still bare. Just like it was when I closed my eyes last night. My phone reads 6:00 am. It's still early and I don't have to be at work for another two hours. Three unread messages pop up in my notifications. One is from Atlas, one from Clara, and the other from my boss. I ignore the message about early morning clients and skip straight to Atlas' reply that I ignored last night.

Everything is fine. Just haven't heard from you since Friday. I feel like I need some clarity.

I sigh. In the heat of everything I put Atlas to the back burner. He didn't deserve that.

I'm so sorry. I'm dealing with shit. I had a wonderful time Friday. I'll explain later.

I don't plan to actually divulge my messy marital problems at a later date. But hopefully I've given him some reason to not give up on me completely.

I open Clara's message next.

I need the details about Friday night. Also, what are you wearing for the event this weekend? I need some inspo.

I guess I also forgot to fill Clara in on my night out. I wasn't planning on telling her much, but I at least wanted to let her know that I had a good time and made it back in one piece. It's the least I could do for using her to vent to. And whatever is happening next weekend, I'm not privy to.

When I go to the bathroom to shower, I notice that Jason's toothbrush is already wet. Maybe he's been up here since last night?

After getting ready for work, I walk down the stairs to the kitchen, and maple fills the air.

A plate of syrupy pancakes and crispy bacon sits on the table. Jason comes around the corner, already dressed in his slacks, and buttoned down.

"I slept in the guest bedroom last night to give you some space." He goes to the drawer to take out a fork and knife and hands it to me.

"I know I have a problem," he says as he pulls the chair out for me.

I sit down and let him continue.

"I've already taken six ibuprofen this morning. I was up all night. I'm a wreck."

"Do you think it's this club?" I ask, my voice measured. I don't want to make him angry, but it's the first thing that crosses my mind.

"No, no. Nothing to do with the club. My mom called me the other day in hysterics. She wanted to talk about my dad." He sits down at the table across from me, poking at his pancake.

I stay quiet, assuming I know where this is going.

He continues, "People from the town are talking. About my family. About my father. She's appalled and outraged, embarrassed. And demanding to know what I've known this whole time. What I've been 'hiding'". He gives air quotes and then runs his fingers through his hair, hanging his head low.

"Hiding? She can't possibly place any of the blame on you," I say.

"Camilla can place the blame on whomever she wants, as long as it's not herself. She kept insisting that I explain what I know when we both know good and well that she was there too. She heard the cries from the basement just like I did. She saw the glances and heard the whispers. Yet she wants to feign ignorance. She is even more culpable than I am. I was a child. I didn't lay in bed with that monster each night."

"Jason—"

"I mean, he's gone. Why can't we just let the shit die with him?" He stabs his fork into the food, and it pokes through, banging onto the porcelain.

"Hey," I stand and wrap my arms around him, "you should have told me that this was going on."

"You don't need to be dragged into this mess any more than I do."

"Yes, but now it's seeping into our marriage. I'm your wife. I'm here to listen and support you." I sink to my knees and lay my head on his chest. The low thud of his heartbeat lulls in my ear.

His voice is little more than a whisper. "I took my frustrations out on you and it's not okay. It feels like it's one thing after the other these days."

"Maybe we just need a little break away from it all," I say.

"Speaking of a break, there's a club event this weekend. We can let loose and forget about all of this work and family drama for a few nights," he says as he kisses the top of my head.

When I mentioned a break, I meant a short vacation with just me and my husband, like a trip to a hotel and spa, but he seems to have other ways in mind to wind down.

"Are you sure it's a good time for that?" I ask, but regret it as soon as I do, already knowing what his response will be.

"When the club calls, you answer," he says with a frown.

I only nod.

"So, what does this event entail?" I ask, moving back to my spot at the table across from him.

"It's Friday night and Saturday night. They have suites booked at the Aviara out in Carlsbad. We will do some golfing, have some time at the spa and then I think they rented out a venue for a shindig Rasheeda is hosting, so bring something dressy."

I think back to initiation night. I struggle to swallow down my bite of pancake at the thought of Rasheeda as a host.

"It's only thirteen of us. A whole venue sounds a bit overkill, right?" I ask.

"It isn't just club members that come to these larger events. Friends of friends of friends are also invited. It's actually a great time for networking."

Maybe the club isn't as private as they make it seem. Or maybe they are fishing for new members.

"Networking? You said no work," I say, playfully.

He ignores my banter.

"It all sounds fancy. And relaxing. Can we afford that right now?" I ask.

"It's already paid for. Courtesy of the thirteen," he says with a mouthful of food.

The thought of being with these people for two days straight makes my face feel hot. Especially considering Haven will be sauntering around Jason while I'm present. But a day at the spa does sound like a dream. The tension in my shoulders from this past week has yet to let up. A massage would be nice. Although if I don't address some of my concerns with Jason before this trip, then I may only wind up with lower back pain to top it all off.

"I better get to work," he says.

I take a few bites of bacon dipped in syrup. "Yeah, me too. Can we talk tonight, though?" I ask.

"About?" He slides out of his chair and grabs our plates from the table, taking them to the sink.

"Boundaries."

"Is that necessary?" he asks, his back towards me as he loads up the dishwasher.

"Yes." I respond loudly over the hum of the appliance.

Jason doesn't like uncomfortable conversations. He avoids them at all cost, letting issues simmer until they've completely boiled over. But he can't avoid it this time. Our relationship is too fragile right now.

After he leaves, I respond to my texts.

First to Atlas.

Sorry for the short response earlier. I think we both need clarity. Want to meet up tonight? I know a place near my house with cheap drinks.

Then to Clara.

Friday night was great! And I'm sure I need inspo more than you do! Shopping trip?

My boss' text will remain unanswered until I get to work. The days of me breaking my back for an underpaid job are over.

My focus at work wavers throughout the day. A stack of patient charts lies in a pile next to my computer, but I have no desire to open any of them.

"Lula? Can I speak with you for a moment?" Sandy steps out of her office and peers around the corner.

"Oh, uh, sure," I say, quickly exiting out of the non-work-related web browser I have open. I spin around in my chair to face her.

"Did you get my text earlier? You never texted me back." She drums her fingers on the wall next to her.

"Text?"

"About the website. It needs some serious updates, and my tech guy has been slammed. He can't squeeze us in." She has the same look on her face that she's had many times before when she's begging for a favor that she knows is above my pay grade, her nose all scrunched up, glasses sliding up her face. To be fair, I never even opened her text. So, I wasn't actually ignoring her. As all the work piles up on top of me, I give her the only answer that I know will suffice.

"I'll get right on that."

But I don't. I spend most of my time at work making a list of questions for Jason. And then another list for Atlas.

<u>Talking Points for Jason</u>

- What do you consider to be your relationship status with Haven?
- Are you romantically involved (physically/emotionally) with any women besides Haven and me?
- What sorts of relationships are you comfortable with me getting into?
- How do you feel about Atlas and I (have I already gone too far)?
- How much information do you want to know about Atlas and me?
- How long are we expecting these extramarital relationships/this lifestyle to last?
- What if I decide that I can't handle this lifestyle any longer?

<u>Talking Points for Atlas</u>

- What do you consider to be our relationship status?
- How does Meagan feel about us/does she know?
- Where do you see our relationship (if there is any) going?
- Do you want this to be anything more than sex?
- Are you comfortable with Jason knowing everything about us?

If I'm going all the way with this lifestyle, I don't want any confusion. My marriage is at stake, and I can't continue to take that lightly. This past month has been a whirlwind and I need to find my bearings.

I get home from work and take a two-hour nap as if I worked my ass off all day with patients and paperwork. But really, I've put my job to the back burner. In reality, I'm just drained from the conversations I have to have tonight. And I'm scared of the answers I might receive. What if Jason has stronger feelings for Haven than he does for me? What if Jason is angry with me for how far things have gone with Atlas? Or worse, what if he wants me to cut things off with him?

On the other hand, what if Atlas sees me as only a piece of meat? What if the connection I feel is completely one sided?

So many moving parts. My head pounds just thinking about it all. I don't want to feel like I'm going crazy anymore. Like the world is spinning, and I have no way to gain my balance. I want to feel levelheaded and certain.

And then there's the whole club event looming in the back of my mind.

I wanted excitement. And adventure. I guess I got it.

Jason walks through the door at a quarter past five.

"Jason!" I call from our bedroom upstairs.

Footsteps tread up the stairs and I can't stop my knee from bouncing up and down. With my list in hand, I swallow and prepare to ask the questions.

"How's my lovely lady?" he asks as he pushes open the door.

"A bit nervous," I say.

He throws his head to the side in confusion until I hold up the piece of paper.

"Boundaries," I say.

He laughs. "Right, right. Well, go ahead." He scoots next to me on the bed and leans back onto the pillow.

"First off, what do you consider to be your relationship status with Haven?" There is a vice grip in my chest and all the possible answers clutter my brain.

A frown stretches over his face. "I think I need a glass of whiskey for this conversation."

I motion to the door. "Be my guest."

Jason comes back five minutes later with the whole bottle of Pendleton and no glass. He sits on the edge of the bed while I stay leaned with my back against the headboard.

He takes a big swig. "I wouldn't call what she and I have a relationship."

"She?" I ask.

Jason clears his throat. It's clear he doesn't want to say her name.

"Haven," he says, his voice crackling.

"Do you love her?" I ask the question that has been burning in the depths of my mind.

"I love you," he says, sloshing the liquid around in the bottle.

"Come on, Jason. All I'm asking for is honesty."

"I love fucking her. She loves the attention I give her. I consider it a win-win," he says.

"Do you love fucking me?" I ask, sounding a lot more pathetic than I intended to.

"Of course, I do. You're my wife," he says.

I try to ignore the ache in my stomach after I listen to him profess his love for Haven's body. It's only natural for me to compare myself to her. What does she do that I don't? Does she play with his ass? Does she give him phenomenal blow jobs? Does the tightness of her pussy send him climaxing in a matter of seconds?

"I read an email. You told her you're in love with her," I say with an accusatory tone and scoot a few inches away so that our skin is no longer touching.

He sighs, sits up, and takes another sip before responding. "I tell her what she wants to hear. I feed into her ego."

"So you're dishonest with her?" My voice shakes, threatening to break. I don't want to turn into an emotional mess.

"No. It's a game she plays. And not just with me but with other men too. It makes her feel sexy, powerful. She knows I love my wife. Our dynamic is weird but we both get what we need from it."

I want to argue, debate whether he's telling the truth or not, but hesitate.

"When did it start?" I ask.

"When I joined the club. Shortly before we met."

"Haven and me. Are we the only ones?"

"I won't lie. I've fooled around with other girls in the club before. That's the whole point, isn't it? But as of right now, she's the only one I'm associating with aside from you, my wife." He scoots back towards me, closing the gap that I created.

Images of girls' faces bounce around in my head. Just how many have there been since we've been together? Since I was brought into the loop?

"And if that changes?" I ask, biting my tongue from what I really want to say.

"You'll be the first to know," he says.

I fold the paper up and toss it to the nightstand.

"Now am I done with the questioning?" he asks, with only a few centimeters of his whiskey left swirling around in the bottle.

"Not quite," I say. I bring my knees to my chest and hold them tight, anxious for my time in the spotlight.

I lump my questions about Atlas into one, strung out mess.

"So… Atlas and I have gotten to know each other a bit. It's nothing serious— But I want to know if you're okay with this," I talk emphatically with my hands.

"We have slept together… outside of the club," I trail off and wait for a reaction but get none.

My voice rises. "I just want to know how much is too much. If you have any questions. That's fine too. I just don't want to overstep any boundaries. I don't need anyone romantically aside from you. I don't even need anyone physically. But this just all sort of happened and I need to make sure that you aren't uncomfortable with it because I don't want to do anything to tarnish our marriage…" Again, I get no reaction, so I continue.

"From the beginning the only thing that mattered was us. And that's still the case for me. But we both are also focusing on our own experiences. And I know what it feels like to be on the other side of all of this and it doesn't always feel the best so please just tell me how to navigate it all."

I finally finish my rant, take a deep breath, and stare at him, eager to get his thoughts.

Jason stares down at the empty bottle now. I can't see his eyes, but I can see his forehead scrunched up at his eyebrows.

Have I said too much already? Was he unaware of anything brewing between Atlas and I?

I hold my breath until he finally speaks.

"I'm not worried about Atlas. Have your fun. I'm sure he and Meagan are having theirs." He stands up and walks out the bedroom door, bottle in hand.

Meagan?

I think back to the call Atlas received from his wife on Friday night. She must have known what he was doing. If not, why was he so comfortable not answering? And initiation night when she joined us…

Am I so deluded?

I wasn't nervous for the talk with Atlas before, but now I am. I hate feeling as though I'm the butt of the joke. The one being duped.

"Wait," I call out.

He turns to face me, his eyes unamused.

"How long are we expecting this lifestyle to last? I mean, what if I decide that I can't handle it any longer?" I say, my voice weak.

"You read the fine print, Lula. Too late to turn back now." His mouth stretches into a smirk.

I shiver at his response. Jason's footsteps pound down the stairs, matching the rhythm of my heart.

I check myself in the bathroom mirror before going back downstairs to tell Jason I'm headed out for a bit.

My undereyes have been darker these past few days. I place a dab of concealer on my finger and tap it into the delicate skin. A few more coats of mascara along with a few swipes of blush onto my upper cheekbones bring life back to my face. A spritz of perfume and clear lip gloss finish the job. Before I leave the bathroom, I grab Jason's bottle of cologne and take a big whiff. It smells good. Bergamot and rosemary. It used to make the hairs on my arms stand straight up every time I caught a hint of it. But now I place the bottle back down and close the door, mourning the feeling that no longer accompanies the scent.

My phone buzzes on the bed. A text from Atlas lights up the screen.

Headed to the bar now. Need a ride?

I take off my work slacks and change into a pair of jeans before I reply.

Thanks, but I think I better drive myself. See you soon.

Downstairs, I'm surprised to see Jason stuff clean dishes in the cabinets from the dishwasher. It's usually my job. A glass sits on the counter next to him, filled with another dark liquor.

"I'm headed out for a bit. I shouldn't be long," I say, swiping my keys off the hook on the wall.

"Tell Atlas I say hi," he replies, raising his glass to me.

I hurry out, trying not to let his sentiment bother me.

On the way to the bar, I recite the list in my head over and over again.

The five questions I have to ask Atlas seem increasingly complex as my tires move me closer and closer to his location.

The beep of my car as I press the key fob to lock it makes me jump. I can't wait to get some liquor in me to calm my nerves.

They are shot. The stress today has me barely hanging on, ready to shut my eyes for twelve hours straight. As I walk towards the entrance, the sharp smell of cigarettes fills my nostrils. It acts as a placebo, taking the edge off. I was never a smoker, but I think that the countless weekends spent at my chain-smoking grandma's house has always left a soft spot in my heart for the smell.

Atlas sits on a stool at the bar, deep in conversation with some older man in a Trump 2024 t-shirt. The scruff on Atlas' face is prominent, like he missed a shave. It looks good on him, though, like he's not trying so hard to be a businessman 24/7.

"Loving the new face," I say, gesturing with my hands rubbing against my cheeks.

He turns to face me, and his smile could light the room.

"Sorry to interrupt," I say to the man seated next to him.

"No worries at all, young lady. He's all yours. Wise man you've got there," the older man says, patting Atlas on the back.

"He is. Isn't he?" I reply.

The older man turns back to the bartender, and I take a seat next to Atlas.

"First off, I want to apologize for running out on you last Friday. It had nothing to do with our night," I say.

"Okay, enlighten me."

"Well, Jason…" My hands fidget in front of me as I attempt to get out the right words.

Atlas nods, urging me to continue.

"I mean there were a lot of things I hadn't talked to him about beforehand."

"Like?" he asks.

"This." I motion to the both of us.

Atlas clears his throat and the bartender approaches.

"Can we get this lady a Midori sour?" he asks.

A smile spreads across my face as I realize he remembered my favorite drink.

"And can we make it a double?" I add.

Atlas small talks with the bartender about football teams while he shakes up all the ingredients for my drink. I wriggle in the barstool and twirl my fingers around the threads from the hole in my jeans. Finally, he sets the glass on the bar top and pushes it toward me. I take two long gulps. The lime makes my face pucker.

"Should I have ordered you something different?" Atlas laughs.

"No, no. This is great."

"Okay, then. Talk to me," he says.

"This might sound a bit silly. But I made a list," I say and pull a neatly folded piece of paper out of my pocket. The crumpling of the paper as I unfold it stands out amongst the voices and subtle background tunes of the bar.

He smirks. "You came prepared."

My cheeks warm. "I'm not always the best with my words. I figured I'd be more thorough if I had a cheat sheet… sound less like an idiot."

He takes a swig of his beer. "You could never sound like an idiot. What's on your list?"

"What would you say this is? Me and you. What are we doing?" I ask.

"We are getting to know each other," he says.

"Dating?" My stomach tenses as soon as I say it.

"That could be a good word for it."

"And where does 'dating' take two people in loving marriages?"

"Marriage is such a flimsy concept in my world," he says.

I look down to his left hand. His ring finger is bare, not even a slight indentation or discoloration to prove there ever was anything there. "Can you elaborate?" I ask.

"Meagan and I are husband and wife on paper. It works for us, and we have an understanding. We care for and respect one another. But marriage doesn't have to be associated with love."

He's right. I've known plenty of couples who just go through the motions, even long after love for one another has fizzled out. I think that's one of the reasons my mom never wanted to be in a marriage. Too scared to feel limited.

I shrug. "I get that I guess. I'm not here to judge your marriage," I say.

"We were in love once. It was such a whirlwind in the beginning, but things changed. I evolved, she evolved. No harm, no foul."

"So why stay together?"

"Why not? We enjoy our lifestyle."

"And you two still have sex?"

"Of course."

I take a deep breath. "Does she know about us?"

"I'm sure she can assume. We don't talk about those things anymore."

I wonder if she's as comfortable and nonchalant about their relationship as he is. It's hard to imagine they are both immune to jealousy.

"But back to your previous question, 'dating'," he makes air quotes with his fingers, "it can take us anywhere. The sky's the limit. If you're willing to ride it out with me." He takes the paper off my lap and sets it on the counter, then reaches for my hand and rubs his thumb in circles.

"Sounds a bit vague," I whisper, looking down at our entwined hands.

"It will get clearer as time goes on. I have no doubt about that."

He lifts my chin and presses his lips into mine. The muscles in my shoulders loosen.

He parts from my mouth and twirls his stool to lean his back against the countertop.

"Now it's my turn for the questioning," he says.

Those muscles that had relaxed just seconds ago tighten up again. I finish off my drink and swirl the straw around in the ice while swimming in his chocolate brown eyes.

"What is the situation with Jason?" His brows furrow at the mention of my husband's name. He crosses his arms over his chest.

"I'm sure you know that this is all new to me. I never pictured my marriage, let alone my life taking this turn. But here we are. Jason and I talked about it."

"You had a list for him too I'm guessing?"

"Yes, I did. And I got the answers that I needed. We have come to a mutual understanding. I suppose we have decided not to hinder one another."

"So, no limitations?"

"Not as far as my marriage goes," I say.

I think back to Haven, her email, and his claims that it's all a game. Even if it is all a lie, who am I to stop Jason from loving another woman? Either way, I may need to get used to the idea that love can't always be contained within one relationship.

CHAPTER 20

Midway through the week, I leave work early and meet Clara at a shopping mall. The sun is shining, and the heat sends sweat beads down my forehead as I walk from the back of the crowded parking lot. Summer has always been my favorite season and I relish in the serotonin boost. Instead of this weekend's events looming over my head like I thought they'd be, I'm actually starting to look forward to it. New experiences and opportunities await. Much better than sitting on the couch all weekend scrolling through TikTok and impulse buying on Amazon. And maybe I'll get to know this world, my husband, Atlas, *and* myself a bit better.

I find Clara laughing with a silver haired man in a suit outside of the Gucci store. He hands her a shopping bag clad with the easily recognizable interlocking G's. She opens it up to take a peek and lets out a squeal that echoes across the second floor of the mall. Clara grabs his scruffy cheeks and kisses both while he places his hand on the small of her back. His palm drifts down lower and I clear my throat.

His hand whips behind his back and Clara turns to face me. "Lula!" she says.

Clara rushes over and links her arm into mine. The man turns and walks away without a second thought.

"What's in the bag?" I ask.

"Just a little something I was owed." She throws her head back in laughter.

We traverse the mall. Hitting all of Clara's favorite shops.

"I've always thought that Atlas and Meagan were a bit of an odd couple. They act almost like business partners when they aren't fucking. So, what he told you makes a lot of sense, actually."

"I guess I'm just scared to be the butt of the joke," I say.

I filled Clara in on my situation with Atlas. I don't know her too well. But she gives off a trustworthy vibe. I don't know if it's her velvety voice or the fact that she's barely five feet tall, but my gut tells me that she's loyal.

Clara wears beige trouser shorts with a white, skin-tight tank and wedges. Her petite figure waltzes confidently through the clothing racks. As if she couldn't be swooped up and carried away by just about anyone in this mall.

My outfit pales in comparison. My black work slacks and faded blouse could easily have me confused with a mall custodian.

"Butt of the joke? What the hell would make you think that?" she asks.

"Jason made some comment the other night about Meagan and Atlas, and it just got me thinking. I don't want to be blindsided again like I was when we first started this whole lifestyle. I don't want to feel like a fool."

"Jason didn't tell you from the beginning?" she asks, mouth agape.

I shake my head. "I mean not right away. I was completely in the dark until shortly after poker night."

"Poker night? You mean the party at Cheyenne's just last month?" Clara hangs back up the dress she was eyeing with a clank.

"That one," I say.

"Asshole," she mumbles. "I always assumed you knew. He never hid the fact that he had a wife. I just figured you had your own extracurriculars going on. I mean Calen has some mysterious wife that no one has ever met who spends her spare time canoodling with women in Paris. I wonder why he didn't tell you sooner. That wasn't fair to you."

I shrug. "It's okay. Maybe he was scared I'd freak out. I did at first."

"No, no. That's no reason to keep a secret this huge from your spouse. And whatever the hell he's spewing about Meagan and Atlas, it's bullshit. I don't know Jason as well as the other guys so don't be offended if I tell you to take what he says with a grain of salt."

"He's my—"

She stops me. "He's your husband. I get it. I get it. I was just telling Ellis the other day that no matter how in love I fall with a man, he'd never get me to jump off a cliff with him."

I give her a quizzical look.

She laughs. "Let's just say boys will be boys. They have an agenda that's all their own."

She whips a hanger off the rack and gasps. "Your legs and this dress! No one will be able to resist you!"

Clara holds up a floral corset midi dress with a slit down the side.

I reach over and rub the fabric with my fingertips. It's soft, and the pale yellow would make my skin pop. I think of my thigh peeking through, teasing Atlas.

I grab the price tag, but the dress is yanked away from me before I get a glimpse at the cost.

"Don't start with that nonsense. We are buying it. I'll apologize to Jason on your behalf," she says.

I end up with several new dresses and beachwear. Clara just about doubles my loot and I'm left wondering how she's able to afford the total.

"What is it that you do for work again?" I ask.

"I'm a social media consultant."

"You work for Stellar?"

"And other similar firms who contract my services."

"Sounds lucrative."

"More or less. Some months are better than others. The people I meet make up for those drier months. Like my Gucci boy, Edward." She brings her finger up to her lips.

Secrecy is just a way of life for these people. I can't even begin to imagine Clara's extracurriculars outside of the club.

CHAPTER 21

Gina Reese: 3 Weeks Before Death

I've turned my bedroom at the cabin into a makeshift office. I moved the creaky bedside table to the opposite side of the room and brought in a metal folding chair that I found stored in a closet, made more comfortable with a throw pillow I found on the sofa in the front room. My improvised desk holds an old laptop I borrowed from Rasheeda, a can of diet coke, and a legal notepad with a list of names drawn sloppily across the pages.

Tessa Aguirre, Victoria Yarborough, Evangeline Anderson, Harper Wilson, Katie King, Sophia Jarvis, Polly Cooper. Name after name scribbled in black lead on the page. Though, one stands out to me amongst the rest. Roxanne Fowler. The first name instantly reminds me of a fiery little girl with crimson hair, a crooked nose, and freckles that I knew from primary school. She was always getting sent to the principal's office for one thing or another. Once she even put bubblegum in some mousy girl's sleek pigtails. Her parents became accustomed to the walk of shame through the school halls each time they were called in for a behavioral conference. Roxanne Fowler, however, isn't a red head and hasn't got a single speckle on her face. I couldn't envision her ever disrupting a class, either. The girl staring back at me in her profile picture on Instagram is doe eyed with a button nose. Her lips jut out in a kissy face and her chestnut brown hair frames her face in the perfect swoop.

Her page isn't set to private, which makes things a million times easier for me.

I resituate the cushion on the chair, balling it up underneath the bony part of my ass and draw a line through Roxanne's name on the paper. One down and plenty more to go.

They are the perpetual runaways. The teens whose missing person posts you share on Facebook only to see two hours later in the comments that they were "found safe." The teens who make the cops roll their eyes when the parents call with the same sob story time after time. They are the boy who cried wolf. Eventually, people stop caring.

But not us.

We are entitled to a finder's fee. I don't need to ask what I'm finding them for. I'd rather not know. I have an idea, though, which is probably accurate. "Inanna offers them up to her loyal servants," Rasheeda said. I didn't like it at first. I chuckled and thought she was joking. And then I had to ask her more than once, "Wait, you're being serious?". I had my reservations, sure. I had my moral dilemmas. But in the end, I had to push past all that and remember why I'm on this path to begin with. Inanna has given me the ticket to my freedom. The strength to leave my poisonous husband, the power to be my true self, the potential to live a life of divine fulfillment. At this point, I won't pass that up for anything.

In the past week, I've been prowling the missing persons posts on social media. My new profile, Olivia Fields, has joined a total of thirteen community groups on Facebook. I've spent my days sleeping and my nights shuffling through the circulating posts of the degenerate and misunderstood teens whose parents are pleading for help all while masking the fact that they're fed up with concern and misery. I scroll through the comments to get leads, learn associated friends, routines, whereabouts, and eventually I find a way to reach out.

Roxanne Fowler doesn't look like many of the others. She isn't rough around the edges. No face piercings, no abnormally colored hair, just the face of a girl who has gotten lost in the pandemonium of the world.

She's perfect.

CHAPTER 22

The breeze flows through my hair, whipping it into my face. I pull it all into a bun atop my head and lean back onto my towel.

We arrived at the resort thirty minutes ago and I ran straight for the beach. The sun is high in the sky and the moisture seeps into my skin. A flock of sandpipers chirp a few feet away from me, unbothered by my presence.

It's low tide and the waves lap steadily ahead. My bare feet bury into the warm sand and the sun rays soak into my face. I can taste the salty air on my tongue.

"Lula?" A voice calls from a distance, breaking through the crashes of the waves.

I roll onto my stomach to see who's coming. Rasheeda walks toward me, holding her sun hat on her head with both hands so it doesn't fly away. To be nice, I wave her over.

My stomach sinks a little. I was hoping for some time to myself before I'd be immersed into the social scene. Some time to bask in peace. So much for that.

"Hi, Rasheeda," I say as she approaches. Her dark sunglasses nearly take up her entire face.

"I was up in my room and saw a little figure down below. My eyesight is terrible these days, but I thought it was probably you. You don't need 20/20 vision to see someone's aura from a mile away," she says, holding her head high.

I chuckle but immediately regret it. Rasheeda isn't smiling.

She brushes off sand from her legs before speaking. "How was your drive up here? I hate going by car these days."

"The drive was fine. I don't mind being in the car. And Jason drove the entire two hour stretch so I relaxed for most of it. Took in the scenery. Did you drive here on your own?" I ask.

"No, no. I had a driver. I get incredibly car sick on these windy roads. I knocked myself out with a handful of Benadryl."

"Smart move," I say.

"Nervous for tonight?" she asks.

"Just a little apprehensive, I guess. I don't know exactly what to expect. But that doesn't mean that I'm not looking forward to it. I'm sure it will be a great time." I try to keep my tone light and optimistic.

"I used to be like that too, you know. Fearing the unknown instead of embracing it," she says with a small tilt to her head.

Sitting up, I bring my knees to my chest. Her face looms down on me but I can't see her eyes because her glasses are so dark.

"Have you ever screamed before, Lula?" Rasheeda asks.

My brow lifts and her mouth turns up into a smile.

"What?" I ask, squinting through the sunlight.

"I mean, really screamed. A howling, screeching, shrieking scream. Stressing your vocal cords to the point of exhaustion, until your head feels dizzy and your lungs burn," she says, her tone haunting.

Now I wish I had my own sunglasses to mask the uncomfortability that I'm sure is strewn across my face. I look down and brush the sand off of my feet instead. "I don't… I mean I—"

My stammering is cut short.

"You want to rid yourselves of those nerves?" she asks.

My head lifts and when I open my mouth to speak, all that comes out is some combination of a cough and a snort.

"Try it. Right now," she says. Her voice is firm. Less like a suggestion and more like a command.

"I don't think so," I say, shaking my head.

I wait for her to say something more but the only sound between us now are the waves lapping up on the shore. Her gaze moves from me to the stretching body of water I sit in front of.

Picking up my towel from the sand and folding it over my arm, I hope she takes the hint that I'm ready to end the conversation and head back up to my room. I clear my throat to get her attention, but she doesn't look my way. Instead, both of her hands grip her stomach as if she's about to be sick.

"Rasheeda, are you alright?" I ask.

A piercing wail emits from her widespread mouth. My body jerks backward and my towel falls back to the ground as my hands clasp around my mouth. I let out a gasp in shock, but it isn't even audible over the straining of her vocal cords. Rasheeda's green veins poke through her forehead and her eyes bulge out of her face. As she presses on my hands move from my mouth to cup my ears. The noise is animalistic, searing. I want to run but my feet stay planted.

Her lips are stretched so far that a few cracks are starting to split, and her uvula shakes at the back of her throat. Just as her brown skin starts to pale, the sound weakens, tapering off until she has nothing left to give.

Rasheeda's wide-open mouth falls back into a broad grin. I uncover my ears and struggle to find my breath. She, on the other hand, takes a deep gulp of air.

"Tonight is going to be a good night," she says in a hoarse voice and turns her back to me, sauntering back up toward the hotel like she didn't just set off cataclysmic vibrations from deep within the sea.

Once she's twenty feet ahead of me, I follow behind her, unable to stop the shakiness that has taken over my body.

Unhinged. The woman is unhinged.

"Have a nice time down by the beach?" Jason asks as I walk through the door to our suite.

"I ran into Rasheeda," I say.

"Oh nice. So, you had some company?"

"That I did," I say, shaking the leftover sand from my sandals.

I don't want to mention my moment on the beach with Rasheeda. I want to wipe it from my memory as best as I can. Her eccentric behavior makes me uneasy, like she has a few screws loose, and is one mishap away from going postal. Maybe I need to get to know her better, but her passion rubs me the wrong way. It's too extreme. Goosebumps still scatter over my skin from the encounter and I'm just ready to rinse off in the shower and get something in my system to settle my nerves.

"I'm going to hop in the shower," I say, walking past him to get to the bathroom.

"Wait. Shall I have a little appetizer before dinner?" Jason asks. He grabs my arm and pulls me close, yanking on the string to my shorts and dragging them down my hips.

"I really just need a shower, babe." I grab the waistband and start to hike my bottoms back up, but he rips it out of my hands and forces them to my ankles.

"You can shower when I'm done." His voice is stern.

Jason throws my shorts across the room and tosses me onto the fresh white sheets covering the bed. He doesn't bother with my top. He kneels and spreads my legs wide, ignoring the flecks of sand scattered around my inner thighs. His teeth clamp down onto my flesh, sending shock waves of pain up my pelvis. I wince, squeezing the bed sheets below me, and he lets out a low groan, wafting the rich scent of bourbon up to my nose.

He must have had at least a few drinks while I was down at the beach.

His tongue traces the bite and then trails closer to my center. When his mouth finds my lips, he sucks them. I moisten as he puts his whole mouth over me. My eyes shut and I let the pleasure fill my body, forgetting about the present.

Fingertips dig into my hips, and I'm drawn out of my trance. I shift a little at the scraping of his nails on my skin and he takes a firmer grasp, keeping my lower half still. My eyes wander to the ceiling. The milky, ornate Victorian tiles leave a subtle reminder of just how luxurious this resort is.

Relaxing my muscles again, I let out a faint moan while his tongue moves up and down, in between my lips. He finds my clit and flicks it a few times before clasping it with his teeth. I shudder and sit up onto my elbows. "Ow! Jason, that's too much!" I scream in pain.

Releasing, he closes my legs shut and scoffs. "Too much, huh?"

He wipes his mouth with the back of his hand and with heavy feet, stomps out of the hotel room.

The lock clicks behind him and I'm left lying on the bed bottomless, wondering what I did wrong.

A tap on the door comes while I'm finishing up getting ready for tonight's dinner party. Jason's footsteps trampled back through the room while I showered, only to leave again before I got out. I'm assuming he came back to get dressed since his slacks and button down are no longer hanging over the leather recliner in the corner of the room.

My bare feet tread across the tile to the door.

"Coming!" I yell out to whomever is behind the door.

Clara stands in the hall in a baby pink miniskirt and a matching bustier top. Her brown hair is parted far to one side and drapes over her shoulder. A mix of florals and vanilla emits from her tiny frame.

"I don't remember you buying that one on our shopping trip," I say, admiring her choice.

She laughs. "Last minute purchase."

I motion for her to come inside.

"Is Jason in here?" she asks, glancing around the room.

"No, he went down with Calen to greet some guests," I lie. I have no clue what he's doing. And with the amount he's had to drink, I can assure he's not greeting anyone. Over at the kitchenette, five mini bottles of bourbon litter the counter. Wherever he is, he's feeling pretty toasty.

Clara pushes past me and darts for the bathroom, her heels clicking on the floor. The toilet seat clangs against the porcelain, and she attempts to bat at the door to close it but misses before the sound of retching fills the entire room.

Could she not have done this in her own bathroom?

"Need me to hold your hair back?" I call out to her.

The only response is a few grunts and liquid splashing into the bowl.

She steps out of the bathroom a few minutes later, face pale and her long hair tied loosely into a misshapen ponytail.

"You, okay?" I ask, "Indulge a bit too much in the minibar? Ours was fully stocked."

She shakes her head. "I didn't even check mine. I've been too queasy to eat or even drink anything all day. I can barely keep down water. I was downstairs at the tiki bar with Ellis and a few of the others. They all begged me to take a few shots. I just kept throwing them behind my shoulder. Each of them was none the wiser. I don't know what has gotten into me," she says.

I go to the sink and pour her a glass of water.

"Maybe you've caught some type of bug," I say.

"Maybe…" she says, and her voice trails off. She stares into the glass for a few seconds, as if she's debating whether or not she should drink it, and then sets it carefully on the counter.

"You know, Lula. There aren't many people in this world I feel like I can trust. I've had plenty of people stab me in the back with zero remorse. Friends, family, lovers. I may seem like an open book but I'm not. I'm so far from it. But with all that said, for whatever reason, I feel like I can count on you. I haven't known you long, but from what I've seen, betrayal just doesn't seem to be in your nature." Clara takes her hair from the ponytail and shakes it out, bringing it back to its glory.

"I consider myself trustworthy. What's going on?" I ask, offering her a seat next to me on the edge of the bed.

"I need to take a test," she says with a flat tone, sitting oddly close to me.

"A test?"

"I'm sure it's nothing. Just paranoia. But I'll feel a lot better if I take one," she says, eyeing me closely.

My voice rises. "Wait, you mean like a pregnancy test?"

"Shhhh!" Clara's arms flail. "Do not say that word again." Her eyes bulge, panic strewn across her face.

"Sorry," I whisper, "I can get you one from the resort market if you're too frightened. I'm sure they must have them."

She nods, seemingly happy that I'm catching on to her request now. "Don't let anyone see you. Please."

Fifteen minutes later, I return with a grocery bag of tests in tow. I'm not even in the room for a millisecond before Clara rips the bag out of my hand and rushes to the toilet, this time the door slams shut behind her.

We have twenty minutes until dinner starts and I have yet to even process what's up with Jason. He can't avoid me the whole night and I'm anxious to know what he's been up to. The thought that he might have gone straight to Haven's room after I ruined the mood has only just now occurred to me. Maybe he satisfied the rest of his craving in her room. I shake the image of Jason's tongue lapping up Haven's perfectly bald pussy from my head.

"Lula!" Clara yells. She runs out of the bathroom with one hand over her eyes and the other holding three separate pee sticks.

"I can't look. I'll be sick again. Please, just tell me they are negative. Oh, please God let them be negative," she says. I can't see her eyes, but wet tears lay on her cheeks.

She sits back down on the edge of the bed, and I grab the sticks from her hand, careful not to touch the spots I know were sprayed with urine. "Just relax. I'm sure you have yourself worked up for nothing. One line, two li–"

My heart skips a beat.

Clara's hand whips off her face. "Two what?"

I shuffle the tests in my hands, looking closely at each line. Each test has a vivid pink streak in the second box.

"Clara. You're pregnant," I say, voice low.

"No. No. No. It's not possible." She stands, ripping the tests out of my hand and eyes them for herself, holding each up to the light when the line is so bold it could be seen from a mile away.

I place my hand on her shoulder. I'm not sure what to say. I've never even had a pregnancy scare before.

"Do you know who the father could be?" I ask. As soon as I say it I want to slap myself across the face for being so intrusive and insensitive.

"Ellis is going to hate me," she says, cascading back down onto the bed.

"I'm sure that's not true. I mean he knows what sex can lead to. He knows what he was getting himself into."

"Except he doesn't," she says, bringing the sticks close to her chest.

I stay quiet and sit on the bed next to where she lays, waiting for her to explain.

"I told him I have the IUD. Hell, I told everyone that I have the IUD. I gave Rasheeda some fake ass prescription for Mirena that I found on the internet. I hate the way the hormones mess with my sex drive. And also… I want to have kids one day. I don't want my chances to be lowered. I knew a girl once who took the pill for ten years and miscarried each and every time she got pregnant afterward. I couldn't take that chance." Her voice breaks.

"Okay so you have to have a talk with Ellis. But it's no one else's business. It isn't the end of the world," I say.

"Lula, I don't think you understand how serious that rule is."

I think back to the packet Rasheeda gave me after initiation. Is Clara really scared of a few pieces of paper?

"All I'm saying is that this is your life. Not the club's. Take some time on your own to think about how you might want to handle this," I stare at the plush carpet below my feet, rubbing my bare heels against it, and continue to make up advice that I have no business giving, "Then have a conversation with Ellis. Ultimately, the choice is up to you. You say you want to have a family one day, what's to stop you from starting now?" I ask and turn to her distraught face.

She laughs but she isn't smiling. None of this is actually humorous to her. She sits up and her face crumbles into her hands.

"What will I tell everyone else?" she asks, voice mumbled. She looks up to face me now, expecting me to spew words of wisdom from experiences that I've never had.

"Nothing. You don't have to tell them anything." My tone is rigid, but I place my hand on top of hers, offering what little comfort I can.

We both are jolted from the winding of the bolt in the hotel room door. Clara leaps up and stuffs the test strips into her bra, the rectangular outline still visible from the outside.

Jason traipses through the entryway, drink in hand. When he sees Clara, he catches himself on the wall to steady his swaying.

"Hey, Clare. Didn't expect to see you here."

"Had to come see my girl," she says, giving me a wink. "But I'm heading out now. I'll see you guys at dinner. Don't have too much fun without me."

She scurries out of the room, leaving me to face my inebriated husband all alone.

His cheeks shine bright red, the alcohol heating them from the inside out. And the hair that's usually styled so perfectly is ruffled, like a strong wind caught hold of it.

"Been busy?" I ask as the door closes behind Clara.

"Very much so," he says, refusing to look at me, "You ready?"

CHAPTER 23

Jason and I walk together to the banquet hall. His arm hangs loosely over mine, only further confirming that there's a problem we need to mend. Maybe he is still dealing with the drama his mother sprung on him. Either way, we can't fix anything until he's sober.

"Do you know what they're serving?" I ask, attempting to lessen the tension.

"Probably something with fish. They hired a local caterer."

At least we are on speaking terms. I squeeze his arm slightly but get no reaction.

I sniff the air as we walk through the open doors and catch a whiff of rosemary. We are surrounded by giant windows that frame the walls, revealing the sky that has already become a deep, dark blue. The ocean is just outside, but hard to see now that the sun has set. The hall is the size of a basketball court, able to host at least sixty people if I had to guess. Quite a few guests already sit at the tables that line the sides, leaving an empty path in the middle of the room that leads to a podium. The tables are draped in red satin cloth, each tied at the ends with a pearlescent cuff. Name cards sit at each spot, scrawled in spirally cursive, and frosted glass lanterns with lit flames rest as the centerpieces in the middle.

Romantic.

The lighting in the room is flattering, not too bright, but not too dim. Enough to see everyone but not too much to where the creases in my makeup will show.

"Lula, Lula, Lula. Looking ravishing as usual!" Calen's boisterous voice booms toward me.

"Thank you. I love the tie," I say, motioning towards his black tie covered in neon pink flamingos. It stands out obnoxiously with his loose, ill-fitting slacks and button up that's two sizes too small.

Calen goes in for a hug and envelops me in his arms. Booze and cigars radiate off his skin. This time I have a sense to pull away before his hands reach my ass.

"I hear Rasheeda's got a full house tonight. You two ready for a party?" he asks and slaps Jason on the back with his palm.

A full house? I swallow hard.

We make our way to one of the tables on the right side of the room, not too far from the entrance. Peering at the name cards, I realize that our table consists of Jason and I, Clara and Ellis, and Greg. I do a double take at the sight of his name and turn to see if he's walking in with the others.

Atlas and Meagan walk hand in hand. Her fiery hair is pulled into a wispy updo, leaving her shoulders bare in a plunging strapless dress that matches Atlas' silver tie. Our eyes meet and my heart skips as his stoic expression curves into a grin. Other singles and couples walk through the entrance. Most I've never seen in my life. From old to young and classy to eccentric, Rasheeda wasn't going for a certain demographic when she created the guest list for this event.

All these people but no sight of Greg Reese.

I turn back around to my table. A plump, brunette girl with glasses, no older than sixteen shows up next to me.

"Can I get you a drink, ma'am? The specials tonight are a Lavender Lemon Drop or a Huckleberry Mojito. We also have a small selection of wines." Her voice squeaks, like she's making an attempt at confidence but failing. There's no way she's old enough to be serving alcohol.

"The lemon drop sounds wonderful, thank you," I say.

I breathe a sigh of relief when Jason only orders water. He definitely needs food in him before he ingests any more liquor. The redness in his cheeks has started to fade, but his eyes are still glazed over.

Chatter fills the room as it begins to swarm with bodies. Clara and Ellis, both as happy as can be. Dimples show through his freshly shaven skin. I never realized how much of a baby face he has. No wonder Clara is head over heels for him. He's a charmer.

As she sits, she leans into my ear, tickling me with her breath. "I'm keeping her," she says, motioning to the tiny cell floating around in her belly.

"I'm happy for you," I whisper back.

I notice Ellis trying to give her a sip of his drink and she shakes her head. She obviously hasn't broken the news to him yet.

Rasheeda saunters to the podium at the front of the room. Her long, black, dress with a high cowl neck and sequins drags along the floor as she walks. Someone from the waitstaff hands her a microphone. A high-pitched screech permeates from the mic. She smacks it a couple times before realizing she needs to step away from the speaker.

"Sorry, sorry. Lord knows I'm not the best with technology," she says. The room gives her a laugh.

"Anyways, most of you know me but for those who don't, I'm Rasheeda Edwards. I first want to welcome our newcomers. I hope tonight you all get a glimpse into the small little world that we have created. I hope you are all able to let loose and forget about societal constraints. This already appears to be a great group of people. You've been invited here tonight for a reason—"

Rasheeda is interrupted by Greg Reese, waltzing into the banquet hall. Everyone, close to fifty people, turns to look and his head immediately drops. I get the sense that he'd like to sink into the floor at this moment, never to be seen again.

"Over here, Greg." Ellis calls out in a heavy voice that I'm guessing was meant to be a whisper.

Greg's heavy feet stomp with each step until he finally slumps down into the chair next to Jason. His hair looks greasy like he hasn't watched it in days and there is a sour stench that emits from his direction.

Everyone turns their attention back to Rasheeda, who gives Greg a death glare. He has yet to look up. She snaps out of it as soon as she realizes all eyes are back on her. Her voice rises. "Anyways, you've all been invited here because you deserve it. Don't let this opportunity go to waste. Tonight, we indulge!

Whether that be in the food, drink, each other, or all three! Make the most of it, please. But remember! What happens in Carlsbad, stays in Carlsbad."

She gives a curtsy, and a few people cheer while others shout and raise their drinks. I clink my glass with the others at my table, aside from Greg who is waiting for his own, and drink.

Our food comes out on sizzling platters. Rosemary salmon, buttered bread, and a Greek salad. My mouth salivates at the dish in front of me.

"I'm just not feeling that hungry," Clara tells Ellis, who insists she get something in her stomach.

"We have a long night ahead of us. At least eat the bread so you don't get trashed," he says, digging into his fish.

Clara's eyes shift to me, then back to her plate. She looks like she might be sick again, her face pale. I hope for her sake she can hold it down.

"Shots for the table?" Ellis yells loudly with food still in his mouth, signaling the waitstaff.

I turn to Jason, hoping he refutes the suggestion, but he doesn't. He only chugs the rest of his water, slamming it down onto the table as if he's ready for another round of drunkenness.

Trying not to make it obvious, I peek at Greg. He pushes his food around with his fork, not actually ingesting any of it. But when the waiter comes around with a plate full of shot glasses, he perks up, reaching his hand out to grab one.

"To long nights and memories," Ellis says as he holds up his glass, taking turns giving each of us a grin before throwing it back.

I do the same. The alcohol's piney taste is strong. My face scrunches up as I swallow it down.

"Oh, shit!" Clara spills her all over the tablecloth, balling up napkins to soak up the liquid.

"Damnit, Clara. Hold on, I'll get you another," Ellis says, holding up a hand.

Clara pulls his arm back down. "No, no. I'll wait. I might have had a bit too much already. Hence the clumsiness."

Within ninety seconds, the liquor hits me hard. I'm no longer antsy about the amount of people. I keep repeating the same mantra over and over again.

It's just like a wedding reception. It's just like a wedding reception.

Greg says very little while we eat, mostly just grunts and mumbles when the conversation shifts to him. Feeling more comfortable, I turn to him, hoping he'll warm up to me.

"How are the kids, Greg?" I ask.

As soon as I say it, Jason kicks me underneath the table and Clara chokes on her water.

"They miss their mom," he says, very matter of fact, finally looking at me in the face.

My face gets hot. "Of course. Of course. I'm sorry," I say, shaking my head, and smoothing out the tablecloth to distract myself from the embarrassment I feel.

I curse myself for being so brazen. I've barely even talked to the guy before tonight. What makes me think it's okay to ask such a personal question? I grab my water and take a long sip, the ice freezing my teeth. Maybe I've drunk a bit too much already.

"Dessert?" The same girl from before comes over with a tray of fudge brownies sprinkled with powdered sugar. I take one and bite into it, the chocolate sparks my tastebuds.

"This is amazing. Try a bite, Clara." I shove the slice in her face.

She shakes her head and I sink my teeth in again, leaving only a sliver.

"Come on!" I say, trying again.

"I can't." Her voice is low, brows furrowed. I give her a quizzical look and pop the last piece into my mouth.

"I know an edible when I see one," she says.

Oh no.

My face falls.

"May your night be more interesting than mine," she laughs and lifts her glass of water.

Jason and Ellis appear to be deep in conversation, so I get up to go find another drink. Maybe I can level out the high that's soon to come if I have a few more drinks.

"Lula!" a voice calls from behind me. I whip around to see Meagan waving me over. She's at a table with Atlas, Wyatt, and Haven. Haven's chair is facing Atlas, her bare, silky, smooth legs are so close they are brushing his slacks. She throws her head back in laughter and my stomach pangs.

I make my way to the group and Meagan grabs my hand, massaging my palm with her fingers.

"Jordan, this is Lula Carson. Lula, this is Jordan Saunders. His company has partnered with Stellar on occasion. I put in the good word to Rasheeda for him," Meagan says. Her eyelashes flutter at him.

Jordan is lanky and stands nearly a foot over both Meagan and me. His chestnut hair resembles a toupee the way it wisps over his forehead. Maybe it is one. If I had to guess, I'd say he's in his early forties. And if I had to take another guess, I'd say he and Meagan have fucked before.

"Nice to meet you," I say with a closed lip smile.

He places both of his hands over mine. "Likewise," he says, "Now did someone mention something about body shots?" He looks from me to Meagan with a wicked grin.

"Get on top of the table, Lu," she says, smacking my ass.

"What?" I laugh.

Both Jordan and Meagan guide me over to their recently cleared table, where Atlas and Haven still sit chatting.

"Ready?" Jordan asks and I lose my footing as he pushes me over the table, my back slamming onto the hard surface.

Atlas and Haven's conversation comes to a halt. "What the hell are you guys doing?" Atlas asks, amused.

Meagan and Jordan stand over me. A bottle of liquor appears out of nowhere in Meagan's hands. I start to pull my body upward, but cold, clear alcohol is poured on my neck, sending my head back to the table. Before I can react, Jordan's warm mouth slurps at my skin, sending tickles across my chest. Squeaky giggles escape my lips. Meagan splashes the liquid onto my cleavage, leaving Jordan to drag his tongue in between my breasts to lap it up. My nipples instantly harden, threatening to show through the thin fabric of my dress.

Meagan grabs my hand and pulls me up off the table. Looking around, I notice Atlas staring at me, but I can't tell whether it's intrigue or indifference. I fold my arms over my chest in attempts to hide my arousal.

"Need a napkin?" he asks.

"Please," I say.

He gets up from his chair and grabs a napkin from a table nearby. Before I can take it from his hands, he comes to me and wipes the mess from my neck and chest.

He keeps his head down, fiddling with my decolletage. "So, I see you've met Jordan," he says.

"I—"

"Come here, hon!" My head turns as Jordan's voice rings out. He grabs the arm of the brunette waitstaff girl. She lets out a nervous laugh and shakes her head, but he doesn't relent and only continues to drag her over to the table.

"Fuck, you're like a sexy little schoolgirl," he breathes.

My stomach turns. Her white button down, navy tie, and khaki skirt resemble a private school uniform, which should only lead to further inferences to her young age. He pushes her down onto the table and her coy smile changes to a grimace. I look around for everyone else's reaction. Meagan's eyes are wide with excitement and others have lost interest.

Am I the only one who is uncomfortable by this?

"Come on now. She's here for work," Atlas pipes up.

"She will get a good tip," Jordan replies.

Meagan lifts her blouse to reveal a pale, chubby belly. The young girl's cheeks flush bright red. The bottle tips over her belly button, over filling it. Atlas rushes in between them and grabs the girl's hand to pull her up, spilling liquor onto her clothes.

"Hey!" Jordan yells.

"I'd like a glass of Pinot, please. And hurry. I'm thirsty," Atlas tells the girl.

She whips her shirt back down, nods and scurries off. I realize I've been holding my breath and I inhale deeply. A calm washes over me and I grab Atlas' hand, squeezing it in my own.

"What the fuck, man?" Jordan raises his arms. Meagan rolls her eyes on the other side of the table. Atlas only shrugs, seemingly unbothered by their irritation.

"He's a creep," I whisper.

Atlas leads me to the hallway outside of the banquet room. A few people linger along the walls, on their phones. None of them are familiar to me.

"I'm sorry if I upset you earlier," I say as soon as we are out of the commotion.

"Don't be sorry. It's not anything that I have the right to be bothered by. I've been in this lifestyle long enough to know how it works," he says.

"Don't say that. Your feelings matter to me."

He grabs my chin and pulls my face closer, pressing his lips into mine. I sink into the kiss and my body melts into his. I feel frozen in time, unable to detach my mouth from Atlas'. He finally releases and pulls me into a tight embrace, resting his head on top of mine.

"I'm so grateful that I've met you," he says.

For the first time ever, I don't feel sexual tension between the two of us. I feel a sort of adoration, a sort of comfort. I don't want him to ever let go. I push my nose into his chest and inhale. His now familiar scent rushes through my sinuses.

"You're a breath of fresh air, Lula. I hope you know that."

"The feeling is mutual," I say.

"Where the hell is my husband?" Meagan's shrill voice travels through the room into the hall where Atlas and I stand. She turns the corner and notices us, clutching to one another. She exhales sharply. If the high wasn't hitting me, I would have jolted out from Atlas' hold, but the all-encompassing tranquility is keeping me still, unbothered.

"Ahhh. I should have known where you'd run off to. Can I have a turn with you now? I want to dance," she says and before getting an answer, Meagan whips around and marches back into the banquet room.

I was so deeply entranced with the man in front of me that I tuned out the old school music that blares in the other room. The walls shake with the beat.

I let go of his body and can feel the heat dissipate between us. "I would hate to make her wait. You are *her* husband after all," I say with a slight sneer.

He shakes his head and smiles as he walks backward off into the room. When he finally disappears into the commotion, I lean back and press myself against the wall. My head is fuzzy and I'm so thirsty I could drink a gallon of water in one sitting. But then I'd probably puke.

Get it together, Lula.

The music continues to seep into the hall. Whitney Houston's singsong voice belts out the chorus of *I Want to Dance with Somebody*.

I chant the chorus softly until the high notes when my voice breaks with a crack. Laughter escapes my lips at the thought of my tone-deaf vocals.

My body wriggles to the rhythm of the song. Soon I'm swaying my hips and drift back into the banquet room by a magnetism in Houston's melody. My feet saunter just past the entryway. The lights have dimmed substantially, reminiscent of the nights at the cabin. The hum of conversation lulls below the music that emanates from a few speakers in the corners of the ceiling. I don't know who is making the music choices, but I'm not mad about it.

The tables have been cleared and pushed against the walls for extra space. Some guests still sit in the chairs, deep in conversation, and others are up dancing. The room feels hotter, steamier, like when you're in a hot car in the winter without the defrost on. In a darkened corner toward the back, a man stands against the wall with his head turned upward while another man kneels in front of him. I try not to stare, but my eyes stay glued on the rhythm of the man on his knees, bobbing his head to the beat.

I snicker, realizing I probably shouldn't be peeping.

Atlas, Meagan, Cheyenne, Haven, and a few other people rub up against each other towards the center of the room, also moving to the flow of the song. Pony by Ginuwine. I twinge and my eyes dart away once I see both Meagan and Haven's grinding their asses up on either side of Atlas. Looks like Meagan is getting the "husband time" she so desperately sought after. Cheyenne strokes her body as she sways, looking like she's lost in her own little world.

Rasheeda and Derrick sit at a table in the back, with a group of older men that I don't recognize. Their stoic expressions lead me to believe it's all business, no pleasure. Rasheeda's eye wanders over and catches mine and my head thrusts downward, leaving me to stare at my strappy heels.

My ears perk up towards a group huddling around a table on the opposite side of the room. There is a gap between a few, allowing me to get a view of what's happening.

Wyatt, the bald guy who was trying to eye-fuck me on poker night, lays flat on his back above the satin tablecloth, blue pants down to his ankles. A small, pale ass bounces on top of him. The crowd snickers as she throws her head back and moans. Another shuffle of feet allows me to see her face. Acne scatters her forehead and chin. Her naked body is thin, without much of a shape. She's got to be barely legal. Probably out on her own for the first time in life and ends up here, fucking some middle-aged average Joe on a dining table in a hotel resort in front of a crowd of onlookers. Just what her parents had in mind, I'm sure. The table rattles and I wonder if it will break under the pressure. I'm sure it wasn't built for two adult humans to play on top of.

Wyatt rolls off the table and pulls his pants back up, getting pats on the backs as he walks off, a smug grin on his face. Just when I think the rendezvous is over, a heavy-set woman with a short, grey bob, parts from the voyeurs and hops up onto the table, laying down in the same position that Wyatt was in. She's got to be in her sixties. The bright red lipstick that lines her thin lips stands out from afar. She's straddled by the girl next and the group watches as she unbuttons the woman's frilly blouse, exposing sagging breasts.

I turn back around now, having seen enough. Everywhere I turn it feels like I'm imposing. Will I ever be used to this world? This world represents autonomy, lust, and pleasure. It promotes seeking out your wildest, deepest desires. The desires that most of the people in this room are probably too scared to admit. These people are here coveting our club, the lucky thirteen.

"There's my girl," Jason says as he comes up behind me, squeezing my waist.

I whirl around to face him and let out a sigh of relief. "What have you been up to?" I ask.

His lip curls. "Just chopping it up with some of the folks around here. It's never a bad time to gain a few new clients, right?"

I shake my head. "You've got to let loose a bit."

"That's what I've got you for," he says.

He pushes me against the wall next to the doors. His fingers inch their way up my inner thigh, sending tickles down my leg, before slipping under my dress. They tug at my panties.

"Jason," I breathe. My eyes scan the room.

"Shhh." His whisper trickles into my ear. He places his other hand on the small of my back and pulls me in closer. Then he lets two of his fingers slip inside of me. I press my face into his chest to prevent a moan from escaping my lips.

"You like that?" he asks in a hushed tone. He pushes in a third with little resistance as I open up to him, already slippery from his touch.

My head falls back, and I let out a long breath. His fingers push farther inside of me, pressing against my sweet spot. My legs feel weak, like I might collapse onto the floor. The euphoria builds up. I'm about to tip over the peak and Jason pulls out of me.

"Don't stop," I say.

He chuckles. "Open your mouth."

His fingers trace my lips, then thrust into my mouth. I lick around each one and my taste buds ignite with the sweet tang. His smile widens as I lap at his fingers.

Without a word, I fall to my knees in front of him, and unzip his slacks, anxious to get him inside my mouth. When his dick falls out, I wrap my lips around it and shove as much of it in as I can before gagging.

"Yes," he says, grabbing the back of my head, "show them all how bad of a girl you really are.

As the next song plays, I suck hard and glide my mouth faster along his shaft, willing him to cum for me. Willing to please him.

"What the fuck?" Jason blurts out, pulls himself away from me, and zips his pants, turning to focus on something behind him.

I wipe my lips with the back of my hand, smearing brown lipstick, and tug at the bottom of my dress before peeking over his shoulder to see what he's looking at.

Greg sits in the same chair as before, but now a younger man with glasses and long, blonde hair sits in the chair next to him, where Jason had sat during dinner. The man isn't part of the club, but Jason seems to have a clue who he is. The look of pleasure has been completely wiped away from Jason's face and is now replaced with a scowl.

"Who is that?" I ask, still standing behind him.

"Andrew Stanford," he says under his breath, more to himself than to me.

Before I can ask any more questions, Jason leaves my side and bolts to the table, fists clenched. He bends down to Andrew's ear and whispers something. Andrew gets up without hesitation and walks out of the room, never looking back. As soon as he's no longer visible, Jason's hands grip Greg's shoulders and lift him up from the chair. Greg stumbles back, nearly tripping over the chair.

"You have some nerve," Jason says, his finger inches away from Greg's pointed nose.

Greg holds up his shaking hands. "He came up to me. I told him I had nothing more to say," he says.

Someone has lowered the music in the room, to the point where it's no longer identifiable, which only amplifies the exchange between the men. My mouth dries up even more. I've seen Jason like this before, the fire in his eyes, the bulging of the vein in his forehead. Nothing good ever comes of it.

"I'm not one to fuck with," Jason warns.

"I don't want any more drama," Greg says.

"Then you wouldn't come here looking like you haven't bathed in months and reeking of stale cigarettes and cheap scotch. You're a shady motherfucker with an agenda."

"No, I swear—," Greg's plea is cut short as Jason takes a fistful of his shirt and yanks him out of the chair, pushing him up against the nearest wall.

My hands move over my mouth. I should do something. I should say something. But my feet won't budge, and my voice is nowhere to be found. The men shift in and out of focus as my mind blurs. The groups around us have all stopped to stare now too.

Greg's eyes bulge from his skull as he shakes his head side to side. I can only imagine the terror Jason's enraged face is igniting inside of him.

Calen rushes over to Jason's side, treading swiftly and heavily. He mumbles something and Jason's scarlet hand smacks the wall next to Greg's head. I jostle in my spot, startled by the sharp noise. Someone else gasps. Jason and Calen each place a hand on Greg's shoulders and push him towards the exit. Greg's sullen face hangs down, probably to avoid the numerous eyes that gawk at him.

The sound of their footsteps fade. The microphone screeches until Rasheeda's voice shouts through.

"Every party has to have that one guy, am I right?" She laughs and other chuckles trail in after hers. "Please, let's continue to have a great time!"

Michael Jackson emits through the speakers and the volume increases, drowning out the chatter.

My rapid heart rate starts to slow.

"Figured you probably needed this." Clara pops up next to me and hands me a shot glass full of clear liquid. I hold it up to my nose to smell. The acrid scent of vodka burns my nostrils.

"This glass looks rather large," I say.

"Thought you could use a double. You're taking mine for me too."

"Thank the gods for you. Cheers," I say, lifting it in her direction and swallowing it down.

"I wouldn't worry too much about it," she says, nudging my shoulder.

I give her a puzzled look.

"The men. Or should I say, the brutes," she says.

"Of course, I'm worrying about it. My husband practically assaulted a recently widowed man. I don't know what has gotten into him lately…" I let my voice trail off. I don't want Clara to know about my recent struggles with my husband. I don't want anyone to know.

"Greg Reese has gone off the deep end. He probably needed a little roughing up to snap him back to reality." Clara shrugs, seemingly unbothered by the violence.

"Hey, do you know the guy that Greg was talking to? Andrew something. Who is he?" I ask, trying to think with my blurry brain of the full name that Jason muttered before going ballistic.

"Andrew? Oh, you mean the blond-haired screwball who loves to show up to places uninvited? Yeah, that's Andrew Stanford. He's a self-proclaimed journalist, digging for something to put him on the industry's radar."

"What is there to dig for?" I ask.

"We are a restricted group of sexually fluid, spiritually conscious individuals. What isn't there to dig for?" she says, whipping her hair to the side.

She's right. These people aren't leading normal lives. When you combine money with scandal, the vultures will come knocking down the door to get a slice of the pie.

"Oh, I love this song!" Clara screams, throwing her arms in the air.

She leaves my side, hurrying to the other dancers, hand still resting on her flat stomach.

I probably shouldn't have taken that double. My head whirls. The mix of alcohol and marijuana have left me dazed, like I'm floating. I think I can make it back to my hotel room. Although, I really wish Jason were here to guide me. Was it Room

201? Maybe it was 203. I definitely remember the number three. I squint to focus my eyes on the exit and make a move, trying to ensure I don't slip in my heels. After teetering to one side, I give up and decide to take them off. No one will even notice if I'm barefoot. Unbuckling my heels and planting my soles on the smooth wooden floor, I feel much more confident in my balance now. Swift and light as air. No heads turn as I make my way through the hotel lobby. The front desk clerk stares down at her phone as I pass. Someone could run through butt naked, and she wouldn't even notice. The elevator dings open, I push the button that reads two, and sit in the corner, closing my eyes as soon as the doors clasp shut. The movement is dizzying, and I swallow hard at the saliva that has built up inside of my mouth.

Just a few more minutes and I'll be safe in bed.

CHAPTER 24

When the elevator dings again and the doors slide back open, I use the mirrored walls as leverage to pull myself up.

"Are you alright, honey?" An older woman stands at the door, waiting to enter.

"I'm fine. Thanks," I say as my arm brushes past her.

The quiet hallway stretches ahead of me like an endless tunnel. My feet carry me forward despite my exhaustion. Doors upon doors line the walls, their numbers blurry. 210, 208, 206… my head begins to pound behind my eyeballs. I rub my temples to soothe the throb. My heels sway in my hands still, close to slipping from my grasp.

The hallway ends with three rooms. Two on each corner and one in the middle. 200 to the left, 201 in the middle, and 203 on the right. I'm pretty sure I remember having a corner room. I shake my head, willing my senses to come back to me.

The door on the right looks promising. I pat at my dress, as if it all the sudden grew pockets, and stashed my key card.

Shit.

I must have left the key with Jason. Still, my fingers trace the door handle of room 203. I press down and it clicks open with little resistance.

I guess I forgot to lock it.

I'm plunged into darkness and the lack of direction throws me off balance once again. A wave of nausea hits me like a ton of bricks and the world starts to spin. I rush to the bathroom and clank the toilet lid open. My head hangs over the bowl and a lock of hair threatens to dip into the still water. I spit the saliva that has pooled in my mouth.

The vomit shoots out into the bowl like a waterfall. I heave with all my might, spilling out the entirety of content in my stomach. Stars appear in my vision as I blink and tears stream down my eyes, which I'm sure smears my makeup. Still in the dark I feel around the porcelain for the handle and flush dinner and the copious amounts of liquor down the drain.

My teeth are gritty and my breath sour. My toothbrush is the one item I forgot to take out and put on the bathroom counter. I pull myself up from the linoleum and navigate through the bedroom for my suitcase, illuminated only by the moonlight that shines through the windows.

I squint through the darkness and feel around on the bed for where I lay my things earlier today. My hand brushes against a duffel bag. I grab the straps and hold it up to the moonlight. Its deep purple color and military style insignia on the front stand out to me because I've never seen one like it before.

Whose duffel is this?

I zip it open, and the contents are all unfamiliar. I reach in and pull out a button-down shirt, size 2x. My blood goes cold, and the shirt drops from my fingertips.

This is not my hotel room.

Even the bed is in a completely different place than before. My heart rate picks up. I shove the shirt back into the bag and zip it closed. Vomit creeps up my throat once again, threatening to splatter all over this stranger's belongings. I cover my mouth, debating on whether or not to rush out the door or rush back to the toilet.

Before I can decide, chatter fills the hall behind the door. A key card scans the lock. The sound of the bolt unhinging from the door booms in my ears. My body is shot with a bolt of electricity. I shift my head from left to right, searching for a place to hide. The bifold doors of the small closet across from the bed call my name. Just as the hotel door clicks open, I fling into the cramped space, squatting next to the ironing board. I try to slow my breath in an attempt to muffle my presence. I'm able to squint through the space between the doors. From my place, the moonlight shines right onto the bed, highlighting the fluffy pillows thrown askew all over the duvet. A man's boisterous laugh travels throughout the room. Clunky footsteps traverse the floorboards. A thud erupts as a body hits the floor.

"God dammit." The voice is so familiar.

Calen.

My eyes widen and I stare through the crack. I listen closely. The two bodies struggle toward the bed. Calen's silhouette comes into view as well as a woman he appears to be half guiding and half carrying. Her long, light hair drapes over his shoulder as they come into the dim lighting. Her slender body plops onto the duvet. The beam shines across her face. She's pretty, wrinkle and blemish free. Plenty of fat still underneath her eyes. Far too young for the likes of Calen.

He stands over the bed, his burly figure staring her down as she wriggles around, obviously heavily intoxicated. His hands trace her thin waist, and she mumbles something that I can't make out. He pulls her shirt up over her head and I see her breasts, small. Underdeveloped. I fight through the shadows to study her features through the small gap. My stomach stiffens. This girl can't be more than fifteen years old.

I sink further back into the closet, terrified I might be spotted. I bring my knees to my chest. My heart pounds onto my thigh. The bed is still visible from my spot. I close my eyes. I don't want to be here. I don't want to witness what is happening.

"Shhh. It's okay," Calen says. His belt jangles just before it clangs to the floor.

"No. No," the girl's faint voice whimpers. Calen doesn't respond to her subtle pleas.

They shuffle around on the bed and Calen's weighty breaths make my skin crawl. I peek through again, unable to ignore what's happening just outside the closet door.

He has her pants down to her ankles, now. He moves her limbs, and they appear limp as they fall loosely against the bed. Calen climbs up to the bed next to her, his billowing white boxers glow as light filters through the curtains. His beefy hands grip her chest first. Then he travels down farther on her body. He slips his hands underneath her underwear. She squirms. Tears tickle my cheeks.

Stop this.

I need to do something. I need to say something. But I sit here, eyes bulging, frozen in place.

Her eyes remain closed, but a piercing whine comes from her lips. She slurs her words, unintelligible rambles. Calen hushes her again and places one of his hands over her mouth while his other is still busy down below her waist. I bury my face into my own hands. I can no longer steady my breathing and begin to hyperventilate.

"You like that, huh? Dirty little slut," Calen says.

Grunts ooze from his chapped lips and drown out her muffled whimpers.

My body lurches as the hotel room door bursts open. I uncover my face.

"Shit," Calen mutters. He scrambles for his clothing.

Feet shuffle on the floor, growing louder with each step. I scan for the source.

"And you're stupid enough to leave the door unlocked? The idiocy." Rasheeda comes into view, her arms folded across her chest.

Rasheeda's deep skin almost camouflages her in the dark room. Her pearly, gapped teeth and sparkly black dress dazzle in the spotlight, courtesy of the moon. Thoughts race through my mind. I expect her to scream, riot against what is happening in this room, in the horrific scene she has stumbled upon. I want to jump out from behind the doors and rush to her side.

Rasheeda sighs. "Put your clothes on, Calen. Nobody wants to see all of that."

Calen threads his belt back through his pants, shaking his head. He laughs, seemingly unashamed of his despicable behavior. Without warning, the girl breathes heavily, like she's working up the courage to fight back, to stand up for herself.

"Where's Gloria? Take me back to Gloria." Her words splutter, barely comprehensible, but louder than before. She makes an attempt to sit up but collapses back onto the bed, too weak to hold herself. Both Calen and Rasheeda ignore the babble.

"They are here for her. Get her dressed. You better not have left any bruises, Calen."

They?

"Alright. Give me a minute," Calen replies.

"She wasn't yours to defile. You imbecile," she says, spitting out her words.

"Don't worry, she's still as tight as she was before we got her."

She looks down at his waistband. "I don't doubt that."

This is dark. Darker than I could have imagined. I need to get out of here. No one can know what I have witnessed. I've seen too much.

My leg has fallen asleep, causing prickles to run up my lower half. I shift my position and accidentally nudge the ironing board. It taps the wall with a faint clunk.

"What the hell was that sound? Do you have someone else here?" Rasheeda asks with a stern voice.

"Of course, I fucking don't," he says.

She creeps over to my hiding place. Her hand grips the knob. I suck in a breath and hold it. The door widens until a phone chimes. Rasheeda releases her grip, leaving the door partially open, just inches from my foot. The chiming stops.

"I'll be down in five. Have the cash in hand," she says. The girl whimpers again. It's entirely possible that she knows her fate. That she's aware enough now to know that this has no way in resulting in a happy ending. Aware that she trusted the wrong people.

"Take her out through the stairway. I'll head out the front and meet you in the back of the parking lot," she says.

Her footsteps fade and the door slams shut. I allow a shallow breath to escape. I watch as Calen struggles to dress the young girl. Her flimsy limbs fall heavily against the mattress as he shoves them through her clothing. He hoists her up off the bed, with little effort from her part. Her arm rests across his shoulders and he supports her waist. His arms are broad but lack any muscle. If she was any heavier, I'm sure it would be impossible for him to make his way down the stairwell while she's in this condition.

The door clicks shut, and I let out an exasperated sigh. My arms tremble as I lift myself from the closet floor. I feel around for my shoes as I hold my breath, ready to make a run for it. I don't want to smell anything that has happened in this room. The quicker I am, the less likely I'll be to absorb the negative energy threatening to take hold and course through my veins. I make long strides through the corridor, glancing for signs of Calen and Rasheeda at every corner. I use the back of my hand to wipe the tear streaks off of my face. The last thing I want is to run into someone who might wonder what is wrong with me. I should be rushing to the authorities. I should be reporting what I've witnessed. I should be doing *something* before it's too late. But I can't. For all I know I could be roped in as an accomplice. Or worse. The thought of retaliation lingers in the back of my mind. The thought of Greg pinned to the wall by Jason's hands comes to the forefront. What have I gotten myself involved in? How far will these people go?

The experience has sobered me up and my mind is less fuzzy. It's clear to me now that it wasn't room 203, but room 213 that was the correct choice. A corner room, but on the other end of the hall. I freeze when I finally reach the correct door. I don't know if Jason is behind it, waiting for me. Will he wonder where I've been or why I look like I've seen a ghost? I run my fingers through my disheveled hair and yank the handle, thankful that it too, has been left unlocked. The room is dark, still, and just how I left it before dinner.

I don't turn on any lights. I don't undress. I crawl onto the spacious bed and curl myself into a tight ball. I pull the covers up over my head, feeling my hot breath surround the snug space. My cries don't sound quite like me. They sound like they are coming from a small child. I keep my volume low, letting most of the noise absorb into the pillow. My tears soak the pillowcase, leaving smudges of makeup behind. I should shower, rinse off the filth from the night. Or at least brush my teeth, the grit from puke still lining my teeth. But I don't. I can't be bothered to drag myself to the bathroom, to expose myself to any part of the world outside of these blankets that cover me.

Before I close my eyes to fall asleep, I think of the young girl, I think of Greg, I think of the fetus inside Clara's belly, preparing to come into this harrowing world. And I think of Andrew Stanford.

I wake next to Jason. Light filters through the curtains. If I had to guess, I'd say it's past nine in the morning. I don't know what time he came in. His naked body is sprawled on top of the duvet. His low snore sounds more like a cat's purr. Clothes lay at the foot of the bed on the floor. He must have taken everything off and passed out as soon as his body hit the bed.

We still have one more night here at the resort. The thought sends chills down my spine. I don't want to spend another minute here. I go to the bathroom to take a quick shower and brush my teeth. One glance in the mirror makes me shudder. The delicate skin around my eyes is puffy, nearly swallowing them up. My eyeballs peer through the little slits, a dead giveaway that I'd been crying all night. Great. I go back and forth in my head as I brush my teeth, debating on whether or not I want to tell Jason that we need to leave the resort. Once I switch off the bathroom light, I have made my decision.

I pull out the pad of paper that sits in the drawer in the bedside table.

Jason,

I didn't want to wake you. My mom called this morning. It's my father. He's not well. I'll explain everything later. I need to go home. I'm taking the bus. Call me when you get up and about.

Kisses,

Lula.

He will find the paper on top of the pillow next to him. In reality, I know that neither me nor my mom have spoken to my dad in decades. But if it were serious enough, I'm sure he would call. He'd love a chance for a sob story. A chance to absolve his guilt for being absent all these years. The thought of the phone call

I'll need to make to my mom to cover my tracks makes me cringe. I don't know what I'll say but I have to figure something out in case Jason ever brings it up. He knows my father is a sensitive subject to both me and my mom. I can't be sure that he'd never mention it, leaving my mom clueless and myself scrambling to make up more lies.

There was an ad for a bus hanging on a bulletin board near the desk when we first checked into the hotel. Our home city was on the list of stops. I didn't think I'd need to make use of it, though.

My feet tiptoe around the room. The last thing I want is Jason waking up and pestering me with questions. Thankfully, I have yet to take much out of my suitcase. It makes repacking easy. The time on the alarm clock reads 7:45 am. Hopefully the bus hasn't left yet for the day. Once I'm all packed, my heart rate speeds up. Behind this door, I could see any number of people I know, all who will wonder why I'm wheeling my suitcase down to the bus stop a day too early.

Exhaling, I shake the fear from my bones, confident that it's too early for anyone else to be up anyways. The door unlatches with a sharp click. Before I walk out, I turn around to take one last look at my husband. He still snoozes in the same position as before, face mashed into the pillow. It wouldn't be surprising if he slept in past noon today.

Closing the door quietly behind me, I head to the elevator. When the elevator doors screech open, I almost scream. An all too familiar face walks towards me, a cool shade of brown plastered on her lips, thin eyebrows arched in a harsh line, with strappy, gold shoes hanging from her hand.

My heels.

In all the chaos last night, I must have forgotten my shoes inside of Calen's hotel room. Rasheeda lets them swing back and forth. Her eyes pierce through my body. She's neither smiling nor frowning. Her face is blank, which makes my stomach quiver all the more. I want to run in the opposite direction, but I know I can't.

Maybe I left them in the hallway, maybe they weren't even in Calen's room.

"Leaving so soon?" she asks.

"My father. Something happened. I've got to get back," I say, my voice shakes.

Her arm stretches out toward me. Long, natural fingernails, grip the heels. I take my shoes from her hand. I wait for her to say something, but she only continues to stare at me. The urge to start crying fills me. Fluid builds up around my eyeballs and I look down, fluttering my eyelids to push away the tears.

"Hope all is well with dad," she says.

I clear my throat. "Thank you."

She continues to stand in front of me, so I step to the side to get past her. My suitcase trails behind me, clacking on the stone. She mutters something under her breath as I walk past. It isn't until moments later that her words click in my mind.

Inanna reserves her most severe punishments for the treacherous.

CHAPTER 25

Jason never calls to check in, which only escalates my anxiety about the entire situation. I text him later in the night, though, hours after the bus has dropped me off and I've made it back home.

My dad is going to be okay. More of a miscommunication than anything. You know my mom. Drama queen. I hope you're having a blast tonight.

The three dots to signify typing immediately pop up.

Glad to hear it. Bet it was interesting to hear from him after all these years. I'll be home tomorrow afternoon.

Relief washes over me. He doesn't seem to sense my lie. And while he may be irritated that I left early, at least he's not showing it. I want out of all of this. And I'm going to have to work up the courage to speak with him about it when he gets home. I think of him and his rage lately. His impatience with me, his built-up anger at his parents, his aggressiveness with Greg. Maybe he thinks the answer to his inner struggles is within this club, but I don't think it's doing either of us any good. We have to find another solution.

I google "trauma counseling" and "anger interventions." As I scroll through the results on my computer screen, a name stands out in an article about the efficacy of the mental health clinics in the area, Andrew Stanford. The man that Jason was so disturbed to see in the banquet hall. I type his name into my search bar and get a plethora of results. Andrew Stanford is a forty something year old journalist who moved here from back East about a decade ago. His forte is a juicy scandal. Even his article of the mental health clinics in Garden Valley offers numerous negative testimonials and hints at inappropriate provider-patient relationships.

My eyes widen when Gina Reese's name pops up in bold. The article is titled "The Reese's: a Tragedy or the Perfect Cover Up?" My fingers click as soon as my mind registers.

Police reports have confirmed suicide. Gina Reese has been reported to have tied a rope around her neck and jumped off of a lounge chair in the master bedroom of her Garden Valley home. Gina was reported to have been suffering from a severe bout of depression in the months leading up to her untimely death. The illness had plagued her off and on for the majority of her life. But where our local law enforcement has failed time and time again is accurately investigating the scene of a death. From contaminating crime scenes to mishandling evidence, is it out of left field to wonder whether this case has been misinterpreted?

Her husband has remained silent, refusing to give a single comment on the state of his wife's mental health, where he was at the time of the incident, or, as sources have recently learned, why he and his wife were separated in the months leading up to her death and why neighbors have been reported hearing loud arguments coming from the home just weeks earlier.

Both police and the husband have also failed to explain why a 911 call from the Reese's residence was made just hours before her body was found. On the released audio, an unidentified male cries into the phone for approximately fifteen seconds before the call drops. Police didn't make their way to check on the source of the call until hours later when Reese's body was discovered.

Many believe a thorough investigation is warranted.

I reread each sentence multiple times, feeling like I'm missing something, wanting to fully ingest each word. A picture of Gina is placed at the end of the article. She appears to be in her late twenties or early thirties in the photo. Her mouth is open, mid-laugh, a candid that I'm sure she never imagined would be in an article about her early death. Her chin-length, ash brown hair is tucked behind her ears. She was beautiful, seemingly full of life. My heart thuds in my chest. I think of Greg, his constant state of dishevelment and unapproachable demeanor. I chalked it all up to him being a grieving husband, but maybe it has more to do with guilt. I shudder.

All the more reason to distance myself from this club.

Later in the evening, I lay in bed, my mind racing with all the different ways I can approach Jason when he gets home tomorrow afternoon. If I lead with the wrong phrase or give off the wrong tone, the entire discussion could go south before it even begins. As my eyes start to become heavy, images of the young girl on Calen's bed weave in and out of my mind. It sends prickles throughout my skin, as if I'm infested with a colony of ants. I can't stay silent with this; it will surely eat me up inside. My husband may have his struggles right now, but if I can trust anyone, it should be him.

Sunday afternoon rolls around. I sit at the couch in the front room, a cup of hot tea to my lips. I stare through the window, waiting for Jason's car to come into view. The weather today matches the storm waging within me, thundering and cold. It's unusually chilly, windy, and wet for an early summer day and the sun has yet to come from behind the clouds.

The sleek, black Jeep crosses the window. I take one more long sip of my tea, relishing in the warm liquid as it goes down my throat. I set the cup down and ready myself for my husband to walk through the door. His keys jangle outside, and butterflies swarm my stomach. I plaster a smile on my face as the door opens.

"Hi, baby," I say. Jason's eyes widen like he's surprised to see me waiting. The butterflies slow as a smile settles onto his face.

"Hi, beautiful." Jason appears rejuvenated. His under eyes are bright and face freshly shaven. Much different from the haggard man I left lying face down on the bed in the hotel room just a day ago.

"Didn't expect to be greeted at the door," he says. I get up from the couch to give him a peck on the lips. He pulls me in for another and then nuzzles his chin on my shoulder.

The thought that has been contained in my head for too long, blurts from my mouth. "I'm scared."

"Scared?" he asks. Jason lays his bags down on the floor and guides me back over to the couch. We sit side by side, facing each other. I curl my legs up under me and place my hands in my lap. Jason's concerned face looks me up and down, unable to decipher what could be going on.

"I thought you said your dad was fine?"

"He is. He's fine. It's just that… something happened."

"Something?"

"At the resort."

We sit in silence. He waits for me to continue. I stare at my sweats and scrape at a crusty piece of cream cheese accidentally smeared from my bagel earlier.

His cold hand lifts my chin to focus back on him.

"If I tell you this, you have to promise to keep it between the two of us." My eyes dart from the window to the archway leading to the kitchen, as if someone might overhear what I'm about to say.

"What's going on, Lula?"

"I saw something. Something bad," I say.

"Where?"

"In Calen's hotel room."

He sighs and leans back against the couch. "What did you see?"

"Calen brought a girl back to his room after the dinner. Not only was she incredibly drunk, maybe even drugged, but she was *young*."

His eyebrows bunch up.

"Like really, really young," I say.

"Why were you even in there?"

"It was an accident but that's not the point, Jason! She couldn't have been more than sixteen and he was touching all over her body!" My voice rises and I shudder.

Both of his hands rest on my knees.

"You're sure this is what you saw?" he asks.

His thumbs rub at my legs. An attempt to cool the boiling blood that's coursing through my body.

"Am I sure? I was there, Jason! What do you mean, 'am I sure'?" My voice breaks. The water filling in my eyes now falls down my face, tears I have been holding in since I left the hotel.

"Baby."

His arms envelop me. I bury my face into his chest as he cradles my body, squeezing tight. The scent that fills my nostrils isn't familiar, but it is feminine, dainty, and floral. Similar to Miss Dior or Marc Jacobs Daisy. The scent of a pretty woman, a desired woman. Audible sobs fill the room. Noises that I'm incapable of holding back. I've allowed evil to take root in my marriage. In my life.

"We can't keep doing this. That poor girl. I don't know what these people are into but—"

"There's no way," he says, shaking his head. His dark lashes flutter over his blue eyes.

"It happened, Jason. We can't be involved in this," I say.

Thunder cracks outside, rattling the windowpane.

"Baby. These people are harmless. Calen might be a horny old bastard, but he isn't a rapist. And he surely isn't a child predator.

I scoot back towards the opposite end of the couch. "You're saying that I'm making it up?"

Another crack shakes the walls.

"No, no, no. You know that's not what I'm saying. I saw you with the brownie, babe. How many of them did you eat?"

"One," I say.

"Are you sure, though?"

"Of course, I'm sure. And what does a weed brownie have to do with any of this anyways?"

"I should have warned you before you even picked it up. Rasheeda likes to lace edibles with hallucinogens. She says that it helps to open up the mind, especially if you are unaware of what's to come. You probably had a bad trip. I shouldn't have walked off from you that night. I should have stayed with you to make sure you were fine. I'm sorry." He shifts closer to my end of the couch.

"You were too busy *handling* Greg," I say in an accusatory tone.

"Maybe the whole drama with Greg set off a bad reaction in you that night. I know how much you hate conflict. The night wasn't supposed to go that way," he says.

The maple trees in our front yard sway violently, leaving trails of green leaves scattered across the lawn. The whooshing sound from the wind seeps in through the loose weather stripping underneath the front door. My eyes shut and I'm enveloped in blackness. Images from the night in Calen's room flood back in but the recollections are fuzzy. The girl's clothes change from beige to gray as my brain fights to remember. Was her hair up in a bun or flowing down her back? And how did I know this girl was young? Was I getting her confused with the brunette wait staff girl that Jordan Saunders had harassed? I think back to that night, traipsing the halls, looking for my room. I think of my lack of judgment, wandering into a random room. Is it possible that it was more than bad judgment, but also a blip in reality?

"I'll ask Rasheeda about it, alright?" he asks.

"No! Don't." I think back to my interaction with her on my way to the bus stop, the unwavering lack of expression on her face. Suddenly, the chill from underneath the door seems to ooze into the room. A shiver travels up my spine.

"I would hate to accuse someone of something I'm not one hundred percent sure of. Let's just forget I mentioned it, okay?" I ask.

His eyes study mine, as if unconvinced that I've given up this easily and accepted my truth as hallucination.

"Okay," he says.

"Can I ask you a question, though?"

"Go for it."

"Did Greg Reese kill his wife?"

The pale skin around his cheeks reddens. "Who told you that?"

"I read an article."

This time, it's him who inches towards the arm on the opposite end of the couch.

"Andrew Stanford?" he asks.

I nod.

"That man is a snake." Saliva flies from his mouth, landing on the gray microfiber cushion on the couch.

My knees squeeze to my chest. "Greg or Andrew?" I ask, my voice timid.

"We are done with this conversation," he says. The couch wobbles as he stands abruptly. His athletic shoes smack the entryway wall as he kicks them off. He takes steps towards the kitchen, his heels stomping into the oak.

I shove my face into my knees to soften the whimpers I know are coming.

A long, drawn-out sigh overpowers me, drawing my attention back to my husband.

"How about I make us dinner tonight? How does chicken and seasoned rice sound?" he asks, his tone sympathetic.

"I'd like that," I say, sniffling.

Dinner is ready in less than an hour. When I come downstairs after my hot bubble bath, I'm overcome with the rich smell of garlic and butter.

Jason hands me a stemless glass of red, probably the Merlot I've stored in the fridge.

"How was your bath?" he asks.

The wine swirls around in my palm. "Entirely uneventful. Just like I needed it to be," I say. A large gulp slides down my throat and leaves a dry taste on my tongue.

We enjoy our dinner at the dining room table as the sun reappears and casts an orange glow through the back glass door. The light touches my skin and my goose bumps from the chill of the afternoon fade away.

Jason hasn't cooked dinner in ages, reminding me of a simpler time when we weren't so bogged down by his climbing of the corporate ladder or tumultuous social circles. The subtle smile lines on his face are proof that my jovial, fun-loving husband is still in there somewhere, hiding behind the stress and expectations.

"What are you staring at?" Jason asks with a chuckle.

"Sorry," I say and shake my head as I bite a chunk of chicken off the fork. "I was just thinking."

"About?"

A grin forms across my face. "Oh, nothing."

In bed that night, we both lie side by side on our stomachs, our faces just inches apart.

Short fingernails tickle me as he moves his fingers up and down the length of my arm. Something I've always loved and another thing that he hasn't done in ages. When we first started dating, Jason and I would lay together on the uneven mattress in my studio apartment, staring up at the shadows cast by the passing cars outside my window and talking about our families and our visions of the future. His touch would lull me to sleep every time. Not too rough and not too gentle. The perfect pressure. It soothes me now, making my eyes heavy and breaths slow.

My yawn is long and drawn out.

"Babe. Are we making the right decision? Being a part of this club?" I ask, my eyes half closed.

"I know it's scary. And I know it hasn't been easy. It has been a leap. A leap that I appreciate you taking with me."

My hand rests over his heart. "I don't want to lose this."

"There's nothing to lose and everything to gain." His lips graze the top of my head.

I wish I believed him.

For tonight I'll forget Calen's room. I'll forget the girl. And I'll forget Gina and Greg. For tonight, I'm just happy to be in my husband's arms.

CHAPTER 26

Gina Reese: 2 Weeks Before Death

News Release:

Tonight, on CBOI 12, a missing teen is sending shockwaves throughout the community as pleas from the public for law enforcement to begin taking runaway teen cases more seriously continue to go unanswered. Roxanne Fowler, a fourteen-year-old from Greenwood left home on the night of April 24th, a little over 4 weeks ago, and never returned. Her parents tell our reporter that initial searches from the Greenwood Police Department have been minimal at best and haven't turned any leads. Becky and George Fowler are now turning to the public to get the word out. Roxanne is a white female and was last seen wearing a brown hoodie, blue jeans, and white tennis shoes. She has brown hair past her shoulders, brown eyes, stands at five feet tall, and weighs just over a hundred pounds. Anyone with information is urged to contact law enforcement at —

The television cord drops to the floor as I yank it out of the wall. My hands tremble. I shove them into the back of my jean pockets to still the shaking. The report was wrong about one thing. Roxanne's hair isn't brown anymore, it's black. Or at least it was black when I last saw her. She's also probably more like ninety pounds now, that is if she's even still out there.

My pale bare feet pace back and forth on the cold floor of the front room of the cabin. Evidence, evidence, evidence. How much can be traced back to me? The computer that Rasheeda gave me to borrow lay open on the coffee table, the screen lit up to show my social media account. The account I used to lure Roxanne Fowler. The account I had planned to use for another young runaway, a girl so wrapped up in teen angst that red flags cease to exist. The black linen curtains hang open, allowing the night sky to peer through the glass windows, or whoever else wanted to peer through for that matter. I whip them closed, ensuring that every last inch of the glass is covered.

Rasheeda's name is the first on my recent call list. The phone chimes as the call rings through the speaker phone. I sit on the couch with the computer in my lap, my shaking fingers hovering over the keys, waiting for her to pick up. She doesn't answer on the first ring, and it goes to voicemail.

Shit.

"Rasheeda. I'm freaking out! Call me back right away!" My lone voice cools the blood coursing through my veins. My eyes dart to each corner of the room, as if I'm not the only one in the cabin and haven't been for days. My fingers swipe hastily on the mousepad.

Profile—privacy—settings—account—deletion—-confirm.

The phone buzzes and I nearly drop the computer to the floor.

"Rasheeda?"

"What's going on, Gina?" Her tone is harsh, bothered.

"She's on the goddamn news, Rasheeda!"

"Who?"

"Roxy."

On the other end of the line, hushed mumbles come through, then silence.

"You still there?"

Another beat of silence.

I jump as Rasheeda's voice comes spitting through the speaker. "Don't you dare say another fucking word. I'll be there in a half an hour. Stay off of the internet."

That thirty minutes lasts for an eternity. With my eyes glued to the floor, I continue to pace the room. I stop every thirty seconds at the window to pull the curtains back just far enough to peer at the long, rocky driveway. My teeth bite at my fingertips. The nail beds are raw and stinging by the time her keys jam into the thick, oak door.

I rush to her, exasperated. "Finally—" Rasheeda's open hand swings and smacks the side of my face. The force whips my head to the side as the slap blares in my ear. My jaw drops in disbelief. A burning sensation lingers. My cheek is hot to the touch.

"What the hell?" I scoff.

"Have you lost your mind?" Her tone is even, measured. Curly, ebony wisps frame her tanned face. Her outfit is hidden behind a full length, wool cardigan. I imagine her pajamas lie underneath, forgotten in a flurry after being woken abruptly from slumber. This is the last place she'd like to be at this moment. If the slap didn't make that clear, her face does.

"I'm sorry. I'm panicking. This can't blow back on me. It just can't."

"Your foolishness is going to destroy everything we have worked so hard to build. I won't hesitate to take out any risk, you'll do well to remember that."

"Are you threatening me?" I ask, now defensive.

"Stay the course. Do what you're told. And keep your fucking mouth shut." She hands me a slip of paper before shuffling out and slamming the door behind her, shaking the walls.

A name is sprawled across the torn scrap in bold, cursive writing, Annie Wilkins. I tear it into little, tiny pieces and let them all fall to the floor. I picture myself in an ill-fitting orange jumpsuit. I wonder how they treat those who commit crimes against children in prison. I wonder what my own children would think of me. My guilty mugshot frozen in their minds forever.

CHAPTER 27

My attempts to block out last weekend's events have proved successful. The more I think about it, the blurrier it becomes. I've started to question my own perspective and the crazy conspiracy theories I made up.

I'm excited for today after suffering a week of being slammed at work. I woke up this Saturday morning to the reddish sun peeping through the slats in the blinds and that sweet, warm, summer air coming through the open bedroom window. My serotonin levels naturally surged, something that I usually have to rely on my medication for.

I've promised Clara that I'd go with her to an ultrasound appointment this afternoon to confirm the pregnancy. She has also made me promise not to mention it to Jason. As if he's going to go report to the entire world that Clara got knocked up by her sex club buddy. I had to force a serious voice when she called me in hushed tones. I get it's a sensitive topic, but it's not the end of the world. Accidental pregnancies happen every day to the most unsuspecting of people.

"I've got to run, babe. Lunch with a prospective client." Jason peeks into the bathroom as I'm getting ready, his outfit more casual than business. His navy polo has both buttons undone and his shorts are a bit too fitted for a professional meeting. I catch a whiff of his "good" cologne. Vanilla and vetiver. The cologne he reserves for date nights. But the smile on his face, the one that's lifted only at one corner of the mouth with a slight tilt of the head, it always gets me. And I realize I don't actually care where he's going, as long as he's coming back to me.

"You look sexy. Where are you off to?" he asks.

The mascara wand swipes black ink across my lashes. "Clara asked me to go run an errand with her."

"An errand? Didn't know you guys were on that level," he says, chuckling, and presses his back into the door frame.

"She just has something pretty serious going on and needs a friend."

"Pretty serious, huh?"

I turn to look at him with my powder brush pouncing on my face. His eyes widen, like he's waiting for me to divulge the rest of the information.

"It's a sensitive topic. She's found herself between a rock and a hard place. And she doesn't want any club members to know yet. Especially not Ellis." I whip back around to look into the mirror, ensuring I've blended my face to perfection.

"What the hell has Clara gotten herself into?" he asks. His question is more to himself than to me.

"Let's just say that the pull-out method is not a reliable form of contraception," I say. Focused more on my appearance than the words coming out of my mouth. Jason stares at my reflection in the mirror, his mouth hangs slightly open.

Shit.

My stomach tenses. "Keep this between me and you, though. Like I said, it's a sensitive topic."

Clara's bright red Audi lurches to a stop in my driveway. It looks as though she just went through the car wash. Not a speck of dirt is present.

"Cute house!" Clara's red lips jut out the car window. They are practically a perfect match with her car.

"Thanks," I say as I take a seat on the passenger side.

The potent scent of cotton candy lingers in the small four-seater. A purple crystal hangs from her rearview mirror. She grips her fuzzy red steering wheel and peels out of the driveway. Soon we are bolting down the highway towards the clinic. I'm not sure where she learned to drive, but I wouldn't be surprised if she has a warrant out for a failure to pay her numerous speeding tickets. My torso lurches forward as we screech to a halt a foot away from the bumper of an SUV. She appears to be completely unfazed, her expressionless face stares at the road in front of her.

"How are you feeling about all of this?" I ask.

"I'm scared shitless." She parts her bright lips slightly, giving me a faint smile.

I rest my hand atop hers. "You're not alone in this. Okay?"

The sterile, acrid air of the waiting room makes me want to get up and leave. The four off-white walls and thermostat set to max AC doesn't help either. This place is entirely uninviting. I get the feeling that Clara feels the same way. Her right knee bounces up and down while wait for her name to be called. We haven't talked since we sat down. Probably because the room is virtually silent aside from the occasional sniffle or clearing of the throat from the other women around us.

My phone buzzes in my back pocket, vibrating on the chair. Everyone lifts their heads to look at the source. My face warms as all eyes fall in my direction.

Hey you. Is it weird to say that I miss you?

It's been nearly a week since I've spoken to Atlas. It was the night before I left the hotel. With all the drama and my hectic work week, I've had little time to think about him. The feelings come flooding back in now, though, as I read the words in his text over and over. I reply.

Not weird at all. I feel confident in saying that I feel the same way. Sorry, I've been absent.

Atlas brings out another side of me. One that's more assured and less worried. His reply comes almost immediately.

Can I sneak you away for a bit? Tomorrow, maybe?

"Who is making you smile like that?" Clara asks as she peeks over at my phone screen.

I turn my phone to the side to block her view.

"It's just my mom." I say.

A little white lie never hurt anyone.

I should be able to get away.

I add a winky face and hit send.

"Clara Montgomery?" The nurse's monotone voice makes us jump.

Clara raises her hand and turns to me. "You'll be here when I get back?"

"Of course," I say.

Every minute that passes feels like an hour. When Clara finally returns, tears well up in her eyes but a smile spreads across her face. She holds a roll of black and white photos. I get up and pull her into my arms where she sobs, her body heaving. Her breathing slows and she releases and wipes her tears with the back of her hand.

"Want to see my little peanut?"

The pictures reveal a tiny little embryo nestled into her uterus. A ball of cells that will soon become a breathing, crying, chubby faced boy or girl.

"Congratulations, Clara."

Clara's tears have been replaced with mania as we speed back towards my house.

"I've always loved the name Penelope. I just know she's a girl. I can feel it. You know how some people say they just *know*. Mother's intuition, I guess. I hope she has her father's chin. I just hate mine." Clara goes on and on without taking a breath, gripping the steering wheel hard.

"Penelope is a beautiful name. But speaking of her father… when are you going to tell Ellis?" I ask.

"I'm not." Her tone is still upbeat, a smile still plastered on her face, eyes still frozen on the pavement ahead.

I stare at her, waiting for her to elaborate, but she doesn't even turn her head to glance at me.

"What do you mean you're not? You're not going to tell him?" I ask with a chuckle.

"We both know I can't."

"He's the father of your child. I don't think 'club rules' apply in this situation, Clara."

"Lula, I think you need to understand that club rules *always* apply." She finally turns to look at me, her brown doe eyes search my face for comprehension. I only offer her a look of confusion.

"I'll pay for this if they find out. Trust me," she says.

"They?"

"Oh, come on. Rasheeda, Derrick, and their henchman."

"Henchman?"

"Do you think they ever get their hands dirty? Rasheeda is far too smart for that. There's nothing she won't do for the sake of the club."

"What are you scared of, Clara? Is there something more going on that I should know about?" I think back to what transpired last weekend, or what I have imagined to have transpired. If anyone fits the description of "henchman", it's Calen.

"I know a lot of people think I'm a ditz. A blonde born in a brunette's body. But I'm not stupid. And you shouldn't be either. This club has its perks, sure. But it's not all sunshine and rainbows. They've taken out the enemy once and they'll do it again." Her voice lowers as she speaks, as if someone sits in the backseat listening in on us.

"What do you—"

She puts her hand up. "We need to stop talking about this. For now, please keep this between you and me," her hand moves to her belly, "I'll figure out the rest."

After Clara drops me off, I pour myself a glass of Chardonnay and take a seat at our dining room table. The house is quiet, the only sound comes from the hum of the running dishwasher that I started before I left. Jason still isn't home from his lunch, which doesn't surprise me. The sun is still high in the sky, but I've closed all the blinds, the only illumination coming from the soft white light from underneath the microwave. I need the darkness.

Clara's words have hit me hard. Is she being dramatic? Or am I forcing myself to be mindless, ignoring the red flags that wave vigorously in my face?

The yellowish liquid sloshes in the bottle I hold, already half gone from when I started. I pour another few ounces and dump it down my throat. It fills my stomach and I take a deep breath, letting the calm take me over. My phone lights up on the table. It's Atlas.

I can't stop thinking about being with you tomorrow.

My stomach flutters. Those three dots pop up on the screen. He's typing again.

I just want to be in your presence. I want to hold you. I want to feel you.

I imagine his large, chocolate hands sliding up my thighs, tickling me as he gets closer to my center. My heart races and my body temperature skyrockets although the air conditioning blasts through every vent in the house.

I reply.

I'll be all yours.

I add a winky face emoji before I hit send.

I lock my eyes on the phone screen, anxious for his next message. My hand tugs at the collar of my shirt, allowing cool air to waft onto my chest. The line of my collarbone tingles as my fingertips glide past it. They wander down my chest until I graze my nipple, which sends shockwaves through my core. I flick the perky nub over and over, aching for the feeling it brings.

The screen illuminates again.

All mine, huh? I think I could get used to that.

My reply is swift.

Me too.

My imagination takes over, as I visualize two of Atlas' fingers sliding up and down my drenched pussy, in between my lips. His mouth curls into a smirk before shoving into my hole, stretching me open.

My own fingers leave my nipple to slide underneath my waistband and past my panties. The need to feel pressure down below is overwhelming. The dining room chair supports me as I arch my back against the wooden slats. My clit is already swollen once I find it. It throbs as I tease it with light touches. Finally, I press hard with two fingers, moving in rhythmic circles, faster and faster. I can hear my heart pounding in my chest. The pressure continues to build, getting stronger and sharper. I keep rubbing. I'm so close. A deep moan escapes my lips, pushing me closer to the edge.

"What the hell?"

My head smacks on the back of the chair and I bolt upright.

Jason stands in the entryway of the kitchen. His hands rest on his hips and amusement is spread across his face. I wipe my wet hand on my pants in an attempt to hide the mess.

"Were you touching yourself in the middle of our kitchen?"

I let out a nervous laugh and saunter over to the sink to wash my fluids from my hands. I'm sure he can tell from my lack of eye contact that I'm utterly embarrassed.

"All his, huh?" There's a tinge of humor in Jason's voice, but it's laced with something else. Something frigid.

I turn to face him. The smile that had just adorned his face has faded. A menacing sneer replaces it. My phone balances on his palm, the text messages between Atlas and I vivid on the display.

"I didn't mean it that way," I say, my tone light.

Jason makes his way over, stopping directly in front of me. My phone waves in his hand, his blue eyes locked with mine. I'm pinned between Jason and the countertop. The cold granite presses into my lower back, sending shivers up my torso. I can smell the sour liquor on his breath, just as he can probably smell the wine on mine.

"Maybe I should let him have you," he whispers and tosses my phone onto the counter. It lands with a sharp clank.

His eyes pierce into mine and I can no longer hold the stare. A crimson hickey rests on the pale flesh of his neck. A mark that wasn't there this morning before he left. I trace it with my finger, and he knocks my hand away.

"Should I let her have you?" I say in monotone, still staring at the mark.

Jason's firm hand grips around my neck. I can feel each finger press into my skin as he squeezes. It becomes harder and harder to suck air into my lungs.

"Not another fucking word. You're a whore. Know your place." His words sting like venom.

I gasp for air now. His grip still hasn't let up. When I attempt to pry his fingers loose, he swats my hand away.

"I said, know your place," he says and digs further into my neck.

Panic rises in my throat. I *need* air. My arms flail as my lungs fight for any bit of oxygen. Tears build up as my eyes water from the tension, clouding my vision. His face is distorted but seemingly unbothered. Not even fazed by the terror in my eyes.

His grasp releases me, and I'm left sputtering for air, taking in as much I can get with each inhale. I use the countertop to support myself, regaining my footing.

"Jason?" My voice shakes, threatening to break.

Before he answers he whips my body around and shoves me forward. My hips smash into the sink cabinet and my stomach into the granite. His bulge presses against my ass.

"J—" I'm stopped before I can finish my sentence. My head is forced down into the empty metal sink. The smell of rotting food wafts up from the disposal as my nose grazes the drain. He has a firm grip on my hair. Any movement could rip strands from my scalp.

"Shut your fucking mouth," he says, his breath hot on my neck.

He fumbles with the button of my jeans, barely able to loosen it with one hand. When he finally gets it undone, his hand shoves inside my panties, cupping my vulva.

"Still wet?" he scoffs.

"You're scaring me, Jason." I whimper.

My words don't faze him. He manages to lower his pants as well as mine and shoves himself inside of me while pressing down even harder on my head.

"Stop!" The drain swallows up my scream.

His other hand grabs my ass. A sharp sting spreads across the cheek as he digs his nails into my skin. I try to wriggle free but it's no use. He's stronger than me and I have no leverage. My body dries up and each stroke becomes increasingly painful, like a rug burn on my insides. If the drain were plugged, my salty tears would fill the sink.

My neck snaps back as he rips my hair from out of the basin, setting my scalp on fire. I wish for it all to be over. I could flail my arms, scream for help at the top of my lungs, beg and plead with my husband. But I don't do any of these things. I stay quiet and wait for it to end, soaking in all the pain.

The all too familiar sound of Jason Carson's climactic groan shakes the walls. This time, the noise makes my stomach churn. He slides out of me and releases his grip on my hair. My back stays turned to him. I can't face him. Not anytime soon.

"I'm going to go shower," he says.

His zipper sounds before his heavy feet stomp up the stairs. He leaves me standing there, pants down to my knees, tears streaked down my face, hair in knots, and staring down the drain wondering if this is something I can ever get past.

I attempt to cover up my bruised neck with concealer, powder, then more concealer. The marks were a royal purple when I finally dragged myself out of bed and made it to the bathroom mirror this morning. Jason didn't sleep in the bed with me. Which I was grateful for. I squirm now just thinking of our bodies brushing up against one another. I assume he slept down on the couch. Judging by his breath last night, he's probably still knocked out, sleeping off his hangover.

If I could put on a scarf, I would. But it's the middle of summer and today's high of ninety-five degrees doesn't allow for any winter accessories. The bruise spans practically my whole neck. It's painful to the touch and as I blend the makeup onto the skin, I can't help but to wince. I'll wear my hair down today, which will help a bit. Another sting ensues as I run the brush through my tresses, tugging at the spot that Jason had gripped between his fingers.

After layer upon layer of creams and powder are caked onto my skin, I decide it's not going to get any better. Surely, I can come up with a reasonable explanation as to why two male hands are imprinted into my neck.

When I sit on the toilet to pee, I writhe in pain from the trauma Jason caused down there last night. I should have thought to ice it last night.

Atlas has asked to meet me for brunch in Athens Park. He promised to bring everything, the picnic blanket, the muffins, the fruit, the mimosas. All I was told to bring was my "pretty little self", which has lightened my mood a bit. I thought about canceling, giving my bruises time to heal and my eyes time to depuff. But I want to see him. I can't be in this home another minute, not after what happened last night. Not with Jason lingering downstairs leaving me to wonder which side of him I'm getting today, the loving husband or the violent predator.

My reflection stares back at me one more time before I shut off the bathroom lights. I searched in my closet for the dress with the highest neckline. This one sits right above my collarbones. Its pale-yellow color offsets the purple bruises just a bit. I place a pair of large tortoise shell sunglasses on the bridge of my nose, a great way to cover up evidence of my late-night sobbing.

When I get downstairs, the room curtains and blinds are all still closed, allowing for little light to penetrate through. My footsteps are practically undetectable as I tiptoe through the hardwood floors, silently praying I won't wake him up. The garage door is farther away from the couch than the front door, so I take that route instead. Atlas had offered to pick me up, but I declined. I couldn't risk Jason seeing his car. I don't know what's right or wrong anymore. I never know when he might snap.

The car stereo stays off the whole fifteen-minute drive to Athens Park. My mind runs wild in the silence, but it's better than any added commotion to my thoughts. I half hope Atlas notices my bruises and half hope he doesn't. Hell, maybe that kind of behavior is normal within their community. I'm not sure I know which way is up anymore.

Athens Park is beautiful today. Children's laughter comes from the brightly colored playground area. Their smiling faces warm my chilled soul a bit, taking me out of my sullied mind. It's still early in the day. The intense heat has yet to take over the air.

My phone pings as a text from Atlas comes through.

Meet me towards the flower gardens in the back of the park.

The flower gardens are in full bloom. Peonies, cosmos, marigolds, petunias, and roses. Reds, yellows, purples, and greens speckle the lawn and spread a sweet aroma around the area.

A large quilt is sprawled out underneath a tree, providing optimal shade and a perfect view of the greenery. Atlas lies on his back with his eyes closed.

"Hey, you!" I call as I get closer. There's a hoarseness to my voice that surprises me, and I realize I haven't spoken at all since last night.

His deep brown eyes flutter open and he props himself up on his elbows.

"Hey, *you*," he says and flashes his usual flirtatious grin.

A smorgasbord of fruits and pastries line a tray that sits behind him, making my stomach growl.

"Hungry?" he asks.

I nod and sit next to him with my legs crossed, picking up a blueberry muffin and taking a bite right off the top. His thumb reaches up and brushes a crumb off my chin. We both laugh and mine sounds as if I'm just getting over a cold.

"You been sick?" he asks.

"No," I say softly to hide the rasp.

He sits up fully now and leans in to kiss me. His lips are gentle and taste like strawberries. I go in for another, craving his taste and the way his lips sink into mine.

"You don't know how badly I've needed that," he says.

He brushes my hair behind my ear then grabs at the side of my neck to pull me in again. I flinch and let out an audible "ow", drawing back from his grasp. I almost forgot about the bruises and piles of makeup on my neck.

His eyes widen as he stares straight at the marks that are still setting off shockwaves of throbs. I pull both sides of my hair over my shoulders and scrunch my knees to my chest.

"What?" I ask him, already knowing the answer.

"Who did this to you, Lula?" His voice is soft, gentle.

I loosen up a bit, relaxing my legs. Atlas lifts my hair, delicately tracing the damage with his fingertip. It feels good to be seen, fawned over. The tension in my neck eases and I let him observe the abuse that Jason committed against me. I swallow hard, trying to fight back the tears that threaten to break through.

"Jason?" he asks.

My face confirms it all. As his lips graze over the tender spots, the flood gates open. Droplets fall onto my cheeks. He kisses every single inch of my neck. When he's done, his face is smothered in a lighter shade of brown, evidence of my attempt to cover up with copious amounts of makeup.

"Sorry." I sniffle and reach for a napkin to clean him up.

"What happened?" he asks.

I sigh. "I set him off."

"Set him off?" His eyes narrow. I notice his hands are balled into fists; the green veins bulge out.

"Just when I think things are going back to normal. Back to the way it was when we started, I'm thrown off again but ten times worse," I say, folding my hands across my chest.

"Well maybe you need to accept that this is the new normal." His tone is harsh. He grabs my hands and massages them with his thumbs. "This isn't okay, Lula. I don't care what sort of freaky shit Jason is into. We all have our own kinks. But this," he gestures to my neck, "is *not* okay."

"I agree," I say.

"Then leave that psychopath," he says, running his fingers through his short, tight curls.

"It's not that simple. He's my husband. We have a life together."

"This is how women end up dead, Lula."

"I know," I say. And I do. I've thought about that a lot.

Do most of the girls killed by domestic violence see it coming? Can they even fathom that the love of their life could do something so heinous? Jason has been aggressive with me, sure. And I'm aware that it's escalating. But deep down, I don't know if he has it in him to be a murderer. Hindsight is always 20/20. And sadly, too many women aren't here to see it. The warning signs are there, so why am I giving him so many chances? Maybe I'm just yearning for what used to be.

We both sit in silence for a few minutes, staring at the petals waving in the soft, warm breeze. A honeybee flies past us, buzzing as it lands on a slice of the watermelon.

"I'm scared, Atlas," I finally admit, eyes still on the garden.

Instead of responding, he holds onto my hand, squeezing it. For the first time in days, I feel safe.

My stomach is in knots when I pull up our street, creeping towards our house. When I reach the driveway, I breathe a sigh of relief. Jason's Jeep is gone. I don't know where he's at but I don't care and I hope he doesn't return until after I go to bed for the night.

I don't have much of an appetite, but my stomach continues to growl, feeling hollow. An old can of Campbell's tomato soup sits in the pantry. Easy to make and easy to ingest. The liquid sloshes in the bowl as I carry it up the stairs to my bed. I've decided I'll draw the curtains and watch trash reality tv for the rest of the day until the sun sets and I'm able to fall asleep.

I settle underneath my down comforter, relishing in the warmth it brings me in this chilly air-conditioned room. I'm behind on a few episodes of Love Island and have been meaning to catch up. It may not be the most wholesome entertainment but it sure will take my mind off of my own messy life. By the time I finally spoon up some soup and put it in my mouth, it's lukewarm. I force a few more spoonfuls down my throat and then set the bowl aside, entirely uninterested.

The jingle of my ringtone startles me but the tension in my shoulders loosen when I realize it's my mother, not my husband.

"Hey, honey. Turn on your television."

"It's already on, mom," I say with a tone that borders on annoyance.

"Are you watching the news?"

"Nope."

"They are reporting on that missing girl from my Facebook groups. Looks like they've found some of her belongings by the old water tower near Sierra Springs. They are saying she's a runaway, but my senses are telling me it's foul play." Her mouth smacks over the receiver. My guess is she's eating her usual nightly cup of berries and two squares of dark chocolate. My irritation grows.

She continues, "I've told you once and I'll tell you again, you can't trust anyone these days. Poor thing was only fourteen. I had a teenager once too, ya know. I would be losing my shit right now."

"Mhmmm," I say mindlessly.

"The least you can do is be on the lookout for her, Lula Jane." Her voice is stern. She can't see my eyes roll but I'm sure she senses it.

"Channel 12?" I ask and fumble with the buttons on the remote control.

As soon as the tv screen clicks onto channel 12, my eyes are glued, and my blood runs cold.

"What did you say this girl's name is?" I ask, my voice low.

"Her name is Polly Cooper. She's a precious little thing, isn't she?"

Photos of Polly run on the screen. Polly in her frilly homecoming dress. Polly arm in arm with children who look similar to her, probably siblings. Polly in a volleyball uniform, smacking a ball over the net. Picture after picture I become more certain. Polly Cooper, the fourteen-year-old runaway, was in Calen's bed that night in the hotel room.

I wasn't tripping from the drugs. It wasn't a blip in reality. I know what I saw that night. This is the confirmation I needed.

CHAPTER 28

How many dirty secrets does this club hold? And how many girls like Polly Cooper have there been? Rasheeda's throaty voice pops into my mind as a vision of that night becomes less blurry. It was a comment Rasheeda made in the hotel room to Calen,

They are here for her.

I feel queasy, like I might vomit the few sips of tomato soup and crumbles of muffin that sit in my stomach onto my bed. Who are *they*?

I remember something else Jason had said about the resort gathering,

It isn't just club members that come to these larger events. Friends of friends of friends are also invited. It's actually great for networking.

I thought they had been fishing for new members. But maybe that wasn't the case. Maybe they were baiting *buyers*. And what do these people want with young teenage runaways? The thought swirls in my head but I can't bring myself to catch it and bring it to the surface. It might make it real and not just a suspicion. An incredibly logical suspicion. All of the lavish parties, luxury cars, and Derrick and Cheyenne's home of grandeur. Rasheeda has a personal driver for fuck's sake. Could all of the money be coming solely from well-paying careers? Would these people stoop so low just for various splendors?

Another fleeting thought passes through. Rasheeda's manifesto. The club packet is stashed somewhere, collecting dust, underneath my bed, pieces of paper I never thought I'd need to see again. I bend over the edge of the bed, hanging upside down, and shine my phone flashlight into the dark abyss. The packet sits next to a granola bar wrapper and a lint filled sock on the rug underneath the bed. Pages shuffle through my fingers while I scan the text. When I find the correct page, the black, Arial font message stands out as if it were bolded, highlighted, and underlined.

We must let go of the pressures and limits that society sets against us and live without fear of sin or damnation. We were meant to chase the euphoric pleasures of the world and through Inanna we can attain the freedom to do so.

Rasheeda has essentially written her own moral code, or lack thereof. To them, there's no such thing as right or wrong, as long as it gets you ahead in the world.

Gina nags in the back of my mind. Is Andrew Stratford right about Gina's death not being a suicide? Did Greg snap? Or did Rasheeda sic Calen on her for not following the rules? For getting in the way of "freedom"? Are they really willing to murder for the sake of the club?

Goosebumps spread across my flesh, and I shiver, shoving my body back underneath the blankets for warmth that doesn't come. My fingers pick at a loose thread on the comforter, twirling it around and around while my thoughts continue to race.

This isn't what I signed up for. But then again, is this what any of us signed up for? I think of Atlas and Clara, I think of Jason. I wonder how many people are turning a blind eye to this corruption. It's possible that they know even less than I do. Or maybe that's just a naive assumption.

Where do I go with my suspicions? What do I do? Who can I trust? The more questions I ask, the more I become a liability. I need to make a slow exit from the club, steadily distance myself from the corruption.

"Lula, baby! You upstairs?" Jason's tone is cheery.

My breath quickens and I jolt upright. I was so lost in thought that I must not have heard him come in. My mouth opens to respond but no words come out. I'm frozen until his feet start stamping up the stairs, pulling me back to reality.

"In here!" My voice cracks as I toss the papers back below the bed.

The first thing I see is his hand extended through the door grasping a bouquet of deep red roses, so fragrant I smell them instantly. Next thing I see as he peeks into the room are his cheeks, flushed as if he just got done running a marathon.

"Can I come in?" he asks.

"It's your room too," I say softly, keeping the blankets as a safety net over my body.

"These are for you." He sets the flowers on top of my nightstand, gently pushing my bowl of soup to the side.

"What's the occasion?" I ask, my tone still faint and measured.

Jason takes a seat on the edge of the bed, his back turned towards me, and exhales. I push my back further into the wall, a weak attempt to get out of my husband's reach. His hands rub on his thighs over and over, as if he's attempting to smooth out his already wrinkle free jeans.

"I've been awful to you. Don't think I'm not thoroughly ashamed by my actions," he says with a break in his voice.

When he turns to face me, I get a good look at his face. Deep, gray bags sit underneath his eyes. His usual bright blue irises are dull, lifeless. Shame is written all over his blood red cheeks. His lips start to quiver, and my first instinct is to embrace him, to make it all better. But I don't.

"I'm sorry, Lula. From the bottom of my heart. I'm sorry." He stares at me, probably acknowledging my protective position. The way I am shielding myself from his dangerous hands.

"Fuck," he groans, "You're terrified of me!" His face collapses into his hands.

"I—I—" I stutter. Once again, I'm incapable of forming a sentence.

"I don't blame you, Lula. I'm a monster," he says with a voice muffled by his hands.

"What is going on with you?" My tone is neither harsh nor sweet, completely devoid of emotion.

He gets off the bed and goes to the corner of the room, facing me. His back hits the wall and he slides down it, bringing his knees to his chest. We sit there in silence for a moment, both assuming the exact same position. I still fiddle with the string. By now I've wrapped it around my finger so many times that it's beginning to cut off the circulation. But it takes my mind off of the bruises that clutter my neck and groin. The bruises that came alive again once my husband entered the room.

Jason clears his throat. "I'm using still, Lula. And at this point, I don't even know what other shit it could have been cut with." He looks to me for a response but I don't give him one, so he continues. "I know I told you I'd stop, but I didn't. When I don't use it, I get irritable and then when I do use it, I get irritable. It's a lose-lose cycle and I don't know how to make it all stop." He runs his hand through his dirty blonde hair.

"Why do you feel like you need it in the first place, Jason?" I ask, a slight whine to my voice.

His defined shoulders sag. My husband is a man that usually has it all together. He doesn't like to be seen as weak. But sitting there, with his back against the wall, head held low and hair disheveled, that's exactly how he looks. Like a fragile little boy stuck in a grown man's body.

"My dad was a bad man, Lula. A disgusting, perverse man. I've told you some, but not everything. I've always left out the worst parts."

My stomach churns. I know how depraved his father was, or I at least know bits and pieces of it. The stories Jason divulged sickened me to the point that walking through their family home for the first time made my skin crawl, like I needed to scrub my skin immediately after leaving. Mr. Carson had a sexual appetite that was not easily satiated. But unsuspecting young boys could usually do the trick. I've always wondered if sexual deviancy could be hereditary. Maybe vanilla sex was never good enough for Jason Carson because it was never good enough for his father. It was my first thought when Jason introduced the idea of the club to me.

"Every day I feel like I'm going to turn into him. Like his ghost is going to possess my body, my thoughts…" His voice trails off.

"You are not your dad, Jason," I say.

"I need help, Lu," he says with pleading eyes that stare at me.

His body trembles as he curls into a sitting ball. Heavy sobs proceed, flooding the room. My walls fall down, and my fear is replaced with sympathy. The cool air further calms my nerves as I slide my legs out from underneath the covers. Sitting on the floor, I envelope my husband in my arms. My body expands and contracts with his as I squeeze him tight, an attempt to take away his hurt.

As much as I want to flee this marriage and everything that's attached to it, I made a vow. *Till death do us part.* But Jason isn't the only one who needs help. I must save myself from this club. But now the question is, do I attempt to save my husband too?

Jason falls asleep next to me in bed, whimpering. With the rollercoaster of emotions that had flooded through me tonight, sleep takes me quickly. As soon as I shut my eyes, I'm back in my childhood bedroom. Heartthrob posters with the faces of Chad Michael Murray and Orlando Bloom line the obnoxiously lavender painted walls. That faint smell of my favorite berry sorbet drugstore candle wafts in the air.

"Honey! Come downstairs!" My mother's voice shrills from down below.

The bedroom door opens to a dark hallway that I don't recognize. My muscles tense. *This can't be right.* My mother's room isn't across from mine. The wall to my right that used to hold a perfectly stained, mahogany door is now replaced with a lone tattered red robe on a hook. The sight takes my breath away.

My feet drag slowly across the floor as I search for the stairs leading down to my mom. I fear I may tumble down them as the lighting gets dimmer and dimmer. Suddenly, I see them. Just ahead of me at the end of the hall. A bright ray of sunlight shines at the bottom and illuminates my path.

I pick up the pace. "I'll be right there, mama!"

I'm practically sprinting when the walls start closing in on me. Panic envelops my body and my throat feels tight as though it might close. My rapid breaths echo off my constricting surroundings.

"Mama!" I cry out.

My arms extend and I use all of my strength to push the walls apart to avoid them from closing in on me. The light at the bottom of the stairs begins to fade and I squeeze my eyes shut, preparing for the darkness.

"Honey. You remember Gina Reese, right?"

When my eyes open, I'm in my childhood living room with my mother, dressed in one of her usual flowy bohemian dresses. She stands next to a smiling Gina Reese.

"Don't be rude, Lula. Say hello," my mother demands.
Something isn't right.

"Hi, Gina," I say with an embarrassing wave.

After one blink her smile fades and once again, the shining light coming in through the windows starts to fizzle out, casting a grayish glow across the room.

Another blink and I gasp, covering my mouth with my hands. Gina's body looks swollen. Her eyes dark and sunken in.

The short, voluminous hair I've seen in pictures is replaced with frizzy strands drooping from her scalp.

My blood turns to ice when I notice her neck. A deep, red, oozing line circles around it. The blood drips down onto her chest but she doesn't seem to notice, doesn't seem to care.

"Have you seen Jason?" Gina's voice is just short of a whisper.

My head shakes. I'm unable to form words, like something is stuck in my throat. Her bare feet inch closer to me, her long toenails lined with dirt. My instincts tell me to back away but my feet are frozen, cemented in place.

"I think we've lost Jason," Gina says in her throaty whisper.

Gina's mouth opens wide, and she starts to gag. Slimy maggots crawl out from her throat. I open my mouth to scream but I can't. No sound comes out. I squeeze my eyes shut, willing it all to stop. I *need* it to stop.

A cold puddle of sweat soaks into the sheets underneath me when I wake in my bed, Jason snoring next to me. I sit up, struggling to catch my breath and a wave of nausea hits me. Barely making it to the toilet bowl, I empty what little I have in my stomach.

CHAPTER 29

Monday morning drags while I sit at work at the reception desk. I cringe as the wheels of my chair squeak as I roll from one side of the desk to another, filing paperwork and entering patient information into the computer. My back aches as I dig my knuckle into the stress knot. I've been begging my boss for upgraded furnishings but once again, it's not in the budget for the month.

My now yellowish bruises are covered up with a turtleneck sweater top. Thankfully the office is kept at a cool sixty-seven degrees rain or shine, so I don't look too silly. The bags under my eyes from tears and stress weren't as easy to conceal, though. They shine through my layers of makeup.

"Goodness Lula. You look like you didn't get much sleep. You alright?" Davina, my socially unaware coworker, leans against my desk with a slip of paper.

Usually I'd play her games, let out a fake chuckle and admit I'd had a rough night. But lately, I'm not in the mood for it. "Is that your subtle way of saying I look like shit, Davina?" I ask with a straight face.

Her cheeks redden and she sets the paper down, shuffling away to continue doing her job. I feel bad. Kind of. She is always making stupid, underhand remarks and expects everyone just to let her get away with it. My mind has been frazzled lately as it is, and I don't need her comments to cloud my mind even more.

"Delivery for Lula Carson?" The office door bangs closed behind a teenage boy holding a cellophane covered basket of brightly colored fruits. I haven't seen an Edible Arrangement in years, but I'm assuming that's what I'm looking at. The boy, with his long side swept hair and scrawny legs, looks at me impatiently, waiting for a response so he can go about his day.

"Uh, yeah. You can drop it off right here," I say.

He brings it to the counter and hurries out the door, without another word. A printed note hangs off the basket, in typed Helvetica font.

We can get through anything together. Thank you for always being my rock. Enjoy, my Sweets. Love, Jason.

The warm feeling that should be spreading throughout my body doesn't come. Instead, I want to beg the boy to take the basket back. Beg him to take it anywhere but here. The cellophane crinkles as I carry it to the breakroom to add to our "free for all" pile. I won't be touching a single piece of this fruit.

"Looks like someone has some making up to do." Davina peeks around the corner, grinning. I'd like to throw a chunk of watermelon at her head. Maybe a few grapes too.

When my tires skid into the driveway after work, I'm surprised to see Jason's Jeep already parked in his spot. I can't even remember the last time he was home before me. The urge to put the car in reverse and speed out of the subdivision hits hard. Instead, I put the car in park, shut the engine off, stare at my sunken eyes in the visor mirror, and scream. The noise scares me at first, but as I allow my vocal cords to strain, there is a release from deep within my chest. I scream until my face turns red and the tension in my temples is unbearable. My rasp that had improved overnight returns and breaks my voice.

I'm left listening to my heavy breaths, taking in the air I just expelled from my lungs.

As the car doors shuts, I notice a young boy across the street, mouth agape, staring at the source of the scream. My Prius definitely isn't soundproof. His wide eyes look at me as if I'm a feral cat, ready to pounce and claw out his eyes. The smile I give him doesn't help and he runs to his front door, slamming it shut behind him.

"There's my girl," Jason says as he greets me at the front door with a smooch on the forehead.

"Didn't expect to see you so early," I say.

"I got all my work done early. I thought we could go to dinner or something. There's this new Pho place I've been dying to show you. You're going to love it," he says.

Is this my life now? Just going day by day, pretending like nothing ever happened. Like the abuse never happened. Living happily ever after with my tortured husband?

I force a cheesy smile. "Pho sounds delicious. Let's go."

He wasn't wrong. The Pho was amazing, and I did love it. The conversation flowed nicely as well. But I felt like I was watching it all from the outside, looking in. Disconnected from my reality. I'm no longer the wife I used to be. And he's no longer the husband he used to be. But we sat there anyway, pretending we were in our past lives. Pretending like the lies, mistrust, abuse, and hatred never seeped into our marriage, causing it to rot from within.

It was nice to pretend for a while. Like a band aid to the wound I have yet to gain the courage to truly properly tend to.

But now as we lay in bed, Jason glued to the far right and me to the far left, ensuring not even our feet brush against one another, the chasm between us is palpable. The tether that connected us, that I clung onto so fiercely, has withered away and now I'm all alone. More vulnerable than I have ever been.

"Babe?" His voice startles me.

"Yeah?"

"You'll always be mine," he says, matter of factly. His tone is neither rough nor gentle, which causes every muscle in my body to tense.

Maybe he can sense my slow retreat from life as I know it. A retreat that I haven't even taken the time to plan out yet. Maybe he wants to let me know that I'm stuck in this cycle with him, with nowhere else to turn. Or maybe, just maybe, it's his way of expressing his undying love for me. A love, that in his mind, is still burning as bright as it ever had. Either way, it spreads unease throughout my mind and a suffocation within my body.

"I know," I reply after seconds of silence.

Throughout the week I go through the motions. A kiss goodbye before leaving for work in the morning, file paperwork and update patient charts throughout the day, come home and make dinner, then get into bed for vanilla sex with my husband before falling asleep to do it all over again the next day. The routine should feel normal. But it doesn't. By Thursday I'm contemplating offing myself. Not seriously, but the thought seems intriguing.

As the soft, warm flow from the shower head hits my back this morning, a feeling of safety washes over me. I wish I could stay here, protected by the thickening steam, slowly fading out all the noise and chaos in the outside world. I get the strong urge to purify myself of all the filth my body has witnessed and endured throughout these past months, and I scrub viciously with the loofah, as if I have vulgar art from permanent marker littering my skin that needs to be erased. When I get to my scalp, I stare in horror at my hands. Clumps of dark strands lie tangled in my palms, winding between my fingers. I fling it towards the drain and pull out another clump. My mother once told me that stress can make your hair fall out. If that's the case, I'll be bald by next month if I don't figure something out. If I don't figure out a way to change this trajectory.

"Lula?" Jason opens the bathroom door, releasing some of the steam that had built up, releasing my sense of safety.

"Yes?"

"It's nine am. Don't you have to be heading out now?"

"Shit." I was in such a trance that I wasn't paying any attention to the time. Over an hour had gone by without me realizing.

"I've gotta go. Just thought I'd come and say goodbye," he says.

"Alright, have a good day. I'll be getting out of here soon, too." Even through the foggy glass I can see that his navy slacks are smooth, without a single wrinkle and his hair perfectly styled, not a strand out of place. My perfectly polished husband. No one would ever guess that he was crying in my meek arms just a week ago, a fraction of the man he appears to be now.

"Oh, I keep forgetting to mention," he shuffles back into the bathroom, "Rasheeda planned a last-minute gathering. She thinks we all need to reconvene, channel some energy. Saturday night."

Before I can answer the door clicks shut, Jason off on his way to work. It can't be a coincidence that the shower water goes cold as soon as the statement sets in. Channeling energy with the club? The thought makes me shiver, wishing for an extra stream of hot water. Just the mention of Rasheeda makes me want to crawl up into a ball on the cold, solid shower floor.

When I finally make it to work, over an hour late, I spend my time thinking of all the excuses in the book. Strep throat, my mom took a tumble down the stairs, I twisted my ankle running after the FedEx man. All sound like blatant lies. Or I could tell him the truth. That crosses my mind as well. The truth is simple anyways. *Jason, I'm scared shitless of this club, and I want no parts of it any longer.* But I know that isn't actually an option. I can't be brutally honest with someone that I don't fully trust.

Saturday night creeps in like a stalker lurking in the shadows. I willed it not to pounce, not to rear its ugly head, but it was inevitable.

It's only twenty minutes before Jason has proclaimed we will leave for the gathering and I'm panicking. I've paced the hallway between our bedroom door and the stairs about fifty times, debating whether or not to jump ship and throw myself out the window. Granted, it would probably only cause a few bruises, *maybe* a broken bone or two. I've dressed the part, though. My plaid, burgundy mini skirt and beige thigh high boots are sexy, yet not too extravagant. Something that garnered me an approving nod from Jason. He wears nicely fitted, tan slacks with a white polo. The outfit is plain, but tasteful. I can only imagine the irrelevance of our clothing choices. Surely, they will be covered up with red robes before anyone even has the chance to notice us.

Last minute, I decide to go with old reliable, the stomach bug.

"I'm feeling a little off," I tell him as I walk down the stairs.

He gives me a curious look as he grabs his favorite watch from the kitchen counter and secures it to his wrist.

"A little off?" he asks.

"I don't know. I was finishing up my makeup and this wave of nausea hit me." I sit at the dining room table, bracing myself. Jason doesn't seem to notice my subtle distress. His focus is on getting us out the door.

"Hold on a second!" I make a run for the closest bathroom across the hall, holding my stomach and slamming the door shut as soon as I get in.

"You alright in there, babe?" he asks.

I have no time to think about it. Without hesitation, I stick two fingers deep into my throat. A few gags, and I push down farther, willing it all to come up. Seconds later my body heaves as the entire contents of my stomach come splashing into the porcelain bowl. I don't make any attempts to hold back, letting out a guttural groan.

"Ah, shit. Did you eat something bad?" His voice filters in behind the door.

"There's a bug going around work. Helene just puked her brains out on Thursday in the patient restroom. And you know that girl doesn't wash her hands," I say, spitting in between sentences.

"You don't feel any better now that you got it all out?" he asks. I can sense his presence leaning against the wooden door.

One more time. I jab fingers back down my throat and bile erupts from my stomach.

"I'll take that as a no. Do you need me to get you anything?" He hesitates for a moment, "I can stay—"

"No, no, no. You go. I'll manage," I say, insisting.

Jason has a weak stomach. Vomit, feces, boogers, blood. It all makes him gag. Being around his pukey wife is the last place he wants to spend his Saturday night, which was the goal.

After the slam of the front door and the crinkle of Jason's tires leaving the driveway, I breathe a sigh of relief. I've gotten out of it this time. But I can't use the same excuse for the next. I can cross that bridge when it comes, but it will nag at the back of my mind until then.

My teeth feel gritty and my throat raw. I spend over five minutes scrubbing the acidic taste out of my mouth and then make a warm cup of chamomile tea to soothe the burning in my esophagus.

I settle in bed with my laptop, needing to focus on a way out of this mess. I have a cousin that lives in Tennessee. Far enough away that the club can't reach me. I think. A one bedroom for rent in Chattanooga is $1,400 a month plus a matching deposit. While our joint bank account isn't hurting, my old Bank of America account, which I never got around to closing, holds a whopping $17.45. Not even enough for gas just to get to Tennessee.

I can't do this without Jason. I need him to jump ship with me. To get away before it's too late.

My phone buzzes next to me. It's Clara.

Where the hell are you?

After consuming myself with everything I'm trying to get away from, I forget about the slight fortunes this club has brought me. One of the main ones being Clara.

Puking my brains out. Hope I don't miss too much.

Her reply comes immediately,

I think they know.

It takes a few seconds for her response to register, but when it does, a weight forms in my chest.

My fingertips hover over the screen, willing a response to form in my head but I can't think of one. I know that Clara had been scared of the truth getting out and I find myself scared for her now. I can only imagine the daggers Rasheeda is shooting her way.

I reply after minutes have gone by.

What makes you think that?

I'm now upright in bed, no longer able to lay down without fidgeting.

I'm not getting rid of her.

They can't make her get an abortion if she doesn't want one. The baby in her stomach is hers, not the club's. Regardless, if Ellis is ready to be a dad or not.

No one can make you do anything you don't want to do, Clara. Don't let anyone bully you into believing otherwise.

Waiting, waiting, waiting.

Her name is Penelope.

All I send back are four question marks. The rest of the night I tap my phone every three minutes to check for another text from Clara, something to clarify her last one, but it never comes. Despite my nerves, I doze in and out, clutching my phone in my palm, waiting for a vibration. Finally, sleep takes me. And I dream of a cute little baby sleeping in a cradle in a dark room. She's the only thing illuminated, with an angelic glow. She's adorable with a button nose and freckles. Curly wisps surround her head. I stare at her from above, watching her little body expand and contract as she breathes. I stand there for a while, admiring, until her body stills. The face that was once so rosy goes pale, almost bluish.

"Help!" I call out, but my voice doesn't penetrate, like it's in a vacuum. No one answers. Then everything goes black.

Jason is next to me in bed when the orange glow from the sunrise, peeking through the blinds, lures me out of my slumber. I didn't hear him come in last night. Who knows, maybe it was this morning. His deep snore tells me that whatever he drank last night, he drank it heavily. My eyes trace the small details of his face, the small mole above his left eyebrow, the curvature of his nostrils, the pink tint of his lips. These days, the only time I get to enjoy the view of my husband is when he's fast asleep. It seems to be about the only time his innocence shines through anymore.

He doesn't sense my gaze, just like he doesn't sense his phone buzzing underneath his arm. At first, I ignore it. He can worry about it later. But when it goes off again, and then again for a third time, I jostle him out of sleep.

"Jason, your phone keeps going off," I say, nudging at him.

"Hmmm?" He squints at me like he has no idea who I am or where we are.

"Your phone," I say, pointing towards it.

It takes him a few seconds to catch on, but he finally manages to get it up to his ear, eyes still half shut.

"Hello?" His groggy voice breathes into the speaker.

Someone on the other end sounds panicky, shrieking into the mouthpiece.

"Woah, woah, woah, slow down. Just calm down and breathe," he says, sitting upright, suddenly alert.

I don't normally listen in on his conversations, but I can't bring myself to leave the room to give him privacy. And he doesn't shoo me away, so I stay. An unnerving wave washes over the room.

"You said Clara?" Jason asks.

I feel cold, like suddenly all the warmth in the room dissipated. I shoot upright too and press my ear next to the phone, forcing my hands underneath me to stop them from trembling. I can just barely make out the voice on the other line. It's Ellis. His gravelly voice is much higher pitched than usual, but I can still tell that it's him.

"She's fucking gone, man. She's gone!" Ellis screams like he's in physical pain, like he's just broken a bone.

"What do you mean she's gone?" Jason asks.

Sobs filter out through the speaker. "I found her in bed in her apartment. Cold as ice. Fucking purple and stiff. They are saying it's carbon monoxide poisoning or some shit, man," his voice shakes.

A whimper escapes my lips, and my hands move from underneath me to cover my mouth.

"No, no. I was just talking to her last night. She was fine," I whisper, pleading with Jason. He shushes me and runs his fingers through his messy hair.

"When did you go over there?" he asks Ellis, ignoring my attempts to reassure myself that this can't be real.

Ellis says something about late last night, about the stovetop, about the fire department, but I don't hear much of it. It all just sounds like gibberish. I can't string the words along to make sense of any of the sentences. My mind turns into mush, and I tune everything out.

When the call finally clicks to end, I realize I've been staring at the blank wall, eyes burning from not blinking. Jason murmurs something but I don't know what it was. His fingers jump around the keyboard of his phone as he texts like a madman, probably updating everyone on the recent tragedy.

While I was sound asleep in my bed last night, awaiting a text that would never come, Clara was suffocating. The thought makes me sick, as I swallow back the saliva that has built up around my mouth. Her body, once so petite and lively, reduced to a rigid corpse.

More buzzing and Jason is back on the phone again, reciting the same story from Ellis. But this time, he adds his own flair.

"We all know she took Vicodin like they were M&Ms she probably was so damn high she forgot she left the damn stove on." Jason's words spit out like venom, stinging me, turning my sadness into rage.

"Vicodin? Clara was pregnant, Jason. She would never be so careless," I say, despite the fact that he's on the phone with someone else. He pretends not to hear me, continuing on with his conversation, which fuels the fire burning within me even more. I can't contain it any longer. Jason's phone is just within my reach, I grasp it out of his hands and throw it at the wall. It lands with a loud thump on the ground.

"She's dead!" I scream.

He doesn't flinch. He doesn't react. He just stares at me with a lack of concern strewn across his face. As if he doesn't want to give in to my irrational behavior. As if Clara dying isn't a reason to overreact.

A thought dawns on me, chilling me to the bone. "You know. You were the only one I told about her pregnancy. She didn't want anyone knowing. She was terrified of anyone finding out. But stupidly, I told you. And now she's dead," I say, my tone flat.

"What are you trying to say, Lula?" His tone matches mine.

Instead of answering I get out of the bed and reach for my robe draped over the ottoman at the foot of the bed. I feel exposed, vulnerable, like I need to cover up. I tie it tightly around my waist and face him.

"Clara was a reckless woman. Recklessness has consequences." His blue eyes seem to turn a shade darker. He searches my face for a reaction. I don't know what kind he's looking for, though. Fear? Sorrow? Understanding? The only one I can muster up is disgust. Pure disgust.

"You know what? I lied to you the other night. You *are* just like your father. A spitting image."

As soon as I say the words, I regret it. Jason is off the bed before I can blink, hurling towards me. His bare feet stomp across the floor and he lunges with his arms out, slamming my back against the wall behind me. A picture frame crashes to the floor next to us, sprinkling glass shards around our feet. I try to wriggle out of his grasp, but he pins me to the wall with both hands, his face only inches from mine. Our breaths are heavy and fast, almost in sync with one another. The stench of his morning breath seeps into my nostrils, foul and putrid.

"Let me go," I say, tearfully. My confident stance has faded and now I'm left cowering, scared of what he might do. I don't trust him anymore, not even a bit.

His pointer finger digs into my sternum, pushing vigorously on the bone. My breath catches instinctively in response to the pain.

"I suggest you learn from that bitch's mistake. Like I said, recklessness has consequences," he says, his finger jabbing into me as he spits out the last three words. I turn my face away from him, unable to look him in the eyes anymore. Whatever form of Jason I used to know, he's no longer in there. Not even an ounce of him. There's no use trying to save something that is irrevocably broken.

When he releases me, I crumple to the floor, as if I was depending on his grasp to hold me up.

It's only me now. I'm all I have to depend on.

CHAPTER 30

Gina Reese: 1 Week Before Death

I haven't left the house in over a week, terrified that I'll be connected to Roxanne's disappearance. I won't survive in lock up, I just know it. The shame alone would kill me anyways. Things with the club aren't helping my paranoia either. The air is different, so offbeat that it's palpable. I was told to sit back for the last gathering, but Rasheeda didn't explain why. My texts are going unanswered, my calls being declined. The only time my phone pings now is when Greg pesters me, begging me to "see reason" and "work things out for the sake of the kids". He wouldn't even want me back if he knew the extent I've gone to for this club. I don't regret it, though. My reward from Inanna will come, maybe just not in the way I expected it.

I'm hoping that after just a few weeks, the dust will settle, and I can go back to building up my new life, back to proving myself worthy. The Annie Wilkins project proved to be unsuccessful. It seems she's just a spoiled little brat who wanted attention from her rich parents. She didn't take the bait. Since then, no more names were sent my way. I just don't think I'm cut out for the heat.

Today, I sit at the tiny table in the kitchen, sipping my coffee and staring out the window at the gloomy sky. I didn't add enough cream but that's okay, I need the caffeine anyways. It's after 1 pm but I'm still groggy and the lack of sunshine filtering through isn't helping. With nothing to do but linger around, I've lost my sense of time these past few weeks. Some days I wake at noon, others at well past three. Some days I don't get to bed until two in the morning and others I'm in bed by six in the evening. It seems the groundhog saw his shadow this year as spring is taking ages to actually rear its head. By this time last year, I was already laying out in my bathing suit, tanning. My skin has gotten so pale, like it has forgotten what sunshine even is.

My phone rings as I take a sip of my coffee and I just about choke on it, taken aback by the sudden noise after so much silence.

"Hello?" I answer without even looking at the caller ID, just happy to have someone to talk to.

"Hey. Long time no talk," he says.

Flutters dance around my empty stomach. I haven't talked to him in weeks, maybe even a month.

"I know, stranger. I guess we have both been pretty busy," I say. It's more of a question than a statement.

"I guess so." His voice trails off, like there's more he wants to say.

We sit in a space of silence for a minute, and I wonder what he's thinking, what's going through his mind. The few green leaves that have grown in on the spindly trees outside the window shake in the chilly breeze. This cabin may have a sort of rustic beauty to it, but the property is dull, and unimpressive. Nothing but dirt and sparse greenery for what feels like a mile. Especially depressing on a day like this.

"When can I see you?" he asks.

My heart leaps. I haven't felt *wanted* in ages. I need to feel wanted.

"My schedule is pretty open these days," I say, taking another long sip of coffee. A light buzz starts to form in my head.

"So I've heard," he chuckles.

A dark figure crosses the corner of my eye. A bird, maybe.

"Gina, we really should talk," he says.

"We are talking." I keep my tone light.

Another streak of motion in the window leads me to get up to go check.

"You know what I mean," he says, his tone deepening.

But I'm no longer focused on our conversation. The dark figure is not a bird at all, but a stocky man dressed in black pants and a black hoodie. His heavy gait is familiar. As he heads to the left of the property, I rush to the same side of the cabin, searching for another window to get a better glance. He's parked on the opposite side of the cabin, probably so that I wouldn't see the car. As he ducks inside, I'm not able to see his face. But I know that beat up Chevy truck anywhere and as it puts away there's one thing that I'm certain of.

Calen is stalking around the cabin, watching me.

"Gina?" I almost forget that I'm on the phone in the middle of a conversation.

"Yeah, sorry. Let's talk."

CHAPTER 31

It's still unreal that she's gone. I didn't get to know Clara for very long, but I felt like she was the type of person that made you feel like you've known her for years. But there are so many things I never got to learn about her. I never learned her parents' names or how many siblings she has. No clue where she grew up or what her zodiac sign was. A whole life shattered and for what?

I don't have many friends left in the world, so I was excited about our budding relationship, but all that is gone now.

I had been constantly refreshing my browser, searching for any news on her death after finding out Sunday morning. But today, the Tuesday following her death, she makes the headlines on our local news website.

Local Woman Dies of CO Poisoning Following a Range Malfunction

A twenty-eight-year-old woman from Garden Valley has died after exposure to high levels of carbon monoxide due to a malfunction in her home's kitchen range. Law enforcement and emergency personnel arrived at the residence early Sunday morning. Despite life saving measures being taken, she was pronounced dead at the scene. No one else was affected during the incident. Next of kin have been notified. For information on safe gas usage and the warning signs of CO poisoning, visit: gvcautilites.com/safety.

It's short, undetailed, and impersonal. Regardless, it makes the whole tragedy feel even more real. Hearing it from Ellis's mouth is one thing but hearing it from a public news source is another.

Clara is dead. Her baby is dead.

Oddly enough, I haven't shed a tear for her. I don't know if it's because I'm dealing with my own mess or if it's because I didn't know her well enough. But that seems silly because I even cried at my best friend's grandma's funeral when I was sixteen. A woman I had never met and had no emotional ties to. Maybe I'm numb to it all. Too much mayhem in too short of time. It's all beginning to feel unreal. As if I'm living in a dream world, ready to shake myself awake.

I called in sick to work today. And yesterday too. I told them that I caught a severe case of Covid-19. When she asked for a doctor's note with proof of a test, I didn't reply. I don't think I'm going back anyways. I have these next few days to figure out my next move. A move that could change the rest of my life, for better or for worse.

Choosing to avoid my marital bed, I take Jason's place on the couch in the front room. This has been my routine since Sunday night. Jason hasn't asked questions because he knows. He knows where he went wrong. He might even know that there is no going back now. There is no repairing what he has broken between us.

This morning, after reading Clara's news article over and over again until I could recite the paragraph by heart, I finally roll off the couch, stretching the tense muscles in my back and shoulders as I stand.

Both yesterday and today I have forced myself to stay asleep until after Jason leaves for work. I don't want the awkward run-in at the fridge or in the bedroom hallway. I didn't hear him leave this morning. Maybe I slept harder last night, or maybe he was quieter, leaving through the garage door. I can't spend today sulking around the house in my pajamas like I did yesterday. The pressure to get things done nags at me, like a tingly sensation in my brain is telling me that I don't have much time left.

First things first, I need a shower. Something to reinvigorate my motivations.

The first thing I notice when I reach the end of the dark hallway to the cracked door of our bedroom is Jason's laptop open on the bed. It's not the laptop per say that catches my eye, but what's on the screen. Gina Reese, at the edge of a bed, donned in only a black thong and the heart pasties that cover her nipples. With one finger in her mouth and another pushing aside her thong to reveal her bald pussy, the look on her face is one of a temptress. The way her glistening eyes seem to glance through the computer screen, able to seduce the viewer in the physical world, is almost haunting.

What sort of fascination would Jason have with a dead woman?

With a quiet shift, I peer further through the cracked door to see Jason. He stands across from the glowing screen, staring. He strokes himself with spastic movements, seemingly lost in the digital realm that Gina resides in. He can't see me because the hallway is so dark, and even if it wasn't, I don't think he'd notice me. He wouldn't want to see the disgust strewn across my face anyways. By the way his body convulses, I can tell that his climax is near. And as he reaches the tipping point, tears stream down his face, dropping onto his exposed chest. I can't watch any longer.

To be sure I'm not heard, I tiptoe back down the stairs, rake my fingers through my tangled waves, throw on some jeans I left in the laundry room, grab my wallet and keys, and head out the door.

I have to talk to someone that is in a similar boat as me. Someone who feels just as marginalized, just as scared.

Someone like Greg Reese.

Greg is at the 129 Saloon in downtown Garden Valley. I drove around for over two hours, stopping at random stores sporadically to try to find contact information for him. I looked through his practically inactive Facebook page for his place of employment. Turns out he wasn't one of the ones that worked for Stellar. A place called Ankenman Systems was listed. When I called them, it took three times to finally get an answer. On the third try, the softly spoken receptionist picked up.

"Greg Reese? He was let go shortly after the tragedy with his poor wife. I didn't think it was right, but there was so much suspicion surrounding everything. We didn't want the press…" She spoke in hushed tones, as if she was being watched like a hawk.

I had thanked her, feeling like I was at a dead end, until she spoke again.

"You know, if you're looking for him, I might be able to help. He likes to spend his down time at the 129 Saloon. You know the place on the corner of Eaglewood and State? It was actually one of the last straws with him. He was caught getting drunk there during a shift," she explained, oversharing business that wasn't hers to share.

The bar is the definition of a hole in the wall. The faded brick building sits in a rundown part of town across from a Dairy Queen and a smoke shop. The nearly bare parking lot is lined with cracks, potholes, and faint yellow parking lines. As soon as the door pushes open, I'm greeted with the thick smell of cigarette smoke and the subtle tune of what I can only guess to be George Strait. I thought all of the bars in the city had reverted to the standard "no smoking" rule but turns out I was wrong. It's broad daylight but there aren't any windows to let the sunshine in, leaving the place basking in a deep orange glow. A pool table, dart board, a couple tables, and a long bar fill the room.

I don't have to look hard for Greg. Only three men occupy the establishment. The bartender, some haggard, bearded man that looks as if he's been smoking for sixty years straight, and a small statured man who could use a haircut and a clean shave. Greg Reese.

"Hiya, ma'am. Ain't it a bit early for a young lady like you?" the bartender asks, looking me up and down.

"Nope. Not too early today," I reply and take a seat on the stool to Greg's left.

He's the only one who even seems to notice another person has walked through the door, which is odd given the lack of social presence.

"What can I get ya? I'll guess something strong?"

"You guessed right. Let's do shots for the house," I say, surprisingly confident.

This gets Greg's attention.

His initial glance is one of shock, maybe with a hint of fear. And then it changes to curiosity, his eyes a bit brighter than they had been when I first walked in.

"I know you." His voice is steady, measured.

I swivel the stool to face him. "You do. I'm Lula, Jason Carson's wife."

The bartender sets shot glasses full of brown liquid in front of us, a smirk lingering on his face.

Greg's laugh is piercing in the lonely space. "You here to beat my ass in the name of your husband?"

"I'm sorry about that," I say, authentically. I know the brunt of Jason's wrath, and I don't wish it upon anybody.

"Nothing fazes me anymore, woman. My wife is dead. My kids need hours and hours of therapy that I can't afford. And my liver is bound to give up on me in the next 2-3 years, according to my doctor." He raises his shot to the old man on his other side and takes the shot, without even a hint of a sour face.

I follow suit, wincing as the liquor burns its way down my throat.

"I'll get the next round, Boyd," Greg says, giving the bartender a wink.

"You still owe me from the last two times you were in here, Reese. You aint getting shit else," he replies, laughing.

I clear my throat. "I did come in here for a reason."

"Well, no shit," Greg says, running his fingers through the mop on his head.

I lower my voice and move in a bit closer to him, catching the smell of stale cigarettes and sour body odor. "There's something going on within this club. Something dark. Clara is dead. Gina is dead. I don't think it was an accident and a suicide."

"You didn't know Gina," he says flatly.

"You're right. I didn't. But something in my gut is telling me that Rasheeda and Calen had something to do with both deaths."

He slaps his hand onto the countertop. His laugh is abrupt and obnoxious, making me shift in my seat. "Let them hear you say that. Oh man would you be in deep water."

I continue, "Andrew Stratford—"

Greg holds up his hand and shakes his head. "I'm going to stop you right there, lady. Andrew Stratford is a fame hungry, piece of shit. He will do and say anything to be the next Anderson Cooper. He didn't know Gina either."

I'm at a loss. Greg doesn't seem to care about the corruption in the club. Even if it led to his wife's demise. And he's right. I didn't know her. I barely know anything about her. For all I know she could have dealt with a lifelong battle with depression.

He continues, "You know someone who did know Gina, though? Your husband. He was the one in love with that bitch. Take your suspicions up with him and leave me the hell alone."

The image of Jason stroking himself to Gina's naked body floods in my mind and I swallow hard.

The bartender fills up another shot and puts it on the counter in front of Greg. "I think you better be on your way now, ma'am," he says, pointing to the door.

CHAPTER 32

A mass email was sent out about Clara's wake. I don't know who added me to it, but I'm grateful I was included. I don't want to be around any of them. But I owe it to Clara to go. To say one last goodbye to a friendship that was just budding.

Jason and I dress for the wake in silence, barely even acknowledging each other. I still help him with his tie, though. And he still zips up the back of my dress, his cold fingers lingering on my back a little longer than necessary.

"Where do we go from here, Lu?" he asks, his presence looming behind me.

I smooth out the front of my dress. "What do you mean?" I ask.

"Are you wanting a divorce?" His question sends a pang in my stomach, even though it's no surprise. We can't keep living this way. I can't keep living this way.

"I think I'll go visit my cousin in Tennessee. Some time away might be good. Maybe we can reconvene after that. See where we stand," I say. Both of us know it's a lie. Both of us know there is no reconvening. We are done.

We take separate cars. On the drive I conjure up scenarios in my mind about Rasheeda and Calen. Will I say hi to them? Will they say hi to me? Will flat out ignoring them be a tell tale sign that I'm now an adversary, suspicious and scared? And then there's Atlas. I should tell him that I'm leaving, break off whatever situation we had going on. So much has happened that he has barely crossed my mind anyways, just a fleeting thought every now and again.

My thoughts carry me all the way to the funeral home, a gloomy, gray building with a hearse parked next to the entrance. People dressed in all black filter in, most of whom I've never seen in my life.

From my rearview mirror, I notice Rasheeda walking in, head held high. Her flowy black dress drags along the pavement as she walks. Sunglasses and a wide brimmed hat cover most of her features, giving her even more of an ominous aura.

Once I see Jason pull up, I sulk in next to him, not wanting everyone to sense the collapse of our marriage.

I'm here for Clara. I'm here for Clara. I'm here for Clara.

I repeat the mantra over and over again inside my head, hoping it will loosen the tension that has taken over my body.

The air in the building is stale, like it hasn't had a window opened in weeks. Hushed voices fill the open space, like everyone is scared that if they are too loud, they will wake her from her slumber.

The casket sits underneath a recessed ceiling light that gives off a warm glow. My eyes dart away as soon as I see the silhouette of her petite body, feeling shaky and a bit queasy. Framed pictures of Clara from a little girl up to a young adult line a table to the left of the casket. Another table to the right is filled with refreshments, cookies, and fruits. Who could stomach anything in a place like this? At a time like this.

Jason leaves my side and heads towards a corner of the room where the club has gathered. I follow but stay off to the side, determined not to engage with any of them. Pamphlets with Clara's angelic face printed in black and white were passed out when we entered. I open mine now, trying to keep my focus on something other than the people around me or the open casket looming in the distance.

"Lula, honey. Such a tragedy, isn't it?" I look up from the obituary to see Cheyenne. She grasps me into an embrace. The mix of fruity perfume and burnt hair smell are overwhelming and I try to hold my breath as she squeezes me tight. Her sniffles are excessive, intentional.

"It really is," I say softly.

"Shall we go say our goodbyes?" she asks me, holding out her hand to guide me.

I'd rather go with someone else than stand there all alone sticking out like a sore thumb anyways. Cheyenne isn't the worst option. We walk towards the casket, pushing through the middle of the group.

"Lula." Rasheeda gives a nod in my direction as I pass, her voice somber, like she's dealing with a great loss. I return a nod, acknowledging her presence as well. Before I get too far, her voice catches my ear, no longer somber, but venomous, with a sharp sting. "Must be your favorite pair. So glad I rescued them from the closet for you."

One glance down at my chunky, gold heels brings me back to that dark, confined space, flooding me with unease. She never found them in the hallway.

By the time I look up, she has already turned her back. Her comment was calculated and it fulfilled the desired effect.

My arm is pulled, moving me forward, and providing much needed distance between myself and Rasheeda.

Cheyenne and I stand in front of the casket, side by side, staring down at the body that Clara used to inhabit. And Penelope too. The air around me thickens, like it's harder to breathe it in and my head begins to feel light.

"She was always such a naturally pretty, little thing. Still so radiant, even in death," Cheyenne says. Her arm links with mine and as much as I want to push her away, I don't. I could use the support if my blood sugar drops any lower.

Cheyenne is lying. Clara doesn't look radiant or pretty. She looks dead. Each of her freckles has been covered with makeup that's two shades too light for her. She's wearing pink lipstick that is chalky and creases in every lip line. And to top it all off, her frumpy, pleated dress covers just about every inch of skin, something that Clara wouldn't be caught dead in.

The irony.

More sniffles protrude from Cheyenne's nostrils. "I need a tissue, excuse me," she says as she leaves me to stand here alone, staring at the lifeless body.

I want to run away. But I also can't leave her side, not with the people who hurt her in this room. They don't deserve to be here, mourning with her loved ones.

"Are you one of Clara's book club friends?" A slim, older woman in a long-sleeve, floor-length, cotton dress grabs my attention. Her small stature and doe eyes are a dead giveaway.

"I am," I lie. "You must be her mother?"

She lets out a slow sigh and grips onto the casket with both hands. "Yes, unfortunately. I'm unfortunately the mother of a deceased child." She sounds detached, looks that way too. Her eyes don't meet mine. She is in another world, one where only her and Clara exist.

"I'm so sorry for your loss," I say, trying to make eye contact with her but failing.

"Losses," she corrects me. "Autopsy reports show she was pregnant. A baby girl. I didn't even know she was seeing anyone."

I scan the room for Ellis. He stands next to Haven at the photo table, her arm draped over his shoulder as they smile at pictures of Clara when she was little. Pictures that might have easily resembled the little girl that was once growing in her belly. Does this thought cross Ellis's mind as well?

Before walking away, I grab her shoulder and lean in close, catching a whiff of her sour, greasy, gray hair.

"Her name was going to be Penelope," I whisper.

She finally turns to look at me but doesn't say another word.

I debated telling her that Clara was probably murdered. That she was wrapped up in a mess that was bigger than her. A mess that she couldn't get away from. But why cause this woman more pain? Her fragility is unmistakable. One more blow and she'd probably break into a million little pieces.

One last glance at Clara's face and I turn away. I can't stand looking at her corpse any longer. She's not in there anyways.

The club has dispersed now, mixed in with the rest of the mourners. Clara's "book club" never fails to keep up appearances. Jason mingles with an evidently tipsy Meagan. She stands wobbly in her heels, catching herself a few times from tumbling over. Drinking before the wake never even crossed my mind. Maybe I wouldn't feel the need to rush out the exit if it had.

"Hey stranger." The voice takes me by surprise.

"Atlas." Without fault, a smile plasters across my face. Probably the first one today. Even though I saw Meagan, I didn't even realize that I hadn't seen Atlas. Or maybe I just hadn't noticed him.

"Miss me?" he asked.

"I'm sorry. My mind is in another place these days," I say. My eyes drift back over to the casket.

"Don't be sorry. I still can't believe it's real," he says, turning his head in Clara's direction as well. "It was just so… sudden."

"Did you feel the same way at Gina's wake?" I ask, not even thinking of the potential insinuation.

He turns his head back in my direction now, searching my face as if he's confused about the question. My eyes don't stray from his, willing him to see reason. To see through the facade.

"Hers felt sudden too. But death just goes that way sometimes, right? We don't usually get a warning," he says, obviously not catching on.

"Right," I say before a long sigh. My response stirs something in him, something like concern. Or maybe sympathy.

"Aside from all this," he motions to our surroundings, "have things been any better?" he asks, and glances over at my husband.

I fold my arms over my chest and shake my head, giving him all the confirmation he needs.

The rolled-up sleeves on his black button up expose his toned forearms. A sight that creates an ache down deep in my stomach. When he opens his arms for an embrace, I sink into it, relishing in the warm comfort that spreads throughout my body. I wonder if he knows how much I needed this. I want to release the floodgates and cry, harder than I've ever cried before. But I don't. It's not safe for me to do that here.

Before releasing me, Atlas whispers something near my ear. It's so soft that I'm barely able to make out the words.

"I think it was all *too* sudden."

The look on his face when he pulls away from me is stern, like he's urging me to speak no more about it and pretend like I didn't hear his hushed declaration.

"I think I better head out. I've paid my respects. Maybe we can talk more later?" he asks.

I agree. I still need to tell him that I'm leaving. Say my goodbyes to another newfound connection. Maybe warn him of what I've seen and gauge how much he knows. Or maybe I'd rather not know. I think I'd rather remember him in a good light.

When we both turn to go our separate ways, our attention focuses on the same scene. Jason and Meagan are no longer casually mingling. The sexual tension between them is unmistakable as Jason's hands tug at her hips, bringing their pelvises together. He grips the back of her fiery hair and pulls, exposing her bare neck, to which she releases a high-pitched giggle that garners stares from other mourners. The discomfort from secondhand embarrassment creeps into my stomach and leaves me wanting to scream at the top of my lungs, *he's my husband but I don't claim him anymore!*

Atlas' feelings must be different from mine. I don't realize that he's left my side until he stands face to face with Jason, leaving drunken Meagan to pout on the side, her lips jut out like a two-year-old who was just told she can't have one last piece of candy.

My instincts kick in when Jason's palms move to Atlas' shoulders, ready to thrust at any moment. As I rush to the men's sides, I can feel the burn from the eyes that surround us, mourners no longer able to focus on the death of their loved one, but on the dramatic show flashing in front of them.

"Do you really think this is the time and place for this shit, Jason? You can't keep it in your pants for one goddamn day?" Atlas' voice is low, but the pent-up anger threatens to seep out.

"You just mad because you aren't getting any?" Jason smiles like he's thoroughly enjoying this, making my blood chill.

"Jason, put your hands down," I say, calmly, and place my hand on his.

Jason throws his head back in laughter. "Are you here to protect your lover boy?"

"I'm here to keep you from looking like a fool. We are at a wake, Jason. Don't do something stupid," I say and place my hand onto his bicep.

"Get your dirty hands off of me!" Jason shouts.

His hands move from Atlas' chest to mine, and he thrusts forward, hurtling me to the ground with a heavy thud. The embarrassment masks the pain my tailbone would have otherwise felt. Gasps come from each corner of the room.

The punch is thrown before I even have a chance to pull myself up off the floor. Atlas' knuckles connect with Jason's jaw, sending an audible crack through the room. A handful of men, none of them club members, grab Atlas, pulling him back from attempting a second blow. Haven is at Jason's side at once, fawning over his injury.

"You can have that cunt," Jason says coolly to Atlas, spitting blood onto the commercial carpet below him.

Without looking back, I race out of the building, almost tripping before I get out the door.

I can't face the shame, the disgust, or the hatred circling around the room and ravaging inside of me.

The house is cold when I get home. I left the thermostat on low, not realizing how empty I'd feel when I got back. How much I needed to be filled with warmth. But instead of cranking up the heat and snuggling under a blanket, I change into some dingy sweats and get down to business.

My cousin hasn't heard from me in ages. Probably since my "thank you" text after receiving her mailed wedding gift, but I text her now, hoping she will take pity on me.

Hey, Sherree. Can you call me when you get a sec? I have a favor I need to ask you.

We have packing boxes stacked up in the garage that we saved from move-in day. I lug them into the house in a pile and keep just enough to fill the space in my car.

Five.

Five boxes to fill my entire life with. The thought makes me sick.

My phone pings.

Lula! I'll be busy at the boys' soccer tournaments all day today, but I'll shoot you a call sometime tomorrow! Hope all is well!

She could tell me no. She could tell me to fuck off, be an adult, and find my own place to live. But she won't. Sherree and I aren't as close as we used to be, but she has never let me down before. I know that I can count on her to help get me on my feet.

The alternative is my mother, and I'd rather be dead, honestly.

I scan the house for items that were mine before the marriage, for items that weren't bought with my mother in law's money or our joint bank account.

My old apartment had the bare essentials. Both my bed, which was a rickety pile of garbage and taken to the dump, and my tv with a crack down the middle that blurred out a quarter of the screen, were taken to the dump. My dishes mostly consisted of thrift store pots and pans and plastic dinnerware that we donated to a women's shelter. I didn't even need a couch since my bedroom doubled as a living room. I watched tv in bed whether it was night or day in my little studio apartment.

I fill the boxes with clothes and shoes, a few framed photos, some books, and some other small items from my single life that once held a special place in my heart. It doesn't take me long and when I'm done, I feel empty. Like I have nothing to show for the twenty-eight years I've been on this Earth.

Maybe it's better that way. A complete fresh start.

As I struggle to stack the packed boxes in a corner of the garage, ready to go when I am, the garage door screeches open, filtering sunlight into the garage and revealing Jason as he climbs out of his Jeep. His eyes go straight to the cardboard pile then up to me and I struggle to keep a hardened face. A face that shows that I'm determined and not backing down. A face that shows that I'm done.

"Where the fuck do you think you're going?" he says as he slams his car door shut.

"I told you that I'm going to stay with my cousin for a while. And seeing how the wake went today, I should probably go sooner rather than later. Give you your space," I say, heaving the last few boxes on top of one another.

He stays quiet and still for a beat, leaning onto the side of his car.

"You know your boyfriend started that shit at the wake. And if I ever see him again, I'll make sure that I'm the one that ends it," he says, venom in his tone.

"You live in the same town, Jason. You're bound to see him again eventually."

"Well, lucky for him, I don't know how much longer he will be here. He's on the streets now. Meagan isn't putting up with that snake. And neither are the rest of us." Jason spits again onto the pavement and as he steps further into the garage, I can see the puffiness in the lower half of his face. The area is scarlet and appears even brighter on his pale skin.

"Have you tried icing it?" I ask before he walks inside, motioning towards his injury.

"Don't pretend like you give a damn." The door shuts behind him.

He's right. I don't feel the urge to mend his wounds anymore. He's got another woman for that now anyways, always has. If it wasn't Haven, it was probably Gina. The thought makes me squirm, picturing the "Gina" from my dreams the other night.

I need to speak with Atlas and say my goodbyes. Especially after what happened today, I should offer him an apology on behalf of my husband. Not like it would mean much. It pains me to know that my marital drama trickled into his life.

With the boxes ready to go, I dust the dirt and grime off my legs. The heaviness in my chest is a little lighter, knowing that I'm one step closer to safety and sanity. I open up a camping chair, position it in a spot where the sunlight hits, and opt to give Atlas a phone call instead of just sending a text. I don't want to wait for a reply. My anxiety is too high for that.

The line trills, and trills, and trills while my stomach tenses tighter and tighter. I almost think it will go to voicemail until someone picks it up.

"Hello," an effeminate voice says.

I almost hang up in fear that I've called the wrong number, but putting two and two together, I realize the woman must be Meagan.

"Meagan?" I ask.

"Lula," she replies with a tone that I can't decide is disgust or indifference.

"Sorry. I'm looking for Atlas. Is he around?" I kick myself for sounding so timid.

"No. No, he's not," she says.

"Okay, can you let him know that I—"

She cuts me off, "Actually, no. I can't let him know anything."

"Okay," I say, letting the word drag off my tongue.

"Listen, honey. I hate to be the one to break it to you, but you were just one of Atlas' toys. You caught his eye for a moment and by now, he's probably on to the next one. It's what he does. I, on the other hand, have no use for him anymore. I threw *his* stuff out onto the front lawn and said, 'good riddance'. Can you guess who pays the phone bill?" Her laugh is more of a cackle, and she gives no sense of remorse.

"Do you at least know where I can find him?" I ask, a slight irritation in my voice.

The phone clicks before I get my answer.

The sun is setting before I finally pull myself out of the camping chair to go back inside the dark space that feels farthest from home to me now, soaking up every last ray for vitamin D.

CHAPTER 33

The night stretched on as each minute felt like hours. The longer I shut my eyes, the more my mind would race, leaving me to spend half of the night staring up at the ceiling. Sleep came in short, infrequent waves and by the time the sun starts to rise and shine through the window in the front room, I'm left with a pounding headache and a weak stomach.

There is a sticky, dry texture in my mouth and my entire body screams for water. On achy legs, I trudge to the kitchen and pour a glass of water, gulping it down in its entirety within just a few seconds. Lately we have been avoiding each other in the kitchen, but Jason's feet patter down the stairs now while I refill my glass, obviously not waiting for his turn. He walks to the fridge in just his linen pajama pants, exposing his toned torso. His neatly shaven chest and stomach prove that despite our crumbling marriage, he's as dedicated to his appearance as ever.

And despite each time he has put his hands on me, threatened me, and made me feel small, I don't feel the need to cower in his presence. Maybe it's the lack of sleep that's dulling my instincts, or the non-threatening sleep in his eyes. He could wring my neck right here, right now, if he wanted. But I still have burning questions that I need answers to.

I take my glass to the dining table and sit, watching him as he pours himself a glass of orange juice.

When I begin to speak, he jerks and chokes on his drink, almost as if he didn't realize that I'm in the room with him. "Did you ever really love me?" I ask.

He sighs, irritated, "Why would I have married you if I didn't love you, Lula?"

I shrug, tracing the water droplets that drag down my glass. "When did things start between you and Gina Reese?"

"What the hell are you talking about?"

"I talked to Greg. I know you were involved with her. Maybe even in love with her," I say, nonchalantly.

His glass slams down onto the island countertop. "Why would you be talking to Greg?"

"I had questions that I thought he could answer. But you aren't denying it. Were you in love with her when she died?"

I stare at him at this moment, trying to decipher the truth from his facial expressions. His fists tighten and tension builds in the veins that line his arms.

"I don't know what you're fishing for, Lula, but you need to stop," he says, wagging his finger. His face contorts, but it doesn't appear to be anger, it's more like fear.

I won't stop. I need to know. I can't leave not knowing. So, I push harder, "Is that why you were jerking off to a picture of her, hoping it would dry your tears?" Without meaning to, a smirk forms onto my face.

"Enough!" he shouts, slamming his hands onto the granite.

"Was she pregnant just like Clara? I could have been a stepmom," I say, avoiding his glare now, knowing that this comment is probably the last straw.

Jason can't take it any longer. With heavy stomps he inches towards me and I jump out of the chair and position myself near the hallway, ready to run out the front door if need be. His breath is thick, almost like a growl. We are at a standstill, wondering who will move first.

My phone chimes in the pocket of my sweats and I release the breath I was holding. I lift it to show him, "My cousin," I say.

Saved by the bell.

"Hey, Sher!" I give Jason one last glance before I walk away, all the built-up fear dissipating from my bones.

One more week. One more week before Sherree has agreed to pick me up from the airport and take me to my new temporary home in Tennessee. Seven days left in this foreign home with my foreign husband. Seven days to end life as I know it. To shed my old skin.

After getting off the phone with Sherree, I have a renowned sense of finality. There isn't much left to do now but wait.

Along with a multitude of emails from my boss, a message from a familiar looking Gmail account comes through my phone.

From: <u>AWashington19@gmail.com</u>
Subject: (blank)
Meet me at Athens Park around noon today. Please.

Despite the sun shining first thing this morning, the afternoon has taken a turn. Charcoal colored clouds fill the sky, casting a subtle chill in the summer air. Park goers must be anticipating rain, because the vast space is eerily quiet aside from an older lady walking her poodle and a middle-aged man jogging along the pathway.

When I spot Atlas sitting on a park bench, I want to run to him. Instead, I pick up the pace a little, adding a skip to my step. Grey sweatshorts and a baggy hoodie are the most casual I've ever seen him. The hood covers up most of his head and his hands are shoved into his pocket, giving him an air of suspicion.

I take a seat alongside him. "Fancy meeting you here," I say, trying to lighten the energy that surrounds us. The smile that I was hoping to see, though, doesn't come. A look of depletion and concern is plastered onto his deep skin.

"I wanted to say my goodbyes. I'm leaving town. There's nothing left for me here."

He pulls his hands out of his pocket revealing cut and bruised knuckles. Jason's swollen jaw flashes in my mind. His hands hold mine and I try not to squeeze too hard, for fear of worsening the wounds.

"Leaving town?" I ask.

"I guess I should say I'm leaving the country. I'm getting as far away as possible from all the shit that's about to hit the fan."

"Should I be worried?"

"I am taking the first ticket to Amsterdam. If that tells you anything."

"I've seen things, Atlas."

"We all have. I'm no saint and if I'm being honest, I've done things that I'm not proud of. But I'm not doing time for this, Lu."

I look away from him, terrified to think of what all he was involved in.

"They are making mistakes. Clara shouldn't have ended that way. It's only a matter of time before everything comes crashing down," he says, his knee bouncing up and down.

The mention of Clara makes the hair on my arms stick straight up. He grabs my chin and turns my head to face him. "I'm not a bad guy, okay?"

I look into his deep, dark eyes and wish I could forget everything and just swim in them. As much as I want to judge him, I can't. We all got into this mess in one way or another.

"I wanted to warn you. You're a good person. He should have never dragged you into all of this," he says.

We sit in silence for a moment, our fingers interlocked again.

"Look. I'm risking a lot by being here right now. But I care about you. I'd hate myself if something happened and I didn't even try."

"You're kind of scaring me," I say.

"Trust your gut, Lula. And get out as soon as you can."

"I'm leaving next week. Going to stay with my cousin in Tennessee. I don't know where I'll go from there. But it's a start."

He nods his head in approval.

"I'm definitely going to miss you, Lu," he says, finally a smile spreading across his now scruffy face.

I return the smile and a warmth fills me in spite of the slight bite in the air. "Want to take a stowaway?" We both laugh, sending a few pigeons flying in fear.

"We both know that isn't realistic," he says with a sigh.

"No part of these past few months has had any semblance of reality," I admit.

"That's how I feel about the past few years of my life. Truthfully, everything is pretty blurred. You aren't, though. All of that was crystal clear. Lula, I don't regret anything that has happened between the two of us."

"I don't either."

"Maybe— hopefully we will cross paths again," he says as he stands.

"Well, if you ever find yourself in Tennessee, hit me up," I say with a smile and stand as well.

His arms stretch over me, wafting his intoxicating scent up to my nose. I breathe in deep, hoping to never forget his smell and the way it feels to be buried against his broad chest.

But as he walks away and fades into the distance, I realize that maybe I don't hope to remember. Maybe it would be easier to just forget it all.

With my talk with Atlas out of the way, the last task on my checklist is to speak to Sandy. Her incessant texts, emails, and phone calls prove that I'm in deep water. But I'm going to need to find a new job when I get to Tennessee, and I'm hoping I can come up with a sufficient and reasonable excuse for my numerous days of being a "no call no show" to rectify our relationship enough for a decent job reference. Sandy might be insufferable at times, but she has always been a good person.

The bell on the front door of the office jangles when I push my way through.

"Morning!" a friendly voice calls out, "I'll be with you in just one sec—"

One of our hygienists, Valerie, is working at the front, probably because their number one receptionist has been dodging her duties. She stops dead in her tracks once she realizes that I'm not a patient.

"Lula… nice of you to show up. Let me grab Sandy," she says, her friendly tone changing in a snap.

Valerie comes back just seconds later and ushers me to Sandy's office, a small utility closet-sized room with no windows and a faint smell of leftover chili.

Sandy spins around in her computer chair, looking less than pleased to see me. Her glasses sit perched on the tip of her nose and her typical, slicked topknot, reveals a hairline that has been receding for some time now.

"Lula Carson in the flesh. I was just about to call and file a missing person report. Thanks for saving me the trouble." She folds one leg over another and places her folded hands onto her knee.

"I'm sorry, Sandy. I really am," I plead.

"You better have a damn good excuse," she says, eyeing me carefully.

"I had a family emergency. Well, I'm still having a family emergency. I have to leave town."

"And when will you be back?"

I clasp my hands together. "Actually, I'm not coming back. I wish I could give you two weeks. I wish I could give you a week.

But I can't come back to work. I can't talk about much, but it's serious. You know me. I would never be this unprofessional otherwise," I say.

"Lula, what is going on? You're scaring me," her strict tone has changed into one of sympathy. I've probably been one of the best employees she's ever had. And deep down, she is going to hate to see me go.

"I'll be okay, really. Just need to make some necessary life changes."

Sandy promises to give me a good job reference and swears up and down that I'd have a job there if I ever end up returning to Pleasant Valley, which I don't ever plan on doing. I lived my whole life here but now all that's left is a dark stain that I don't think I'd ever be able to wash away.

"Bye, Val. Sorry for all the trouble," I say timidly as I walk back past the desk. She only waves and gives me a few seconds glance. I guess not everyone is as forgiving as Sandy.

As I reach the door to leave, the bell chimes before I can open it and a familiar face pushes through, almost colliding with me. I spring backwards and my breath catches in my throat.

Rasheeda lets out an unsettling laugh. "So sorry. Did I scare you?" Rasheeda lets out an unsettling laugh.

"Wha– what are you doing here?" I stammer.

"Morning! Are you here for an appointment?" Valerie calls behind me.

She's never been a patient at this office before. I do all the patient records. I would have noticed her name.

"I'm here to schedule," Rasheeda says loudly, smiling and baring her slightly gapped front teeth. She continues, "I've heard such great things about this dental office, so I decided I'd better make the switch."

"I'll be with you in one moment," Valerie says as she hurries around the desk busily, oblivious to the awkward shift in the room.

Rasheeda is still positioned in front of the door, blocking my way out. I inch a bit to the side in hopes that she will take the hint and move, but her motives appear calculated as she looks me up and down with her narrow eyes.

"So nice to run into you, Lula."

Is she following me?

I force a smile and she finally steps to the right, clearing the doorway. With both hands on the door, I'm ready to bolt out until she opens her mouth to speak again.

"Oh, Lula?"

I turn back to face her, dread emanating from my face.

"If you speak to Greg again, do tell him I have some theories of my own," she says with a wink before turning around to speak with Valerie.

My stomach flips and with a slam of the office door, I speed walk to my car, jabbing the lock button with my finger over and over again before I put the car in reverse and speed away from the building, my tires screeching on the pavement.

She knows about Greg. She knows I was in Calen's room that night. She knows that *I know* far too much.

The words of Atlas ring through my head.

Trust your gut, Lula. And get out as soon as you can.

I need to leave tonight.

CHAPTER 34

I drive home in complete silence aside from my audible prayers, or
mantras, for Jason to be gone when I get there. Maybe if I pray
hard enough, *he* will hear me. The clouds have deepened and
finally release heavy rain drops that patter onto the windshield. My
fingers strain from gripping the steering wheel so hard.

Relax, Lula.

As the car creeps up our street, there is no sight of Jason's
jeep, allowing my tightened muscles to relax a little bit. I back my
car into the driveway and open the garage door to make it easier to
load up all my stacked boxes. One by one I carry them to the trunk
and my backseat, struggling to stuff the final few in so that the
doors can all close.

The rain seems to get heavier, and I finish with soaked hair.
I'm too nervous to feel the chill, though. It only motivates me to
move quicker.

As much as I avoided it, I'll need to stay at my mom's until
I'm ready to head to Sherree's. It's not ideal, but it's the safest

place for me. I can't guarantee my safety if I wait out the days here.

Now I just need my toiletries. The house is warm, much warmer now that I'm soaked in rainwater. I rush up the stairs to the bedroom and grab an old duffel bag from under the bed. Face wash, hair spray, perfumes, flat iron, makeup bag, toothbrush. I swipe it all into the open zipper pocket, hoping I don't damage any of it with my carelessness.

I dial mom's number. No answer.

I try a second time, but still no answer. A text will have to do for now.

Hi, mom. I tried to call. I'm coming over. I'll explain everything when I get there. Just didn't want to blindside you.

I send the message, but not without second thoughts. I send another.

I love you.

She will be thoroughly confused. But that's okay. It's all confusing right now.

The duffel bag slings over my shoulder. I take the stairs two by two, ready to get out of this house and quell the thumping that has been building up in my chest.

Once I reach the landing, I glance around, taking in all the memories from my first home. I dreamed of this for so long and now I'm ready to wish it all away. Every room, every corner, holds a reminder of life the way it used to be. My fingers brush along the walls, feeling the soft, matte texture that I picked out myself. I wonder if Jason will continue living here. Maybe he will move another woman in, start a family, make this house what it was meant to be. As sentimental as it all is, I can't say I'll miss it. The bad times have soaked it with a deep, dark stain.

I swipe my keys off the kitchen counter and slide the one to the house off the ring, setting it back down and positioning it in the middle of the granite so that it's easy to spot. A loud sigh leaves my body.

I'm done.

An eruption of creaks from the garage door opening breaks the silence and my short sense of calm.

Jason is home.

I really, really wanted to be gone before he returned. I swallow hard, as my throat muscles tense up, forming a lump.

With my bag still hung on my shoulder, I brace myself for the awkward run in we are about to have in the doorway. The door flings open as I approach it. Jason's startled expression and dilated pupils remind me of a cat caught scouring the house late at night. It wouldn't be stupid to think that he's moved on from cocaine to something stronger, something more unpredictable.

"I'm heading out," I mumble, my attempt at avoiding any sort of dramatic exit.

"Out where?" he asks, as he shoves his jittery hands into his pants pockets.

"I talked to Sherree. We figured it out," I say softly and take another step towards the door.

Jason pushes the door closed behind him with a gentle click, pressing his back against it. "I can't let you leave, Lula," he says, eyes locked with mine. The blue of his eyes are barely there, just a thin ring circling the widening black pupil.

He must notice the look of confusion that forms on my face because he continues. "You just couldn't leave it alone. You just couldn't shut up and enjoy the splendors you were so graciously given," he says as his voice amplifies with each word. His gaze doesn't let up as his head shakes from side to side, like I'm a toddler being scolded for throwing a toy. The thumping in my chest intensifies again.

"Jason, are you high right now?" I keep my voice measured, careful.

He chuckles and I instinctually take a step back. "I think that's the least of your worries right now, Lula."

Something inside of me is telling me to scream. To run. But that's not logical. The rational part of my mind is telling me to relax. I've dealt with threats from this man before. I just need to get it over with, once and for all.

"I'm leaving, Jason. Get out of my way." With all my might and both my hands, I trudge forward, pushing his body out of my way.

My hand is nearly on the doorknob when I'm yanked backwards by a handful of my hair, stinging the nape of my neck. The hardwood floor connects with my lower back as my hands only partly catch my fall. I barely recognize the scream as my own and he quickly muffles it with his sweaty palm, filling my tongue with a salty tang that makes me want to gag. His name protrudes from my mouth over and over but never makes it past the clasp of his fingers.

The young boy across the street crosses my mind at this moment. The fear and concern in his eyes while he watched me in my car. He has heard my screams before. Maybe he will hear them again.

"Shut the fuck up!" he screams, his voice thunderous. The temptation to bite the pudgy flesh of his fingers is strong, but I'm scared to anger him more. His grip loosens as one hand leaves the back of my head and travels to his pockets.

"Don't make me use this, Lula," he says, pulling out a silvery blade. My body goes cold despite the sweat that glazes my body. I recognize the knife as one from our unopened kitchen set. His aunt bought it as a wedding gift, but we were already gifted one from his mother. The box collected dust in the garage, waiting for the day we might find use for it. I guess he decided that the day is now.

I force my body to still, abandoning resistance.

"I need you to get into the Jeep," he says, much quieter now. The blade hits the dim lighting just right and gives off a reflective shine. It looks sharp, with such a fine point that it could puncture just about any body part with little effort.

I allow him to hoist me upwards, his hands digging into my armpits. "Where are you taking me?" I ask, my voice shaking. I can't keep it steady any longer.

"Just get in the fucking car," he says and gives my back a shove towards the door that leads to the garage, "Don't even think about making a run for it either." The knife grazes my side, a reminder to cooperate.

The Jeep is parked in the garage with barely enough room on either side to pull the doors open. We don't ever park the cars here, for this very reason. Always in the driveway. He had this plan before he even entered the house tonight. The thought makes me sick to my stomach.

He has lost his mind.

He puts me in the passenger seat before getting into the driver seat. The locks click, the garage door opens, and the Jeep backs into the driveway, plummeting us into the dark of night. The tires screech as he takes off, not bothering to follow the speed limit. Jason's fingers tap the steering wheel as he glances back and forth between me and the road ahead of us.

"Put both hands on the dash and keep them there," he demands. I do as I'm told.

My phone.

I shift in my seat, hoping to feel the cellphone in one of my pockets. Each feels empty. I can't remember where I last had it. In my car? Up in the bedroom? In my duffel? Jason's phone sits in the middle console. If I can get a hold of it, I can call for help. But I can't do anything with my hands so visible.

"Where arc we going?" I ask, searching his face for an answer to the madness, even though I'm not sure that I want to hear it.

"You'll see soon enough."

"Why are you doing this?" My voice breaks. I swallow hard to hold back the tears that threaten to cascade down my face.

He doesn't respond. "Are *they* telling you to do this? Is it because I accused Rasheeda and Calen of killing Gina and Clara? I can't do anything with those suspicions. I have no proof!" I scream at him, no longer able to hold in my cries.

"Rasheeda didn't kill Gina!" he yells, a slight rasp in his throat.

With a whimper Jason says, "I killed her."

Gina Reese: Last Day

I'm in a dizzying limbo. With Calen sneaking around and Rasheeda giving me the cold shoulder, I have a feeling that I'll be pushed out soon.

A liability.

But they need to trust me. I'm nothing if not loyal. I'd never sacrifice what I've been given for a deal with the police, for a leg up. I won't allow the government to impose their version of morality on me. I just need a chance to plead my case to them, to prove that I'm valuable.

The rhythmic knock at the door is familiar and as I rush to open it, a warmth fills my entire body, my body that has been icy cold for weeks now.

"Long time no see," Jason says, his sexy smirk plastered onto his face.

I throw myself at him, hungering for touch and comfort. He doesn't disappoint. His arms wrap around me and lift me inches off the ground, like I'm weightless. We stay like this for minutes that feel like ages. When he puts me down it's like I'm snapped back to reality.

"Come inside, it's chilly out here," I say, grabbing his hand and pulling him into the cabin. The sun is setting, only further adding to the bite in the air.

"I've missed you. I'm sorry I've been distant," Jason says as we sit next to each other on the couch.

"It's okay. You've got your own life going on. I understand."

He nods. "It's getting harder to explain my absences. *She* is always on my case." His huff says it all. He doesn't talk about her often and when he does, it's just a passing mention or a complaint. Sometimes I forget that she even exists, like she's living on an entirely different plane.

"How have you been?" he asks.

"Things have been… weird," I say. The intangible cold fills my body once again. I grab the throw blanket that's draped over the couch and cover up my body with it, bringing my knees up to my chest.

His eyebrows raise, expecting me to elaborate.

"Rasheeda is questioning my dependability and my devotion. I don't know how to prove my worth to her and the rest of you. I thought by my being here, focusing on Inanna and her wishes, I'd flourish. But that isn't what's happening. Maybe I'm losing sight of things."

He shakes his head and grabs my hands. "How long do you plan on being out here? Maybe all this isolation isn't the best. Especially after your fall out with Greg."

"I can't go back *because* of Greg. Not until I'm able to stand on my own two feet. I won't go back with my tail between my legs," I say, exasperated.

"Go back to him temporarily. Get a job, something stable. Save up enough money for your own place and leave him after that. You shouldn't be out here all alone, Gina." He squeezes my hands and searches my eyes.

A few stray tears fall down my cheeks. Jason uses his thumb to brush them away.

"I'm not meant for that type of life, Jason. He will put me back in a box. I don't want to start that routine again. I have a plan. I need to see it through. I just need you all back on my side," I whimper.

His hand moves to my thigh and the idea sparks like an ignited furnace. I don't need to plead to Rasheeda. Rasheeda is only a conduit, but I need to tap into the source. I need to plead to Inanna.

"I need you," I tell him with a whine. No time is wasted as I throw the blanket to the floor and straddle his lap. Pressure grows as I glide my clothed pussy over the bulge forming under his jeans. When our mouths connect, our saliva joins and becomes one energetic substance. Bonded fluids. His dick becomes as firm as a rock as I move my body back and forth, the aching in my pussy becoming unbearable.

My lips move from his mouth to his ear. "Fuck me. Harder than you ever have before," I whisper.

He takes off my top first, then I kick off my shorts, leaving me stark-naked. Undoing his pants takes a bit more effort as I fiddle with the button, eager to get him inside of me. His dick springs up from the confines of his jeans and he forces my body down on top of it, the shaft sliding in with no resistance. Groans of pleasure emanate from our mouths synchronistically. My body was in agony for a lack of sex, a lack of connection. I needed this to heal me. And the warmth finally washes over me again as he slides in and out of my body. I allow him to fondle my breasts, relishing in the tingling sensation as he smothers his face into them.

My pleasure builds and I know that it's time. Time to give it up to *her*. My head falls back, and I shut my eyes, ready to focus all my energy.

"I give myself to you Inanna! Use me! Take me!" I'm louder than I meant to be, but I don't care. Jason slows his momentum, probably taken aback, but I move faster, forcing him to pick up the pace.

"Choke me," I say. His eyes widen as if he's confused. "Don't let go until after I cum."

I grab his wrist and place his hand on my neck, giving him a nod of assurance. His fingers squeeze around my neck, and we continue to fuck, moving me closer to climax. My body tenses as I reach the peak and his grip gets tighter. His moans lead me to believe he's close too.

Take me. Take me. Take me.

Eyes closed, I recite the words in my head, ready to give her my energy.

Tighter, tighter, tighter.

I forget all about the need for oxygen, almost as if I don't need it, almost as if she's channeling my life force, breathing for me. The wave comes in heavy, crashing into me, dispersing pleasure throughout my body. I soak it in, channeling it as a sacrifice to her.

And suddenly, she takes it all away. All the fear, all the emptiness, all the pleasure.

I listen to his story, without a single interruption. As the tears flow freely from his eyes, I gain a slight sympathy for him once again. He couldn't have known what was going to happen. It was an honest mistake.

"Gina was on another level with the club. Devoted is an understatement," he says, "We wrapped her body up in a tarp and drove it back to her house in the bed of Calen's shitty ass truck. From there, we staged the suicide, wrote a note, I called the police, and we all moved on. Rasheeda was probably going to off her anyway. She was losing her mind, bat shit crazy."

"Greg knew about this?" I ask, my tone gentle.

"He said he didn't want to know any details, but he'd keep his mouth shut and go along with whatever."

"And Clara?" I ask.

"She reaped what she sowed. But I didn't have anything to do with that. I'm not a fucking murderer." His tears are dried up now and rage has stained his face once more.

"I know you're not. Deep down you're a good person, Jason. That's why I know you won't go through with this. You loved me once; you won't let this happen." I speak as though it's a fact, willing it to be true.

"I don't think I've ever loved anyone. I don't think I know how to love." This makes my stomach turn. All the hope that was starting to build drains from my body.

"You're a liability, Lula. They won't let that go. They have too much at stake."

"Then let's leave together. Somewhere they won't find us. We can work on our relationship. We can work on your deep-rooted issues, together." My pleas sound stupid. We both know that there is no fixing us. No fixing *him*. I touch his thigh anyway, an attempt at some form of connection but as soon as my fingertips brush the fabric of his pants, his whole body shifts.

"I said both hands on the dash!" His voice thunders through the narrow space of the car and I jump in my seat, bringing my hands back to their original position.

"I don't need your help. I don't need therapy. At this point, there is only one solution," I don't ask him to elaborate but after a beat, he continues on anyway, "The pain, the burden, and the shame. The sins of my father have haunted me my whole life. It's like flecks of his darkness seeped into my soul, leaving speckles of irreparable stains, stains that can only be removed by the grace of Inanna." His hunched shoulders appear to have relaxed a bit.

"And how do you plan to receive this grace?" I ask, trying hard to not let my voice shake.

"A suitable sacrifice," he says as he turns his eyes away from the road to glance at me.

"You're willing to throw my *life* away for some woo woo lunacy?" My voice shakes now, cracking at the end of the question.

"They were going to take you out regardless, Lula. At least you will have died for something." His tone is so rational for spewing such nonsense.

We are on the highway now. The speedometer reads sixty-five. If I jump out now, will I have any chance of survival? I picture my body colliding with the solid pavement just before a passerby's tires crush my skull. It's not an option.

Through the window, even in the dark, I start to gain a sense of familiarity.

The cabin.

Dread overtakes me. Images of blood, hoods, a knife, consume my mind.

"No, no, no. Jason, please turn around," I plead but he doesn't answer.

Cars don't litter the asphalt at the start of the path like before. Could it be that we are the only ones here?

"Get out," Jason demands, knife held up high for me to see.

I do as I'm told, and he places the knife in his left hand so that he can grab mine with his right. His hand is clammy. Or maybe it's mine. He pulls me forward on the path, the dirt crunching under our feet. The sun has now fully disappeared, and the clouds block out the moon, which is the only source of light out here.

"Are we the only ones out here?" I ask in a low voice, as if I'm attempting not to wake whatever wildlife lies in this expanse of bare land.

He doesn't answer but tightens his grip on my hand and pulls harder, nearly tripping me. His direction is illuminated only by the dull light of his phone. He knows this route by heart by now, I'm sure.

I can't shake the sinking pit in my stomach that I may not see the light of day again. Buried deep out in this land of nowhere underneath a pile of dry earth. Or will they make my death look like a suicide? An accidental poisoning? The possibilities are endless. But they can't keep getting away with this. Tears make a silent stream down my face, leaving a salty taste as I lick my lips.

Through squinted eyes, I focus on the amber lighting that suddenly appears in the distance. The curtains are closed, but the glow filters through.

As we get closer, the cabin appears more run down than before. Or possibly I was too focused on other things that night to notice it. Rotting wood, paint peeling from the shutters, the faint scent of mildew permeating through the crevices; dilapidated and seemingly desolate aside from the light signaling human presence. No one would even believe this place was habitable from the outside. No one would come looking for anyone out here.

Movement catches my attention in the windows, glimpses of dark figures. Shivers travel down my spine but not because the temperatures have dropped. My body shakes in pure terror as we inch closer to the door.

Cobwebs line every corner of the entryway. Jason's knuckles rap on the door, knife still firmly grasped. We stand in silence for what feels like ages. The only noise comes from our shallow breaths. Footsteps thud from behind the door. My stomach clenches and I feel frozen; my feet glued to the ground below me.

Now is my chance to run. Maybe my only chance. I should run. Tingles radiate through my legs, itching me to move.

Run. Run.

*F*ight or flight kicks in and I turn to make a run for it. Jason loses his grasp on my sweaty hand, and I take large strides, trying to gain distance from him. But he's faster. Jason lunges for me and latches onto my hair, sending a searing pain to my scalp and whipping me backwards.

The creaky door flings open, and I'm thrown into the cabin, my body smacking the faded hardwood.

"Dumb cunt!" Jason yells.

Nine red robed, hooded individuals stand above me. They all peer down at me with straight faces. Faces that I recognize even in the dark room lit only by a lampshade in the corner. All stay silent as Jason turns around to undress, folds his clothing nice and neat, and is handed a robe with which he swiftly dons, covering his tousled hair with the hood. Soon he stands over me as well.

I wonder if they can sense the terror in my eyes. I remember the hanging woman and how brutal these people can be.

"Take her to the table," Rasheeda commands.

"You don't have to worry about me! I'm leaving town and I won't tell a soul about any of it!" I scream as their hands work together to lift and carry me towards that infamous door at the end of the hall and like each time, I have no idea what lies in wait behind it.

"No! No!" My shrieks are muffled by a hand that smells like an unwashed armpit.

The hallway is dark, but the door opens to the crimson-lit room. The bronze Inanna stands behind a large oak table in the center of the room, where the hanging woman had been all those weeks ago. The group hoists me up to the table, flat on my back. My stomach muscles strain and I attempt to sit up, but I'm quickly forced back down, left to wriggle around on the table.

"Don't fight us," Jason says as he puts the knife to the pulsing vein on my throat.

"Inanna might be ruthless, but she isn't spiteful. Open up." Haven shoves a pill into my mouth, but I don't swallow. It flies out of my mouth with my next scream.

The robed members circle around the table with Jason at my side and Rasheeda above my head, closest to Inanna. With the blade so close to an artery, I try to still my body, despite my rapid breaths and uncontrollable shaking.

"Rasheeda, I swear. I won't ever speak about any of this. Gina, Clara, the girls. Any of it. Please, just let me go," I say with a shaky voice, tilting my head to look up at her tapered eyes. She has coated her lips with red lipstick, obviously prepared for this whole situation. How long had they been planning this? Just how naive had I been?

"It's out of our hands now, Lula," Derrick says, like a voice of reason. His face is the first I've seen holding a sense of pity for me, but it doesn't last long, seconds later he's just as stoic as before. My whimpers don't faze them. Soon I feel like I'll drown in a pool of my own tears.

"Inanna! We give you this sacrifice in exchange for your protection. Protection from those who threaten to destroy us, control us, and limit us!" Rasheeda's sing-song voice thunders throughout the room.

Hums of assent follow. They're all on board. All wrapped up in the same ideology. Or so consumed with the lifestyle that they don't care what the cost is. Most of them will pay anything at this point.

Our kitchen knife pales in comparison to the dagger that Rasheeda pulls out from the inside of her robe. The sight makes my whole-body lurch, my arms flailing at the bodies standing next to me, forgetting the knife held close to my neck. Numerous hands hold me still, my efforts pointless. Jason presses the tip just underneath my chin, slightly nicking the skin, a clear warning. It stings and I fear what may come next, the pain that awaits.

"Undress her," Rasheeda says. Collectively the group tears off my clothes, leaving me naked. Goosebumps scatter over my exposed body. Eyes scan my frame, leaving me vulnerable.

"We must drain her of her life force," Rasheeda tells Derrick in hushed tones. He nods, taking the dagger from her hands. He looks to her for guidance and direction. He couldn't do this alone. Rasheeda is the true driving force.

My eyes dart back and forth between Rasheeda and Derrick, the leads of the show. Her head bobs at him, giving him the go ahead.

"We give this sacrifice to you," he says. The sharp point pierces through the thick skin of my stomach as he drives it down, sending a searing burn throughout my middle. A deafening howl leaves my lips as the blade cuts through flesh, fat, and muscle, narrowly missing the lower portion of my ribcage. I fight against their restraints as he slides it back out, the sounds of my slippery insides bringing vomit up my throat. I turn my head and the contents of my stomach pool on the table beside me, the sour stench mixing with the scent of the blood that's protruding from my belly. The fluid is thick and warm as I instinctively use my shaky hand to cover the wound.

"Who's next?" Derrick asks.

"Me." Haven's face shines as she answers Derrick's call, as if she's been asked to officiate the wedding of a lifelong friend. "I told you to take the pill," she whispers to me. Derrick hands her the dripping dagger and she thrusts it into my side, hitting bone this time with a perceptible clank. I gasp but no sound follows, and I'm left sputtering for air. The pain is so agonizing that my whole body quivers.

"Here, baby." Haven hands the weapon to Jason next, then caresses his cheek with her bloody hand, a thick red smear.

My eyes flutter, and I try with all my might to keep them open. Jason's coated face stares down at me.

"Please, Jason. Don't do this," I whisper, barely able to get the words out of my mouth. But he's already told me his deepest, darkest secret. He has too much to lose with me being alive. My pleads are useless.

He brings his finger to my lips, "Shhhh. I have to, Lula. I already told you. It's the only way." Haven comes up and kisses the back of his neck as he glides the knife down my body, just barely grazing my skin. He stops at my vulva and sweeps the tip around my labia.

God, please. No.

He loses interest in his sick game and a bit of tension releases as he moves the knife away from my lower half.

Blood pools down by my side now and I use my other hand to cover it, pushing with what little strength I have left.

"Just finish it, baby. End it," Haven whispers as she nibbles at his ear.

"One last time, Lu?" Jason asks. He bends down and places his warm, open mouth on mine. He sucks and kisses my trembling lips.

"Holy shit! That's a lot of blood," a voice says from the side.

My hands aren't stopping the blood that flows from the wounds any longer.

"Enough!" Rasheeda's voice booms as she snatches the knife from Jason's hand. "Her life force must transfer with ease. One more slice and you'll sour it all. Let her bleed out."

I'm freezing. The warm blood that oozes from me isn't enough to lessen the chill that creeps up my body.

Rasheeda hovers over me like a sleep demon ready to pounce. Her gapped smile stretches at the sight of what they've done. She relishes in the blood that seeps from my body and with a gentle swipe, her hand is covered in it. With a backwards tilt of my head, I follow her footsteps behind me, where she covers Inanna in my fluids.

One by one the members come up to me, soil their palms in crimson, and cover themselves and each other. The air in the room switches from one of somber and vigilance to temptation and desire. Robes fall to the floor as each one bathes in what was once a part of me and the rich scent of blood becomes overwhelming. I try not to watch as hands stroke breasts, waists, and thighs. Moans of pleasure erupt from their mouths. Rasheeda only watches in amazement, the only one still covered with her robe.

Vomit comes up again.

The feeling in my toes start to leave me as I wriggle them back and forth.

It's almost over.

I don't feel ready for it. But I'm sure that nobody ever does. There is so much that I haven't done yet. I've never before yearned to bring another life into this world. But suddenly, I envision what my swollen, brown belly would look like it were to hold an unborn baby. I envision what it would look like to find my father again, reconnect, forgive. To rebrand and rebuild. To have a second chance. But I'm too late and second chances are never promised. Jason was my beginning and now he's about to be my end. And despite my will, my heavy eyes beg for me to stop resisting, so I close them, my body wishing it all to be over.

With so many sensations happening at once, I almost miss the cool metal pressing up against my skin.

Jason's knife from home.

In all his eagerness he must have forgotten about it when he was handed the blade from Haven. This may be my only chance for escape. I don't know how I can pull it off in this condition, with this many people against me, but I have to try.

With my hand against my belly, I lift myself onto my elbow first. The feat feels nearly impossible, like my abdominal muscles have been severed. Just a bit more effort and I'll be sitting upright, from there, I have to move quickly if I have any chance. With trembling hands, I grasp the wooden knife handle.

Now.

In one motion I sit up and whip my body off the table. My feet feebly plant on the solid ground. Heads turn as I move to run, leaving a blood trail as I go. They all seem frozen in place, too surprised and taken off guard to make a move. I keep my steps strategic, continuously checking behind me for movement.

"Someone grab her!" Rasheeda calls out.

I turn to walk backwards towards the door in the rear I have yet to go through, both eyes on the people in front of me. Jason takes the lead, making quick strides to grab me., but I'm too scared, too hurt to turn around and sprint. He reaches for my arm, not noticing what's in my hand.

"Stop!" I scream and swing the knife, connecting with flesh. A fresh slice lines his neck, right above his Adam's apple. The cut must be deep. His hands immediately go to the wound, but it doesn't prevent the blood from spilling out. His eyes are wide, as if he's in a state of shock. It comes in a spurt and pools onto the floor below him and seconds later he falls to the ground with a thud, sending gasps throughout the room.

His naked body twitches at my feet. Blue eyes that were once so full of fire, now dull and lifeless. I don't have time to feel sorry or sad, or even relieved. All eyes are back on me again and I must continue to move.

Haven's howl is so piercing it could shatter glass. I brandish the metal, keeping it held out in front of me, hoping Jason stands as a warning to the others.

"Stay back!" I yell.

Derrick and Calen make a run for me. With no time to spare I turn my back and sprint, holding my bare torso as I go for the door.

Both men pick up the pace and slip in Jason's blood, hitting the floor hard. But I don't turn to watch. I keep my eyes focused and my feet moving, blocking out the pain that each step escalates.

The shouts behind me fade as I burst through the door. It opens to a room that's almost pitch black, aside from the moon light that seeps in through a tiny rectangular window. From the fresh linen smell, I assume it's a laundry room. Panic rushes in when I realize there might not be an exit. With arms out, I feel my surroundings. There is a bang when my palms hit the aluminum washer and dryer. They are easy enough to push in front of the door I just entered through, maybe buying myself a bit more time.

I feel next for a door out of this hell. There has to be more than one way out of this cabin.

The commotion outside the door strengthens as the men grow near. They try to push the door open, but the appliances stand in the way. Shoulders heave at the wood as the men attempt to barge through.

Time is running out.

A fire burns inside of me when my hand brushes up against a metal knob. I waste no time in giving it a quick twist and push. The fresh air smacks me in the face and I run against it, with no direction, just lengthening the gap between myself and the danger behind me. My body threatens to give out, but I can't slow my pace.

Squinting through the moonlight, I think I see the silhouette of a vehicle. I can only guess I'm at the back of the cabin now.

"Which way did that bitch go?" I hear from a short distance.

Running out. Running, running.

It's an old, faded Chevy truck. It could belong to anyone. My last-ditch effort. I stumble to the driver's side as dirt crunches under feet behind me.

The door squeals as I open it just enough to squeeze in before slamming it shut and jabbing the locks down. They will have to pry me out of this steel box if they want to finish what they've started.

It's a long shot but if there's a key in here, I'm going to find it. The center console is full of crumpled up receipts and candy wrappers. Nothing but napkins and envelopes of mail in the glove box. And only crumbs and beer cans underneath the seat. My thumping heart dulls as breathing becomes more challenging. I pull the visor down and metal clanks down onto my lap.

Keys.

A hand smacks the driver's side window. It's Derrick, eyes ablaze.

"Open the fucking door, Lula, or we are busting the glass," he warns, tone level.

Calen positions his beefy figure at the front of the truck, glaring at me through the windshield, visibly winded. Both men are naked and stained in blood, their limp dicks dangling between their legs.

I shove the thickest key into the ignition and twist. The engine revs but refuses to start.

The men outside get nervous, banging on the window and hood of the truck.

On the third attempt the truck sputters to life. A laugh escapes from my lips, relief and hope building. A rock smashes into the windshield as I mash the gas pedal, sending glass flying inward. Calen's heavy body thumps onto the hood before quickly rolling off as the truck lurches forward. I keep my foot planted on the gas. The truck reaches seventy miles per hour before I reach the road, the cabin getting smaller and smaller in the rearview mirror.

As the distance between me and the club grows, the pain suddenly hits me like a ton of bricks. My hands struggle to grip the steering wheel, the vitality draining from me. Miles of barren land stretch ahead of me and my eyes won't focus any longer, the pavement turning fuzzy.

My body tries to shut down, luring me into a dreamy slumber. The sharp swerves of the truck knock me back to consciousness.

I can't give up. Not now. Not now…

I allow my eyelids to droop, and my hands relax near my wounds as I give in to the magnetizing oblivion.

A sharp wail rings through my brain. Red and blue sparkles dance beneath my closed lids.

It's over. It's all over.

CHAPTER 35

"They'd like to speak with you, if you're up for it," the mousy nurse in Pooh Bear scrubs says as she hands me a cup of water with the little pebbled ice cubes.

I nod and take a long sip.

They have been in at least three times since I've gotten out of surgery. Each time my mom kicked them out. Today she's out running errands, doing things she's been putting off for over a week while I've been in the hospital.

"They have all the time in the world to get your statement. Now is not the time. You'll pop a stitch," she told me.

She hasn't left my side. And for once, I'm grateful for that.

She has also gotten in touch with my absent father. She thought he deserved to know what was going on with his daughter, considering the extreme circumstances. I suppose that was valid. He took the first flight into town, dropping whatever life that's gripped him so tight and stopped him from being present for the past decades. He'll visit tomorrow. A day that I'm both dreading and hungering for.

"So explain this to us again. You were all intimate with each other?" Detective Hanover asks, arching his left brow. He sits in a rigid, weathered hospital chair across from my bed.

The media has jumped on the case. The secrecy. The sex. The trafficking. The *murders*. It's the type of drama that no one expected in their own backyard. Andrew Stanford has even reached out and asked me for a comment.

"How is that relevant?" I ask.

"Ma'am, it's all relevant to this case. Our first step is to peel back each and every layer of this cult," he says. His southern accent proves that he isn't from here. At least not born and raised.

"We shared partners," I admit.

Detective Hanover nods in understanding. I know the questions are going to get deeper, more explicit, more uncomfortable. I know this journey is far from over. Hell, I may even be charged when it's all said and done.

A uniformed officer informed me of Jason's death while I was in post-op. But I knew that already. I saw the look of his eyes after I sliced his neck. I saw them lose their light, their radiance. The officer gave his condolences, despite the fact that I'm the one that killed him.

"Calen Banks is dead," he says plainly, waiting for me to react.

I can't stop the smile that creeps up on my lips. I didn't realize how hard the truck hit him.

"What about the rest of them?" I ask, lack of emotion back on my face.

"Some have been taken into custody. Others are being questioned, just like you are," he says, eyeing me closely.

"Am I being considered a suspect? Or a victim?" I ask in an accusatory tone.

"There are many victims in this story, Mrs. Carson. Too many to count, I'm afraid to say."

"They were trafficking women. Girls. But I'm sure you have some knowledge of that already," I say.

He ignores my assertion and continues, "Do you have any information on the whereabouts of Atlas Johnson?" Detective Hanover crosses one leg over the other and leans back in his seat, as if we are two friends having a casual conversation about the latest drinks at Starbucks.

"To be honest, I didn't even know his last name until just now. So no, I can't say I know anything about his current location."

The detective scratches his bald head. I can't quite read him. I don't know whose side he's on. I don't know what the others have been saying.

"Do I need a lawyer?" I sit up straighter in the bed, not wanting to appear weak any longer.

He shrugs. "Only if you think it's necessary. We have persons of interest but have yet to rule out any potential suspec—"

I cut him off, knowing where he's going with this. "Look, detective. I want these people taken down as much as you do. But I won't be made out to be an accomplice. They turned my life upside down, shattered every semblance of reality I had. I want justice just as much as you do."

"What do you know about the deaths of Gina Reese and Clara Montgomery?"

I breathe a sigh of relief. "Maybe I should start at the beginning."

And as I spew the dark contents that have been eating at my brain, I clear space for the future that can potentially be mine. A future that isn't predictable, safe, or even comfortable. But a future that is all my own.

ABOUT THE AUTHOR

BRISTOL ROSE is a writer and author of the new novel Club 13. She graduated from Southern New Hampshire University with an MFA in Creative Writing in 2025 and since then has spent her time plotting her next story.

Bristol writes in the psychological thriller genre. Through her writing, she aims to expose the darkness of the human condition through stomach-clenching, heart-racing stories that envelop readers and give them a break from reality.

When she's not tapping away on the computer, Bristol can usually be found outside or curled up with a book. Bristol lives in Idaho with her family.

FIND BRISTOL

Instagram: @bristolroseauthor

Also at: *Bristolroseauthor.com*